Knight School

BY

Andrew Mayne

AndrewMayneBooks.com

03052013p

Special thanks to Justin Robert Young for his help.
Thank you to Brittney Davies for her copy editing assistance
(all mistakes are my own).

Dedicated to the Paladin Society.

CHAPTER ONE

Ghosts

The helmet had a finger-long gash across the top, ending in a broken face shield. The dull-gray plastic resembled a skull in the pale moonlight; the only color was a fine spray of blood that had dried on the outside. The tall man gently set it aside and aimed the narrow beam of his flashlight at the ground. The light made a cone in the cold mist. Just beyond the circle of light, things moved. He knew there were eyes out there watching – some of them perhaps human.

His companion used the edge of his shovel to knock a branch aside, sending a dry log down a small ravine.

"Quiet," scolded the tall man.

The shorter man tossed the shovel to the ground, took a

Beretta from his waist and pulled back the slide, making a metal click. "I thought your snitch said this area was empty?"

"They did. That doesn't mean plans don't change. Put that away before you hurt someone."

"That's what guns are for."

"Not out here."

"Then why you packing the 12-gauge?"

"That's different. And it's not for them..."

The short man picked up the shovel and stabbed it into the ground. "If I have to dig much more of these, I'm going to start putting the little bastards into them."

"That's not how we do things."

The short man looked over his shoulder at the tall man. A layer of dirt and grime masked his face. He pointed a crusted fingernail at the shattered helmet. "These little bastards made their choice."

The tall man sensed something more than greed in his companion's voice. Beneath it all was a deep-seated anger and a desire for revenge.

CHAPTER TWO

Venn

Everything goes black in the library. The boy asking the odd questions vanishes in the shadows.

Red eyes appear in the darkness and stare at me – glaring eyes, filled with rage.

The first footstep is like a thunderclap as it slams the floor. The second brings the eyes half the distance toward me.

Two more and it'll be upon me.

I see a huge silhouette in the dark. There are horns above the eyes. Not devil horns. These are the horns of an animal. The horns of a bull.

The Bull Man is almost on me. He grips the edge of a table and flips it into the air. Dictionaries and papers go flying. Chairs fall over and it lands with a CRACK, knocking into a shelf.

He's one pace away from me. His shadow falls over me like an eclipse.

His shoulders lower as he prepares to run straight through me with his horns.

My first day here is about to be over less than an hour after I arrived.

I knew this school was weird the first moment I laid eyes on it.

I had no idea this was only the beginning.

An hour ago I was behind a bush a block away, changing out of my tight dress slacks into a pair of my dad's old jeans. I had made a quick exit out of the apartment in the slacks so Mom wouldn't notice they came above my ankles. There hadn't been time to take me shopping and I didn't want to make her feel bad. She cried enough already.

The jeans used to be Dad's. He stopped wearing them after he got sick because cinching them up with a belt made them look like a potato sack. We all joked about the "farmer pants." It was the kind of laugh followed by secret sadness.

When Mom sent me to the Salvation Army to drop off Dad's old things, I slipped the pants out of the box and hid them in my moving stuff. I wasn't being sentimental – just practical. Mom had more important things than taking me shopping. She had just started her job at the hospital, and money was tight and I was growing out of things fast.

I was terrified of showing up for my first day in high-water slacks. The jeans were way too loose and out of fashion, but at least they covered my ankles. Putting them on, I accidentally brushed up against the shrub and got treated to last night's rainfall as the leaves dumped their water on my leg. It looked like I pissed myself. Fantastic. Great first day. It was only going to get worse.

Fifty minutes before the Bull Man came charging toward me, I was in the main office waiting for a student to show me around.

Everyone ignored me. Kids walked by without even a nod or a glance. The secretary didn't ask me about my name. Nobody wanted to know why I was called Marv. I was dreading having to explain to people at the new school that it's not short for Marvin. Now that no one cared, I wanted to grab someone randomly and tell them my dad was a big comics fan.

There were no annoying jokes, only silence. The silence was killing me. Of course I would have rejected the attention. Not having it makes me feel even more like a loser.

When I first saw the school straddling the hill, with tall redwoods looming over it, I got a chill as I noticed the morning fog clinging to the trees like a mysterious gray blanket. That was nothing like the chill I got when I stepped inside.

I used to have dreams where I was invisible and nobody

noticed me. I'd trade that for this reality in a heartbeat.

As I walked up the path to the front doors, everyone seemed to look right through me. This was worse than being invisible; I was just the fog passing by.

There was nothing friendly in their eye contact. It wasn't exactly hostile either. I was just a thing carried by the wind. A piece of trash blowing down the hallway.

The secretary who was uninterested in my name handed me a schedule and told me to wait for someone to come get me. I sat quietly and looked around the depressing office. It was tiny compared with my old school. The trophy case in the hallway was half empty and looked forgotten. The school was old, but not run down. The place kind of felt like something that slipped out of time. It was like an old wooden ship in a forgotten harbor where someone cleared the barnacles and repainted every couple years, but there wasn't any love in it.

I felt a sinking feeling when I realized this was going to be my school for the next three years. Three years of being a nobody. Three years of haunting the halls like a forgotten echo.

Forty minutes before the Bull Man came charging at me, I was contemplating my boring future when I noticed a tall shape in the doorway. This was my student guide, Carrie.

Taller than my almost six-foot frame, she was an Amazon. Dressed in old jeans and a flat green army jacket, you could almost mistake her for a man from behind. She wasn't the kind of girl who tried to act like a man. She just looked like she was trying to mask her femininity. When she handed me a photocopy map of the campus, I could see the remnants of nail polish on her fingernails. It was like she had tried it on then wiped it away out of embarrassment.

Athletic, yet awkward, with her high cheekbones, she was what my mom would call a late bloomer. She could be an Olympic champion or one of those models who have what they call an interesting look. It's the look we make fun of in high school and then slap ourselves on the forehead later on because we couldn't see the real her. I thought she was kind of pretty, but didn't make eye contact.

Model, athlete or hitchhiking serial killer, as a tour guide she sucked.

"Lunchroom," was all she said as she pointed through the window in the door.

I leaned in to look and couldn't think of anything observational to say other than that there were more of the blue plastic chairs that hurt your ass than the red plastic chairs that hurt your ass. "Interesting," I mumbled.

I think I got a flicker of her eyes as I made my comment. I sounded like more of a wiseass than I meant.

She moved down the hall in quick strides. I had to increase my pace to keep up.

"Computer lab," she said in her monotone.

"Library?"

"Not yet," she replied.

I should have known there was something about the way

she said "not yet." She knew what was coming. I was too busy trying not to feel depressed by the strange way people were acting and how much smaller this school was than my old one.

Smaller, yet it felt bigger – more intimidating.

We walked through a courtyard. A kid with long bangs that came over his eyes lifted his head up from his calculus textbook and stared at me. I saw what may have been a slight nod. Whether it was for me or for Carrie, I couldn't tell.

A black fabric guitar case sat at his feet. Only there was something odd about it. The fabric was bent in where the base should be. At the top, a broken zipper revealed a handle inside wrapped in leather and ending in a pommel.

When he saw me looking at the case he slid it under the concrete bench. A raindrop landed in the middle of his equations and he turned back to his book.

Carrie was already through the doors into the next building. I hurried to catch up. Two girls, maybe fifteen like me, were coming the other way. I held the door open for them and they walked through without saying a word.

A sarcastic "Your welcome" died in my throat.

Both of them were wearing jeans and shirts that looked kind of plain. I had yet to see any of the fancier brands kids at my old school wore – the kind of stuff you bought at the mall where the salespeople looked like models.

All the shoes I'd seen were for the most part discount store brands.

After I had left my bush and headed toward the school, I noticed a neighborhood on the other facing side filled with three-story houses. My stomach did a little panic as I realized it was a wealthy neighborhood. And here I was walking in wearing sagging pants that were out of date even when my dad wore them.

Inside the school, however, I didn't see anyone who looked like a rich kid. I thought about that as Carrie walked me down another corridor. Something hit me.

"Hey, um, is there another high school near here?" I asked.

She flung open a door. "Parker Academy is up the road."

Ah, I got it. Parker Academy was the rich kids' school. There weren't any rich kids here because their parents sent them all there.

I felt slightly less self-conscious about my pants. Not that it changed how people were looking past me.

"Gym," said Carrie, in case the sound of bouncing balls and smell of sweat weren't enough of a clue for me.

I pretended to study the gymnasium. A group of teens playing half-court basketball stopped for a moment to look at me, then turned back to their game.

"Um, play any sports?" I asked Carrie.

She lead me down the hall as she thought about the answer. "Field hockey," she finally replied.

"Cool. I didn't know they had a team here."

"They don't," she answered in a clipped tone, as if it was a stupid question.

Pretending we were having an actual conversation, I continued. "I do some martial arts." I didn't say which one, allowing her to ask me.

She didn't. Instead she replied, "I know."

That was interesting. How? I'd deleted all my online accounts a few weeks ago. I was tired of everyone telling me how sad they were and offering their advice.

I had to know. "Um, how do you know?"

"Venn," she replied.

Venn? "What's a venn?"

She stopped and faced me. "He's who told me."

Oh. "Is he a teacher?"

Somewhere under her high cheekbones and mouth carved from ice she cracked a smile. "He thinks so."

We walked down the hallway and she turned to a set of double doors. "Here's Venn."

It looked like a library to me, but through the small window I could see a boy about my age sitting at a table with his fingers folded, looking back at me.

It wasn't the blank stare I got from everyone else. He was looking at me. Almost into me. And he was smiling. It wasn't a comforting smile. It was the smile of someone who knows something. Something important. Something about you.

I was ten minutes from finding out what the joke was all about.

I stepped inside and met Venn.

That's when my life changed.

That's when things got weirder.

That was minutes before the Bull Man tried to kill me.

CHAPTER THREE

Study Hall

Venn has that kind of knowing look that scares you. You can tell he sees things you don't. He knows weird facts that seem random then form a pattern. We're about to have a conversation about martial arts and nuclear annihilation that will end in a way I never could've imagined.

"Marv Whitlock, I've been waiting to meet you," says Venn. His light brown – almost yellow – eyes follow me as I sit down. He's half a head shorter than me. Brown hair falls down to just above his face as I take my seat. There's a faint hint of a slant to his eyes. Somewhere he probably had an Asian relative.

He's my age, but there's something about him that seems older. He's incredibly self-possessed. He doesn't use the unsure "um" I use before every sentence. When he said he had been waiting to meet me, I got the impression he didn't mean he'd been waiting in the library – rather, he'd been waiting a much longer time.

I wasn't sure if he was another guide or the head of some club. I look around a little unsure. The library is abandoned. The lights in the librarian's office behind the check-out counter are off. It's just Venn and me.

A large manila folder sits in front of him. I see some photocopies sticking out from the edges. He reaches inside and pulls out a newspaper clipping. I recognize the black-and-white photo on the other side through the thin paper. It was a small article about one of the tournaments I'd won. The clipping wasn't part of my transcript. It was something he must have pulled from online.

"So you're into judo?" asks Venn.

I nod.

Venn pulls a few more clippings from the folder and looks them over. "Looks like you're pretty good."

I shrug. I still wasn't sure where this was going or who he was.

"Ever break any bones?" asks Venn.

"A couple toes, a nose," I reply.

"Did it hurt?"

"I wouldn't know. You'd have to ask them."

Venn smiles, getting the joke.

"Are you into the martial arts?" I ask.

"I dabble," says Venn, with the confidence of someone

who does more than dabble.

I notice his wrists and forearms. Although he was skinny, they're corded like thick cables.

Venn pushes the folder aside and leans back, crossing his arms. "Do you know the problem with tests?" he asks rhetorically. "People can prepare for them. All you know about someone is what they're like when they show up prepared. You don't know anything about their character. Character is who we are when we don't think anyone is looking."

"What's this about?" I ask.

"Right now? Character. What are you like when nobody is around?"

"Um, usually I'm alone when nobody is around?"

Venn lets out a small laugh. "What this is about is this: You don't know anyone here. I doubt you had much of a conversation with Carrie... Everyone else is trying to figure you out. The only person who knows anything about you is me." Venn pats the folder. "And that's all theoretical. I think I know you. I think I have a pretty good idea about you. I think you could matter."

"Gee, thanks. Matter? How?"

Venn shakes his head. "That's not important right now."

The conversation felt weird. "Why does this feel like a job interview?" I finally ask.

"In a way, it is."

This is all weird. "For what? To see if I'm cool enough to be friends with you guys?"

"Marv, whatever passes for cool is the farthest thing from me and my friends. We care so little about cool it makes apathy look hip. What we care about is character. In this school if you don't have it, you're a nobody. I think you have it. My friends aren't so sure."

I feel blood rushing to my head. Who the hell is he to talk about me being judged? I hadn't even been here an hour and already I'm getting pulled into some kind of clique crap. I wanted to call him out on it, but the truth was, I didn't know what to say. I didn't have a friend in the world here. This was the longest conversation I'd have. If I pissed him off, then what? Three years of cold stares?

Venn notices the expression on my face. "Marv, it may sound like I'm speaking in ellipticals, but I'm actually going in a spiral."

Ellipticals. "I have no idea what that means." I couldn't hold it in any longer. "You sound like a very clever guy, but I don't know where this is going and I have to get to class."

Without looking at the clock he replied, "You have thirteen minutes until the bell rings. Your next class is 80 yards down the hall. It'll take you ninety seconds to get there. Right now we're having a conversation. I'm the closest you have to a friend right now. Hear me out. We're having a conversation about character."

It felt more like a lecture, but I relaxed and let him continue. There's something about the way he speaks. It wasn't forceful, just persuasive.

Venn's eyes look up as he thinks of something. "If you

heard over the PA system an enemy power had launched a thermonuclear missile at Portland, what would you do?"

"Find my mother," I replied.

"Right here, right now. Do you run to the hospital where she works? You don't own a car."

"I'd steal one."

Venn smiles. "So your first act in the case of an emergency is to commit a felony and deny someone else the use of their car who might be trying to help someone else?"

"If it's to help my mother, yes." The fact that he knew my mother worked at the hospital washes right over me.

"Noble. You wouldn't think about asking a friend to use their car?"

"I don't have any friends. Remember?"

"At this moment, maybe not. Maybe you could ask me."

"You're not old enough to drive."

"True, but my brother is. I also know where my parents keep a spare set of keys to their other car. Maybe I'd risk a minor infraction and help you."

"All right. Would you?"

Venn's eyes dart to the right as he thinks the question over as if he were doing a math problem. "Yes. Right now, I would. But that's all hypothetical. Me saying I would do a thing isn't the same as me doing the thing. Isn't it?"

"No."

"No," he repeats. "And that's what brings us back to the question of character. If you knew me, you'd know the answer. But you don't. And all I know about you is hypothetical."

"Let's hope the Chinese don't decide to blow up the West Coast," I reply.

"My friends and I would survive," says Venn without hesitation. "So short of immediate nuclear annihilation, my friends and I need to know your character."

"Why?"

"For reasons I can't get into until I know you have character."

"Sounds like a Catch-42," I say stupidly.

"I believe it's a Catch-22," corrects Venn. "It's not. Although I don't presently possess a thermonuclear missile, we have other ways."

"Of testing me..." I say hesitantly.

"It's only a test if you know what comes next."

"So what comes next?"

Venn grins. He raises a hand and snaps his fingers. All the lights go out. His last words before the red eyes appear are, "Fear. Fear is what comes next."

That's when the Bull Man comes charging toward me. He's less than a yard away. I can hear breathing and feel his hot breath on my face. The horns are headed straight toward my chest – right at my heart.

I only have a fraction of a second to react...

CHAPTER FOUR

The Bull Man

The red eyes streak toward me like two hell-bound meteors. Underneath the sound of crashing tables and the Bull Man's footsteps I can hear metal clanking.

My shock flies away like ropes slipping from my wrists and instinct takes over. That's what judo is all about. You practice something so many times that you don't even think about it. When your body feels your opponent's balance change, you pull them off their footing and sweep them to the ground. Like a finger retracting from a hot stove, there's no time to process. It's all instinct.

Dad never trained me for a demon Bull Man charging at me. He did teach me momentum. And he taught me how to take a losing situation and turn it into my advantage.

I raise my legs before the Bull Man can close in on me completely. My calves explode and I kick him with both feet in the chest. His momentum is transferred between us. I go backwards, and he lifts into the air for a moment. I hear a loud groan as I fly over the back of my chair.

The first day of judo, and for most of your early lessons, all you learn is how to fall. You learn how to fall sideways. How to fall forwards. How to fall backwards.

You learn how to fall without getting hurt. You learn how to fall and then land on your feet.

I fall over the top of my chair and go into autopilot. I'm on my feet before I can think.

Something flies past my face and I hear a loud CRACK as it strikes a table. A shape swings past my eyes. I jump back. The Bull Man has a sword! He strikes again and I duck. Wood chips sting my cheek as the blade lodges into the veneer top.

The Bull Man reaches over with his other hand to free the sword. I step back and my butt slams into a table. I jump backwards and land on top of it. The legs quiver under my weight.

Through the helmet, under the red points of light, I see human eyes. This doesn't make everything any less terrifying. When the Bull Man was a demon, there was hope this was just a dream. Now it's real.

The Bull Man yanks his sword free and swings it toward me on the backstroke. I jump backward to avoid the metal edge splintering my shins.

I land hard behind the table. The Bull Man is on the other side across from me. I hear him snarl. He raises the sword into the air with both hands and brings it down toward my skull.

The edge comes a hair away from my nose and slams into the table like a cleaver. He doesn't wait to pull it free from the tabletop. The Bull Man grasps the edge of the table and starts shoving it toward me, trying to pin me to the bookshelves.

I shuffle back to keep from getting mowed under. A row of chairs get swept up by us and start sliding back. I see the shelves getting closer from the corner of my eye. I'm about to be trapped.

A few feet away from the oak bookcases, I dig a heel into the carpet and push back.

The Bull Man is a mountain and much stronger. But I resist for just a moment. His shoulders flare and metal squeaks as he prepares to make a powerful thrust with the table and pinch me between the wall.

I wait for the moment when he can't pull back his body and let go. The table slides back without resistance.

I leap on top of the table. The sword handle grazes my thigh just inches from my nuts. I forgot about it in the dark.

I run across the table and kick the Bull Man in the head. His helmet makes a sound like a bell and he staggers backwards. I continue up and over him and land on the ground behind him in a squat.

Before he can face me, I wrap my arm around his head

and throw him over my hip in a move that's been forbidden in tournaments for fifty years. The move could break the spine of an unprotected man. The Bull Man's neck doesn't break, but the table behind us does as we fall into it, his metal armor acting as a sledgehammer.

I pull myself over his body so he can lessen my fall. We break through the table and hit the ground. His metal shoulder guard slams into my face, stinging me. I had never tried that throw on someone in armor. Now I know why it's a bad idea.

We're both stunned, but I recover quicker. My arm is still around his neck. I grab my wrist and put him into a chokehold.

"Submit!" I shout, not really sure what you say to demon Bull Men with glowing red eyes who come charging out of the dark at you.

His gauntlets try to pull away at my arm. I feel sharp edges dig into my skin.

I give his neck a tighter squeeze, bringing pressure on the two arteries that pump blood to the brain. Another few seconds and it'll be lights out for him.

I've felt that feeling a hundred times. You think you can fight it, but it's not about holding your breath. When the blood stops going to your head, the corner of your vision begins to go dark and you feel yourself passing out.

He thrashes and I give him a second of a really tight squeeze, then ease up a fraction.

"SUBMIT!" I scream it into what I think is his earhole.

A metal glove slaps the ground and a pained voice shouts, "I yield!"

I don't let go.

"I YIELD!" he shouts louder.

I release him and get to my feet before he can grab me again. He gets to his knees and punches the broken table.

"GODDAMN IT!" he yells at me, but doesn't come closer.

Behind the glowing red eyes is an angry teenager.

I'm blinded as the emergency exit opens and sunlight streams inside. Dark shapes swarm into the library and people start picking up the tables while others put books back on shelves. The Bull Man vanishes through the exit.

I see their silhouettes go back out the door as the cleanup crew leaves, never making out any faces.

The lights come back on.

I'm all alone in the library.

The Bull Man is gone.

Venn is gone.

The broken tables have disappeared.

It's like it never happened.

Except the red scratches on my arm and the adrenaline coursing through my body tell me otherwise.

The bell rings and the sound of people shuffling into hallways echoes down the corridor.

A freshman girl with a ponytail and a stack of books in her arm enters the library. She sits down at a table and opens a book without looking at me. I'm about to say something, but can't think of what.

I can't understand what just happened, let alone describe it. I shake my head and try to find my next class, hoping to find Carrie in the hall so I can ask her. I'm afraid to find Venn. Not because of what I might do, but because of what he might have planned next.

Part of me remembers something I didn't notice when I was fighting off the Bull Man. Now it's getting louder in my memory as I replay it, sorting out all the details.

After I flipped the Bull Man and we broke through the table there was another sound after the crash.

The sound of someone laughing.

CHAPTER FIVE

New Kid

I stumble into the hallway. Bodies stream around me like fish avoiding a rock in the middle of a river. I get a few stares, but still I'm an outsider. I don't quite exist in their world.

Part of me wants to grab the nearest person and scream at them, "What the hell is going on?"

Of course I don't.

I keep walking, hoping someone will stop me and explain. No one does.

It was a joke, right? A weird, cruel prank?

The metal sword and the crashing table weren't very funny. The horns aimed at my chest weren't a barrel of laughs.

What if I hadn't moved? What if I'd stayed in my chair paralyzed? What if my head had been an inch forward when the blade cut through the air?

In movies, things are all clear-cut. You know when someone is getting mugged or beat up. Life isn't always like that. Two people across the street yelling at each other could be friends joking or someone about to get shot.

I don't know how to react to this. I keep walking through the crowded hallway, searching for faces, for someone to look back with recognition.

I find myself standing in front of the glass window looking into the office. The secretary taps away on her keyboard with her fingers. The door to the principal's office is wide open. I can see his elbow holding a phone.

Do I go inside?

And say what?

So...I go in there and say I was attacked by a demon Bull Man with red glowing eyes and a sword in the library? But I'm really sorry, the broken tables and all the chairs were cleared away so there's no evidence. Just believe me!

Great first impression.

They'll have me peeing in a drug test kit and talking to the school shrink before my mom gets here.

Mom.

Jesus Christ. I can't let her know. She'll freak out. She'll know I'm not high or going crazy. She'll believe me. She'll pull me from here and probably try to move again. She doesn't need that right now. She doesn't need another thing to cry over.

I can't tell anyone.

I have to just deal with this.

"Are you okay?" asks a woman's voice.

I turn around and face the teacher asking the question. She's got short, graying hair and a butterfly pinned to her blouse.

"Do you need the nurse?" she asks.

"She's at work," I say mindlessly, thinking about my mom.

"I'm sure she can see you. Do you get nosebleeds often?"

"What?" I inhale and smell the metal taste of my blood. In my reflection in the window I see blood dripping from my nose. It's falling in globs and splattering on the floor. I say something stupid. "It's the dry air."

She raises an eyebrow. Oregon is anything but dry.

"I mean, I tripped," I correct myself weakly. Why not just say I pick it too much, for crying out loud?

She hands me a tissue from a pocket. I wipe the blood away and hold my nose. "Shnanks," I reply. "Mime mokay."

She gives me a nod with a worried look then leaves for her classroom.

I go to the bathroom and clean up the blood. Even I avoid my own reflection. When the bleeding stops, I find my next class.

The teacher, Mr. Pressman, a short man who looks too young for the beard he's wearing, gives me an angry look when I enter late, before he realizes I'm new and don't have a clue where I'm supposed to go.

"Over there." He points to a desk. "I'll bring you a class packet tomorrow. Starting two weeks into the school year?" he says with a dismissive tone.

With my back turned, under my breath I mumble, "I'm sorry my dad took so long to die. If he'd done it at the beginning of summer instead of the end, it wouldn't have been such an inconvenience for you."

Only I didn't say it under my breath.

Everyone heard me.

I feel all the eyes on the back of my neck. There's a gasp. I'm not the partially invisible boy anymore.

I take my seat and avoid looking up. I don't want to know the expression on the teacher's face. I feel bad for him. I'm horrified that I just laid it out there.

My head is still trying to figure out Venn, the Bull Man and all the crazy stuff at this school. I didn't mean to be the moody, sulking kid. I don't want anyone feeling sorry for me, not that I'm sure anyone here is capable of that.

"Turn to Page 83 and look at the sample quiz," says Pressman, deciding to ignore my outburst.

I open the textbook on the desk and pretend to read the questions. I sense Pressman staring at me from the other side of the room. We both may be pretending that didn't happen, but neither of us will forget it. Is he the kind of guy who feels embarrassed? Has he marked me as a troublemaker? Is he going to hold a grudge?

I try to think of how my dad would handle this situation.

He'd probably wait until after class and apologize for the comment. That's what I have to do. I'll just wait and then tell him I meant no disrespect – even if his comment that started it was stupid. It's not like I get to decide when to enroll.

I sit through the rest of the class thinking about the library. Around me people steal glances in my direction. Do they all know about the prank already? Maybe it was an assault, but in their eyes it was just fun. Right?

I can imagine them laughing at me behind my back. On top of that, I'm the moody crybaby who feels sorry for himself and has to mention his dead dad when he walks into the room. Pathetic.

I'm pathetic.

I have another horrible thought. What if I wasn't supposed to hit the Bull Man? Crap. I think about haunted houses on Halloween and how some kids can't control themselves.

My judo club used to run one for charity. Every night you'd get some kid who would flip out when you jumped out in a rubber mask from behind a stack of boxes and the kid would kick or punch you. We never hit back. We knew the rules.

I kicked the Bull Kid in the head. I nearly choked him to death.

Jesus Christ. What if this was a prank that went too far – only I'm the one who took it too far?

I couldn't imagine feeling any more horrible a minute ago. Now I'm the biggest idiot in the universe.

I bury my head in my book and shut out the world. God, I'm a screwup.

When the bell rings, I pull myself out of my loathing and wait for the other students to leave. I go up to Pressman's desk to apologize. He doesn't look up from his book.

"Um, Mr. Pressman," I start to say.

"I said I'll have your packet tomorrow."

"Um, yeah. I just..."

"Goodbye," he says coldly without even lifting an eye.

"Yeah, I just."

He snaps the book shut and glares at me. "You know what goodbye means? Did they teach you that at your last school?"

"Uh, yeah, it's Old English for 'God be with you,' " I reply automatically.

"Well then. I'm sure that's a subject you've thought about a lot lately given recent events. Now if you're done pouring your heart out, maybe you should go to your next class?"

His coldness stops me dead. I can't feel the scratches on my arm or the blood in my nose. I lock eyes with him then back away from his desk. My skin burns with rage.

I no longer feel like the biggest jerk in the world. This guy just beat me for first place.

I'm afraid to ask how this day can get any worse.

I make it through the rest of my classes. There's no sign of Carrie or Venn in the hallways. The two conversations I tried to strike up in other classes go unanswered.

At lunch I eat my sandwich in the corner of the

lunchroom and watch everyone else. There are some whispers and thumb gestures toward me. To hell with them.

The most interesting thing was when I saw a large kid, built like a keg, walking down a row of tables. He had a ponytail and goatee, yet still probably wasn't old enough to drive. Dressed in all black, wearing a duster and boots, he carried his tray in my direction, then stopped and went the other way when he laid eyes on me.

But not before I saw the metal emblem hanging from his bruised neck: a horned bull.

CHAPTER SIX

Mr. Wilson

The handcuffs are cold around my wrists, but I'm so red with shame, I don't even notice. Behind me, through the office window, I can hear the sound of students gawking as they gather around to see the new kid who got arrested on his second day. In the principal's office, he and the sheriff are talking things over in harsh tones. Neither of them has told me what this is about, but I can guess...

Any minute now I expect them to ask me about what happened in the library. Somewhere I imagine the Bull Boy is having photographs taken of his neck – physical proof of what happened. What story is he spinning? The sheriff gives me a sidelong glance every now and then as the principal shakes his head.

Today was supposed to be a better day than yesterday. The first day is always the roughest, I told myself. That was a lie...

Yesterday, when the last bell rang I felt a wave of relief. It was gone as soon as I reminded myself I had to come back here tomorrow morning. But I wasn't worried yet about what new hell tomorrow would bring. I was worried over whether Bull Boy and some of his friends would stop me on my way home.

Hell, I was even worried Mr. Pressman might decide to drive his car off the road and send me into a ditch.

I was out the front doors and onto the sidewalk faster than if the place had been on fire.

Between the school and the apartment block we moved to, there was a large forest that seemed to go on forever. The trees were tall and kind of eerie-looking. I thought about cutting through, but figured that would be the worst place to go if I wanted to avoid getting murdered. My mind was filled with visions of my head split open in a dry creek bed and Venn laughing over me.

I was better off sticking to the sidewalk and keeping an eye out for Pressman and Bull Boy.

The walk home was a paranoid journey of constantly looking over my shoulder. Every passing car made me duck out of fear that someone was going to throw something at me.

I got home at last and went straight to my room. Mom

wouldn't be home until late, so I just climbed into bed and tried to think of some lie to tell her about how great the day was and how I was making lots of new friends and had awesome teachers.

Maybe the other teachers were okay. After the encounter with Pressman, I kind of just kept my mouth shut. They probably thought I was aloof – another word for a quiet jerk.

I stared at the ceiling and replayed what happened, trying to understand what I did wrong. The Bull Man thing had to be a prank. My haunted house theory was the only thing that made sense. It was some kind of hazing or gag and I just flipped the hell out.

Whose fault was it? I may have overreacted, but it had to be done at Venn's instigation.

Venn.

He's at the center of this. Carrie lead me to him. Bull Boy appeared when Venn snapped his fingers. He's the ringleader.

Who was Venn?

What kind of ring?

Mom came home and went straight to her room after wishing me a good night through the crack in my door. I could tell she was real tired. Normally she'd want to talk about the day. Right now she just has way too much on her mind.

I stayed in my room trying to understand what was going on. It all came back to Venn. He knew all about me. I knew nothing about him. I needed to know more.

Sometime after midnight I left my room to use the bathroom and saw Mom's laptop on the kitchen table. Internet had been hooked up the day before, so I decided to do my own research on Venn.

I didn't know where to begin at first. Ellison High didn't have an online student directory. I wasn't even sure how to spell Venn's name.

Finally I did a search for "Venn" and "Ellison High." The top hit was a link to a Portland newspaper article. The photo in the article was a younger version of the teen I'd met in the library.

Crap, I thought as I read the story. My stomach sank. He wasn't just some smart-ass kid. My nemesis was scary smart:

> Thirteen-year-old Ellison City student Venn Maddox became the youngest person to ever win the West Coast Junior Chess Championship. He beat out more than 20,000 students from Washington, Oregon and California who entered via an online tournament that lead to the invitational.
>
> Despite the chess title, the incredibly articulate teen is no geek. Venn credits his win to his interest in unusual strategies and hobbies including the martial arts. He holds a second-degree black belt in jujitsu (the state's youngest) and has competed nationally in kendo (Japanese sword fighting).
>
> Venn says chess is just a hobby and he has no plans to pursue it beyond the title. "I'm kind of bored by the

> game, to be honest," he explained. "I respect the game, but at the end of the day it's just pushing pieces around on a board."
>
> Chess Grandmaster Joseph Pushkin, who was on hand for the tournament, was somewhat dismayed by the comment. He referred to Venn as an "arrogant little pr-ck" and chalked Venn's win as a statistical fluke.
>
> The title was previously held by Venn's older brother, who won the title last year at age 16.

So, Venn has moved from pushing plastic chess pieces around to toying with people.

I fall asleep determined to seek him out and tell him I want no part of it.

Game over. I'll just forfeit. I don't care what anyone thinks.

All I want is to just be left alone. I don't need his puppet master games.

Venn had other plans for me...

My second day starts off like the first. I take the long walk up the hill to the school with the giant redwoods towering behind it. There's the morning fog that still clings to grass. The other students walk past and around me as if I'm just a piece of trash to avoid.

Inside the school, I find my way to my first-period class and take a seat in the back of the room. The teacher, the woman who'd asked about my nosebleed, points to a chalk drawing of a sunflower on the board and explains how we're going to dissect it.

Dissecting a sunflower? Okay. Whatever.

We split off into groups and a kid comes over to my table.

"Hi, I'm Benny," he says with a grin that looks bigger than his face.

Wide-eyed with one of those perpetually cheery faces, Benny is just a little shorter than me and a bit lankier. He's wearing the same kind of dull green army coat Carrie had on. There's a button on the collar that says "Zombie Rights, NOW!"

"I'm Marv," I reply gruffly.

"Cool. I love comics." He takes the seat next to me and drops his books on the table. "Flower dissection. Um, awesome." He lifts the sunflower and eyes it skeptically. "I hope these flowers were raised in an ethical greenhouse and given anesthesia before they were removed. I don't think I could deal with the guilt if I thought the poor thing was boxed up in one of those horrible factory farms."

Benny's sarcasm lifts my mood. I crack a smile. "I'm sure it was free-range and died of natural causes and willed its body to science."

Benny lets out a laugh. "Damn hippies. Taking the fun out of everything. My dad says they once dissected a dead dog he'd found on the way to school when he was a kid. Can you imagine Mrs. Peters losing it if we brought in a dead cat and asked to carve it up?"

"The newspapers would be all over us. We'd be hated by everyone on the internet."

"Let's not do that," says Benny.

"Yeah. I got enough problems."

Benny lets the comment slide. We take turns with the scalpel cutting off parts of the sunflower. Benny names him Mr. Wilson.

When all of Mr. Wilson's parts are laid out on the table, we make illustrations of the flower and little diagrams explaining the different functions. My drawings are rather straightforward. Benny's has small artistic flairs. He gives the sunflower a tie and the petals a part like hair swept to the side.

For the final touch, he draws a bee with a lusty expression staring at the sunflower. A word balloon says, "Hot damn! I got to get some!"

From behind us comes Mrs. Peters' voice. "Some what, Benny?"

"Carbohydrates. It's the exchange. The bee gets sugar. The flower gets to rub its...pollen all over the bee's leg which it'll go spread. Circle of life," Benny grins.

"You're quite the romantic," replies Mrs. Peters before going off to look at the next table.

Benny nods to me. "She's cool. As long as you know your stuff, you can get away with anything. Don't know it, and she'll make you pay."

"Good to know." I try to find a way to bring up Venn.

"So, um, do you know..."

"Venn?" says Benny. "I kept waiting for you to ask. Of course. Everyone knows Venn."

"So you know about..."

Benny shakes his head and interrupts me. "I don't know anything. Leave it at that."

"Yeah, sure," I nod my head, pretending I understood.

Benny slides a book over to me. "You can bring this to him. He has study period next hour, same as you."

"He does?" I look down at the book. It's Le Morte D'Arthur, Malory's book on King Arthur.

To be honest, I'm not sure if I'm ready to confront him yet, but Benny has already pushed the book toward me and headed back to his table. Mr. Wilson is pinned to his collar behind the zombie button.

After the bell rings I follow everyone out the door. I'm halfway to my other class when I see the principal and the sheriff standing in the middle of the hallway. The principal, a tall bald man with a large mustache and a serious expression, is pointing in my direction.

I look over my shoulder to see who he's pointing to. Everyone is staring at me.

Oh crap.

The sheriff pushes through the other students and takes my bookbag and clenches my shoulder firmly. I reflexively want to shrug it off, but I don't when I see the 9mm at his side.

"Face the lockers," he says. "I know you know martial arts, so for your safety and mine, I need to place you in handcuffs."

Holy crap!

My head is pressed against the metal vent on the locker. I can smell dirty gym clothes and a rotten sandwich. The sheriff pins my arms behind me and I hear the ratchet and click of the cuffs on my wrist.

Holy crap.

I've been arrested.

He grabs my elbow and pulls me toward the front office.

Everyone clears the center of the hallway to make room. It's like a goddamn parade and I'm the center attraction.

A cute girl with curly brown hair puts her hand to her mouth. I can read her mind. She thinks I'm a criminal. I'm some violent thug they're busting.

I look at her, pleading with my eyes. I don't know her. I just want to explain that it wasn't my fault. I didn't know it was a prank.

Damn. Damn. Damn.

My heart sinks when I realize they're going to have to call my mother.

HOLY CRAP.

They drag me into the office and push me into a chair. The sheriff and the principal go into his office with my bag.

On the far wall, a poster of a missing girl stares back at me. Green stripes in her hair, a piercing in her nose, she has a lost look about her. The photo was obviously taken before she went missing, but something about her says that was her destiny. What would my photo look like right now? What was my sad destiny?

The secretary gives me a dirty look and shakes her head. She says something under her breath about keeping out the trash and how Ellison is no place for drug dealers.

Drug dealers?

The sheriff walks toward me. He's holding something in his hand. It's a book – only there's a compartment in it. Inside is a plastic baggy with something green.

OH!

CRAP!

It's Le Morte D'Arthur.

The book I was holding on to.

It's the book Benny gave me a few minutes ago.

It's Venn's book.

CHAPTER SEVEN

Snitch

The sheriff is waving the book under my face. Principal Knudson is standing behind him with his arms folded. His face is red with anger.

"I don't know what you got away with where you came from. But we don't tolerate this here. You're out of here," says Knudson with a growl.

"It's not mine," I plead as I look down at the bag.

"Your backpack. Your book," replies the sheriff.

"It's not mine," I repeat weakly.

The sheriff flips through the pages in front of the cut-out section and turns to the inside of the cover. He turns it toward me. "What does that say?"

I read the inscription:

Property of Marv Whitlock.

My face goes numb. I look up at the sheriff, searching for words. "It's just writing."

"Your name. Your book."

It was Venn's book. I'm about to say so, but something holds me back. I don't know that it is Venn's book. Benny gave it to me. He only said it belonged to Venn.

Benny.

Benny the bastard.

He set me up.

A few minutes ago we were joking around, playing out a little death scene for the sunflower. All the while he was planning on setting me up. It was all a lie. My first friend here was just another person making me for a fool.

I took the book without question.

I am a fool.

It was too good to be true.

This was payback for yesterday.

Venn and Bull Boy weren't planning on beating me up. They had something far more devious planned. They got me busted for drug possession.

Holy crap.

"I don't even use drugs," I plead. I can't bring myself to point out that Benny gave me the book to give to Venn. Maybe it was an accident. Maybe I wasn't supposed to get caught. I'm nobody's drug mule. But still.

"You don't use marijuana?" asks the sheriff.

"Never. You can test me."

"So this is for selling?" he replies.

"What? No," I snap. I feel dizzy and can't keep things straight.

"So you admit that it's for your personal use?" he asks tersely.

"No!" I keep thinking I should ask for a lawyer. But I don't have one or any idea how to get one. And isn't that what guilty people do?

"You just said that it's not for selling. So that must mean you use it. Which is it? Personal use? Or for selling?"

"Neither," I reply.

"But you said it's not yours. How could you know then?"

He stares at me without blinking. He's trying to trip me up. The problem is, I don't know where to fall.

Tired of waiting for me to answer, he asks, "Does it belong to someone else?"

Knudson is glaring at me, challenging me to name another student. He's convinced this is all on me.

All I have to do is say Benny's name and mention Venn. They'll drag them in here and grill them, too.

Then what?

I say they did it? They call me a liar. Two against one. The chess champion and the teacher's pet against the new kid nobody likes.

I'll be an even bigger jerk.

No one will believe me.

I'm going down either way.

Besides, maybe, just maybe, Benny didn't know. Maybe it was an accident. Maybe Benny didn't know what was in there.

Maybe I'm a fool.

But I'm nobody's rat.

If I saw them hurt someone, I'd do something. This is different.

I'm no rat.

This is on me.

There's no advantage to me saying anything right now. The sheriff and Knudson have their minds made up.

"Did someone give this to you?" asks Knudson.

I could say the name...

"If you cooperate, it'll be a lot easier," says the sheriff. "Was this meant for someone?"

I could tell them Venn...

I don't.

He lifts the baggie out of the book and holds it under my nose. I've never been this close to pot before. I look away.

"Time to go to the police station." The sheriff turns to Knudson. "You call his mother."

"Don't!" I blurt out.

"Give us a name," says the sheriff.

I know they're going to call my mom anyway. I think she'll believe me. Maybe. I'll have to explain the setup to her. I'll have to tell her about Benny and Venn.

This is going to kill her.

I've heard stories of kids getting sent to real jail by judges wanting to make a point. Jail with bars. Jail with kids who look like they're in their thirties and have done some horrible things. Violent people who just like to cause pain...and do worse.

My life just got more horrible. If someone tried to touch me in jail I'd hurt them. I'd break an arm. I'd fight back. But that would make me the violent offender in the eyes of the law. It would only get worse. My life would be over.

"Just tell us who it belongs to," repeats Knudson. He's daring me to name someone. "Where did you get it?"

I say nothing.

"Where did you get it?" asks the sheriff.

I stare past them and keep quiet. I won't fall for their interrogation method. I refuse to talk. I won't play along.

"All right, get up. We're going to the station," says the sheriff. "You don't want to cooperate and tell us where you got it."

"The forest," comes a voice from the doorway.

We all turn and look at Venn. He's standing there with his arms crossed.

"It grows there. All over," he replies.

The sheriff waves the bag at Venn. "You know about this?"

"Yeah," he shrugs. "It's mine."

WTF?

"This belongs to you?" asks the sheriff.

"Sort of," replies Venn.

I sit there speechless. With my hands cuffed, I have to slide sideways to see Venn's face.

Knudson points to the hollowed-out book. "This book

says Marv Whitlock."

"It was a gift from me," says Venn.

The sheriff waves the bag. "This is a gift?"

"No. The book. My brother made one for me. He uses it to hide condoms."

The sheriff's face turns red. "Funny, Maddox."

Something transpired there I don't understand.

The sheriff continues. "So you're saying this belongs to you?"

"What I said was 'sort of.' Actually, that belongs to Mrs. Peters. She asked me for it."

Knudson's jaw drops. The sheriff is at a loss for words.

Venn gives me a wink.

Holy crap. What the hell is going on? Did Venn just say that he was selling pot to our science teacher?

Why?

"I think you need to have a seat," says the sheriff. He points a finger at my chest. "Did he know what was in there?"

"Heck no," said Venn. "It was a mix-up. I wasn't going to show him where it grew until later. Until I knew he could be trusted..."

Knudson's lips move as he tries to find the words. "Maddox...have you gone insane?"

I can tell he wants Venn to shut up in front of the sheriff. He was all too eager to have me spill my guts. Now he's afraid one of his star students is going to be hauled away in handcuffs.

"Insane? No more than usual." Venn confidently strides over to the sheriff, pulls the bag from his hand and holds it up in the light. "Keel moss. It grows in the north end of the forest. Mrs. Peters asked me to collect some. Used in a tea, it's a folk remedy for arthritis. She says it helps." He opens the bag and holds it open for the sheriff to smell.

The sheriff inhales then looks up at Venn. His face slackens.

"Oh boy!" says Venn with a grin. "You didn't think? Oh man! My apologies. Seriously?" He shoots a glance over at me. "And you thought this poor kid was a drug dealer? And here I am naming Mrs. Peters. The thought of her being handcuffed and hauled from school. Good God."

Knudson takes a whiff of the bag and shakes his head. "I'm calling Mrs. Peters in here."

"She'll be here any minute. As soon as I heard Whitlock had been arrested, I kind of deduced why and sent for her," replies Venn.

"This isn't funny, Maddox," barks the sheriff.

"No, it's not. Harmless, but not funny. Not as harmless when Parker Academy's star basketball player got caught with an ounce of cocaine at a party two weeks ago you busted up. But that didn't make it into the papers, did it? I don't even think he got a suspension, did he? Weird? Not funny, either."

The sheriff glares back at Venn. "I don't know what you think you heard."

"Only what he tells everyone when he brags about it,"

replies Venn. "But they have different rules over there, don't they? Apparently at Ellison a student can't even bring moss to a science teacher without the local police thinking he's the head of a drug cartel."

I'd never seen a teenager talk back to an authority figure like that before. He wasn't being a wiseass. He was talking like he was an adult making a case for how foolish they were acting.

"Why pick on poor Marv?" asks Venn.

"We got an email from his old principal telling us to watch out for him," says Knudson with a grouchy tone.

"An email?" asks Venn incredulously. "An email that can have a fake header and return address?" He shakes his head. "Let me understand this. The internet told you he was a notorious drug dealer?"

"That's enough, Venn," snaps Knudson. He turns to the sheriff. "I think we should let this go."

The sheriff hands the bag to Knudson. "Square this up with Mrs. Peters." He shoots me and Venn a look. "Something doesn't add up here." He turns to Knudson. "Deal with your students." Shaking his head, he leaves.

"Excuse me, sheriff," says Venn. He reaches down behind me and pulls off the handcuffs. "Let's not leave poor Marv here shackled up." Venn tosses him the handcuffs.

I rub my wrists, not sure how Venn got the cuffs off without a key.

The sheriff pockets them and walks away. Knudson goes back to his office and shouts over his shoulder before closing the door, "No more games, Maddox. The sheriff is already no fan of yours. Don't make things worse."

I look at Venn for an explanation. He's already left the office.

I stand up and try to build up the nerve to knock on the principal's door to ask for my backpack and books back.

The way Venn handled it, I knew everything was a setup. But for what? I didn't get hauled away to jail. He came in at the last moment and stopped that from happening.

What was the point?

What did he accomplish?

What was next?

If I had known, I would have run home right then.

CHAPTER EIGHT

Berserker

I feel the spider's legs as it crawls down my arm and heads toward my neck. It itches like tiny pinpricks traveling down my arm. Every step brings the sensation that it could be the prelude to a sharp bite as its fangs deliver poison into my veins. Even with the hood over my head, I can sense Venn's eyes watching me.

I fell for his little trap.

Again.

He didn't even wait until the next day. The Bull Man attacking me in the library, getting busted in the hallway by the sheriff and handcuffed in front of everyone, it was all a prelude for what was happening now.

Venn was sliding me around his chessboard at his will. I

couldn't avoid him because I didn't know where he'd be coming for me. I never thought I'd step into it so willingly.

I should have ignored the note.

I should have gone home.

But I didn't.

I had to know. I was curious. Right now that curiosity has manifested itself into a black widow spider that's crawling down my forearm. Sweat streams into my eyes as I try to remain perfectly still.

Try not to breathe...

The bell rang, emptying the halls, and I was spared the looks of the other students over my arrest. While that helped avoid short-term embarrassment, they didn't know I was exonerated either. As far as everyone knew, I'd been hauled away in a police car with flashing lights and was getting fingerprinted and was about to be shoved into a cell with muggers and rapists.

Everyone who saw me get busted in the hallway had undoubtedly told all their friends. Either I was a dirtbag drug dealer or the fool who fell for Venn's little pranks.

He had to be some kind of sociopath. The two times I'd seen him, he'd been well-spoken, polite – not a plotting monster. You could see the intelligence behind his eyes, but I never saw a stray look or a nervous glance that betrayed something more sinister.

He was like a politician. He has complete control of himself – and even the people around him.

Was the fake pot payback for what happened in the library? Was it a threat – next time it'll be real?

He did it so easily. Benny seemed like a good guy. Why wouldn't I take the book to the next class? I never suspected him.

Carrie, Benny and the Bull Boy were all part of his network. Who else? I couldn't trust anyone.

Walking back to class, I glance through a classroom window at dozens of faces illuminated by light reflecting from a screen. They appear ghastly. All similar. All pale white and expressionless.

How many of them were in Venn's circle?

A row of classroom doors stands before me. Each one could be harboring dozens of allies of his. Each potential friend I make could really be one of Venn's. Every one of them, trying to get my trust so they can do something to me – make me into an even bigger jerk.

What for?

Make me quit school?

Get me to do something even worse?

When people talk about the high test scores kids in Japan and other Asian countries get, they leave out the darker side: the shaming and bullying. Fail a test and bring your class average down, your classmates will gang up on you afterwards. The teachers hold them responsible for making sure you fall in line. Bullying is encouraged.

It's not as bad as it used to be. But their test scores aren't as high as they once were. Kids didn't kill themselves there over broken hearts. It was because their peers drove them to it. On purpose.

I take the same empty table in the back of the lunchroom. I reach for my bag in my backpack and remember I forgot to pack a lunch. My stomach growls, telling me that $5 bill I've been holding onto needs to be broken.

Money is so tight, I don't bother Mom about an allowance. For lunch I just make do with what's in the fridge. She's doing her best. I'm old enough to look out for myself.

I see the other kids with their lunch trays filled with steaming pasta and salads. My belly protests the unfairness of it all.

I walk over to the checkout and buy two chocolate milks. That'll leave enough money in case of an emergency.

What kind of emergency will a couple dollars help me with – I need to buy a Band-Aid and a bag of Skittles?

On top of all this, I need to get a job. It'll have to be something within walking distance. There isn't much around here. Between the school and my apartment, there's a convenience store and little else.

No money. No friends.

All I have is enemies right now.

This town sucks.

I pay for my milk and sit back down. The chocolate milk placates my stomach for a little while. The sugar will give me something of a boost until I get home and crack open a microwave dinner.

A laugh echoes across the cafeteria. My head snaps up from my thoughts. That was Venn's laugh.

He's sitting at a table with Carrie, Benny, the Bull Boy and a few other kids I don't know. Nobody is looking in my direction.

I guess it was a private joke.

Hah hah for them.

I think about walking over there and confronting them. I'm not afraid of Venn. Not physically.

Maybe he's like some martial arts master. I can still do some damage.

That's the secret to winning a fight: Don't worry about winning. Just focus on causing the other guy a lot of pain. If you don't care how much pain you get, then you'll always win a tit-for-tat fight. Maybe not bodily, but mentally.

My stomach is still growling. I finish my first chocolate milk and crack open the second carton.

I notice a white envelope sticking out from under my backpack on the table. Somebody placed something underneath.

Crap.

I left my bag alone when I went to the counter.

I'm so stupid. An hour ago I was about to go to jail for holding a book I didn't bother to look inside. Now I leave my bag by itself.

I think about the warnings in airports not to leave your bags unattended. God forbid you leave your duffle bag alone to go stand in line at Starbucks – some drug dealer might plant a kilo on you or a terrorist could shove an explosive tube of toothpaste in your side pocket.

My bag has me afraid. Jesus Christ, it's my own bag. Now I don't want to touch it.

I feel like calling over a teacher and telling them I accidentally left it alone.

They'll think I'm nuts. Then what? Is this how paranoia starts? Next I'm saving my pee and refusing to leave my room?

I slide the envelope out from under my bag. Part of me is saying, "Blow up already. Get it done."

It's a fancy-looking envelope. The kind one of my mother's friends would send with a wedding invitation.

On the front is written my name, Marv Whitlock, in fancy script.

I glance over at Venn's table. Nobody is watching me. The envelope doesn't feel thick. That doesn't mean it couldn't hold an acid blotter, a death threat or photos of my mom. Hell, where'd that thought come from?

I slide out the card inside. It's an expensive paper stock. The writing is in gold letters.

It's an invitation.

> Marv,
>
> You're cordially invited to Room 142 as soon as the bell rings.

If you decide not to attend, your presence will be missed, but will be understood.

We invite you to join us with the promise of adventure and mystery revealed.

Sincerely,

V.

What. The. Hell?

It was the kind of thing you got to go to the prom or a tea party. Or a funeral...

Things happen in threes, Dad used to say.

Going by the last two acts, I can't even imagine what the third will be.

My funeral?

I couldn't think of anything stupider than going to that room. Doing that would be the dumbest thing in the world. Dumber than that.

I turn the invitation over, looking for some other piece of information, some clue as to what it's all about.

The bell rings.

I head to Room 142.

Fine, let's play this out.

I'm ready for anything. If they all jump me, I'm going to do some damage. SERIOUS DAMAGE.

They caught me off-guard with the Bull Boy.

The sheriff and fake weed came out of nowhere.

Now I KNOW something is going to happen.

If I'm going down, I'm taking some of them with me. Venn may be a little badass himself. But he doesn't have my rage.

What he forgot is this: I've got nothing to lose.

In the last 24 hours I've faced fear, public humiliation, and the threat of being expelled and going to jail.

There's nothing left.

Nothing except my anger.

I stomp down the hall toward 142.

Part of me, no, all of me, wants them to try something.

Anger at Venn.

Anger at the world for taking my dad away.

Judo is known as the "gentle way," but there's nothing gentle left. That died with Dad.

These mothers have no idea what's coming.

CHAPTER NINE

N.E.M.

Room 142 isn't a classroom. It's just a door between 140, the art room, and 144, a supply closet. There's no window on the door, just a metal vent at the bottom. I turn the handle and look inside – prepared for anything. At least I think I'm prepared.

It's dark. There's a staircase.

Room 142 is the entrance to the basement.

At the bottom of the stairs I can see some light from beyond the pipes and girders.

A basement. It had to be the basement. Nothing good ever happens in basements.

Hell, you can get assaulted in the library. Lord knows what goes on down here.

I walk down the steps. Somewhere a furnace kicks on and pipes begin to rumble. At the bottom of the stairs is a stack of boxes and chairs piled onto one another. Beyond this is a ring of light.

There's a group of people standing in a circle. Maybe a dozen of them. They watch me as I walk down. Venn is sitting in an old wooden desk in the middle. There's a metal lunch pail in front of him.

"I'm glad you decided to join us," says Venn in a friendly tone, as if this was a school picnic.

I reach the bottom of the steps with my fists clenched. I give everyone a wary look. Carrie and Benny are toward the back. Bull Boy is standing a few feet away from Venn, leaning on a laundry cart filled with deflated dodgeballs.

"You know Carrie and Benny," says Venn. He nods to Bull Boy. "I think you know who Rhode is. The rest of us you'll probably get to know a lot better in the near future."

I glare at him. "Why the stupid games?"

"Stupid? I'm hurt. A lot of planning went into all this. How about we play one more and I tell you?" says Venn.

"What if I refuse?"

"Then why did you come down into the dark basement? You didn't come here to say you quit, Marv. You came here to see this to the end."

He keeps using my first name as if we're old friends. Everyone else is watching me without any expression. All the tension is on the pail sitting on the desk.

"The next game is in here," Venn says as he touches the

pail. "But before we start, I'm going to tell you a quick story. I'll then give you a chance to go back up the stairs and we'll all be done. I'll never bother you again. None of us will. In fact, it'll be like we don't even exist."

The last sentence sends a chill up my spine. Like they didn't exist? The atmosphere of the basement has my mind going to all kinds of weird places. The expressionless faces all around me seem like something from another world. I'm spooking myself out, making this more sinister than it is. These are just kids with a cruel sense of humor.

"Nathan Edward Miles," says Venn. "Does the name mean anything to you? It shouldn't. He died at 18. He never really grew up." Venn points to a carving in the desk. There are letters etched into the top. "N.E.M. This was Nathan's desk. He carved his name here a long time ago. It's the only mark he left on the world. Not long after he made this he died in a place called Kham Duc. It's a soggy piece of ground in Vietnam.

"Nathan was stabbed in the stomach by a bayonet and then dragged off into the jungle as a prisoner of war. He survived three days before dying of infection.

"What do you think Nathan's last memories were? This high school? Some chick he made-out with at a Led Zeppelin concert? The family he'd never have?"

Venn traced his finger around the name. "We don't know. Nobody knows. Nathan is gone. He died just a few years older than you and me. You can bet 19 doesn't feel all that different than 15. He was a kid. We're just kids. We're about to enter a world we didn't make.

"Nathan got sent off to a part of that world he didn't know or understand. The reasons were irrelevant as he died in the jungle. He was a teenager dying for a world he didn't create. Dying for a cause that was forgotten and ignored. All that's left of Nathan is these three letters. There's not even a body. Just a pair of dog tags handed over at the end of hostilities. Nathan wasn't those dog tags. He was a kid like you and me. Bored one day, he carved his name here."

Venn sits back and stares at the letters. "If I hadn't found it, nobody would even know his name today. Think of me as his ghost as I sit here. I'm telling you what Nathan could have said when he was dying in the jungle, trying to keep his guts from spilling out, knowing he was about to die.

"When you leave this place and move on to the adult world, you're stepping into a world not of your making. You can't change that. You just have to accept that. Until then, I want to give you an alternative. Something Nathan didn't have. Something he could have looked back on in the jungle as he lay dying and be glad for. Something more than anyone else has."

"What?" I ask.

"I can't tell you just yet. We have one more game. It's the worst one of all. But I can tell you this: It's not worse than what Nathan went through. You'll probably survive."

Venn opens the metal pail and pulls something out of a bundle. He opens it on the table. It's a chain mail glove. "Pick it up."

I hesitate.

"The glove won't hurt you. It's just that. Don't be afraid."

I pick up the glove to prove I'm not scared. I try to ignore how ghastly he looks in the light right now. His eyes are in deep shadows.

"Here's the way the game works," Venn explains. "You can drop the glove anytime you want. If you do, the game stops and you go your way. You don't find out what I'm talking about. We don't exist for you and vice versa.

"If you hold onto it and endure what's next, then you pass. Got it?"

"What happens?"

"No more questions," says Venn, shaking his head. "Just drop the glove now and leave if it's too much."

My hand is clinching the glove. I can't back down. I can't run away.

Venn smiles. "Let's begin." He nods to someone, the sour-looking one talking to Rhode yesterday. "This is Richard, he's a bit of a sadist. Don't worry, nobody will be shoving marker pens up your privates or making you grab things in a toilet. This isn't about latent homoeroticism or demoralizing power fantasies. This is about willpower. This is about pain." He raises an eyebrow on the last word. "Understand?"

"Yes."

Everything goes black as a hood is pulled over my head. My hands are grabbed and raised up. Someone is wrapping my wrists in duct tape. A moment later I'm hoisted into the air so only my toes are touching the ground.

"Let go of the glove if you give up," says Venn.

Something strikes me hard in the pit of my stomach. I lose my breath and pain radiates from my chest.

"Here's the rule," says another voice, I assume Richard's. "I can't leave a big bruise. If I do, you win. If I make you drop the glove, I win. Get to the end and we all win, eh?"

Before I can answer, something whacks me in the back of the knees. The sharp pain makes me buckle.

"Just drop the glove," says Richard.

"Why don't I shove it up your ass?" I snarl.

"Oooh. So you do like those kind of games?"

"Go to hell," I grunt.

Something makes a loud crack. There's the smell of ozone. The sound and smell aren't a good combination.

Oh crap.

He's got a taser.

Metal prongs touch my ribs.

ZAP!!!!!!

I spasm as every nerve screams out. My feet slip and I feel my arms yanked out of my sockets.

"Like that? Kind of a modern hot poker, you think?" Richard taunts.

I say nothing. The metal rings of the gauntlet I'm holding dig into my palm. I'm not letting go.

"Got any piercings?" he asks.

Richard jabs the gun into my nipple and pulls the trigger.

ZAP!!!!!!

"Damn it!" I shout as my pectorals spasm.

"Again!" he shouts before shocking me in the stomach.

ZAP!!!!!! ZAP!!!!!! ZAP!!!!!!

The milk I drank feels like it's boiling and about to explode. I lose my balance again and fall to my side before getting yanked by my wrists.

Richard shocks me again in the thigh. I spasm, but say nothing.

A calm passes over me.

The ZAP!!!!!! begins to change to a muted roar.

I'm not afraid of the shock anymore.

I'm past the pain now.

I'm calm.

I flinch at every touch, but I don't care.

In judo we practice all kinds of pain points. Points between your fingers, under your jaw, gaps between your joints. Your body is full of them. One of the worst is just behind your ear. If you grab someone by the collar and jab the knuckle of your thumb there, you can tip them over as they try to avoid it. We called it Mashi.

Mashi hurts like hell.

Dad showed me that point once. He showed me how to use it on an opponent. He then showed me how to not let it be used on me.

The secret to Mashi is to do it to yourself. You push that point again and again. You endure. You learn to live with it. You learn to not care.

The secret to any pain isn't to run from it – it's to run

head-first into it.

This kind of pain is only temporary. It's not chronic. It's not cancer...

"You're pathetic," I shout at Richard.

A fist slams into my kidney.

"Does that feel pathetic? How about this!"

Something slams into my balls. I see sparks. I think I can hear yelling. The blood rushing in my ear is too loud for me to be sure.

This pain is more than I can endure without crying out, but I don't let go. I can't. I deserve this pain...

There's a low voice behind me. It's someone different. Someone I haven't spoken to before. "You're going to feel it crawl down your hand. If you remain perfectly still, it'll make it to the floor and over to its nest of eggs. If you move, or flinch, it'll think you're a threat and it'll bite you. If that happens, you have about four minutes to make it to the nurse's office. Tell her specifically it was a spin haired black widow. If they treat you with the wrong serum, you'll go into cardiac arrest. Repeat after me, spin haired black widow."

I'm trying to focus. The words sound long and drawn out.

"If you can't say the words, then let go of the gauntlet."

"NO!" I shout. I can't let go. I can't give in. I have to fight it.

"Then repeat the words. Spin haired black widow."

"Spin...haired...black...widow..." I mumble. My leg is beginning to quiver. Pain shoots out from different parts of my body.

"Last chance."

"No." It comes out as a whisper. "Spin haired black widow."

Something touches the back of my hand. I feel tiny feet walking across my skin.

It's on my wrist. I try to remain still. Stinging beads of sweat fall into my eyes inside the hood. My leg won't stop quivering.

The spider crosses my wrist and passes over the tape holding it bound. I relax until I feel it on my forearm. My fingers are twitching.

The spider passes by my elbow. It walks over the faint mark where I give blood. Every time I visited the hospital I went to the blood center and donated – as if my small sacrifice would give my dad extra time.

I went every day, waiting for a different nurse so they didn't recognize me. On the fifth day I passed out in the chair. That's when they realized what was up. After they told Dad, he asked me to stop in slow, exasperated breaths from his bed. There were tears in his eyes. He feared what was happening to me more than him. He made me promise to stop doing that. His face was so gray. His eyes so withdrawn.

"No more, Marv," he'd told me.

The spider is on my bicep. A chill moves across my skin. It's heading toward the cuff of my shirt.

My heart beats furiously as I try to will the spider to go outside my shirt and not inside.

Tiny feet walk under the sleeve.

The spider is trapped under my shirt.

I close my eyes and try to remain perfectly still, hoping the fabric doesn't move and crash down on the spider, making it angry.

The spider reaches my shoulder. It crawls over to the nape of my neck. My upper back trembles. I can't stop it.

The spider is agitated. It's stopped moving. It's just below the hood.

Does it want to crawl inside?

Oh God.

I can let go of the gauntlet.

Then what? They'll swat it away?

Didn't the voice say it was too late?

The spider walks down my back. I can feel it going over my spine as if it were a huge mountain range. Each tiny step only takes it a little further. My body is a vast continent.

My breath is coming in short gulps. I forgot to breathe and have started hyperventilating.

"Spin haired black widow. Spin haired black widow," I whisper over and over as a mantra.

The spider is at the small of my back.

My pants are loose. I'm afraid it's going into them. I lose touch with the spider for a moment.

I relax when I think it's on the outside of my pants. My dumb baggy pants.

Something touches my stomach.

The spider is crossing the hair near my navel. My belly

begins to spasm. The spider stops.

Oh crap.

Something bites into my skin.

Waves of pain ripple across my body.

My hands jerk at my restraints and I fall to the ground. Somehow they untied me when I wasn't paying attention.

I pull away the hood. The basement is empty.

I don't have the energy to stand up. I crawl across the dusty floor toward the stairs.

I keep repeating, "Spin haired black widow."

The stairs might as well be Everest. I can't climb them. I make it three steps then feel the black curtain closing around my vision.

CHAPTER TEN

The Sound of Poison

The sound of poison rings in my ear. I know it doesn't make any sense, but I'm not quite lucid. My head is ringing. I feel a tingling sensation.

This must be what happens when it gets to your brain. The top of the stairs is a million miles away. I'd have just as much chance jumping to the moon.

I pull myself up a step. The poison still rings.

Then it stops.

The ringing goes away. I can think a little more clearly.

The ringing was the school bell. It wasn't the poison.

My hand goes to my stomach and touches where the spider sank its fangs. The skin is smooth. In the dim light I can't see as much as a bump.

My legs can move. I don't feel the radial sensation of numbness. Somewhere I find the strength to lift myself up to the railing.

One step after another I climb toward the top.

Shadows move past the vent on the door to the basement as students hurry to class. I'm going to be late, but that's not really my concern right now.

Every point of my body cries out. I can still feel where I was shocked. My balls are sore and wrapped in a gauzy numbness.

The bell rings again and I reach the top of the stairs. The handle is too slippery for my sweaty palms. I lean against the door and fall into the hallway.

A boy in a wheelchair rolls past me. He shoots me a glance then hurries on to his class.

I lie in the middle of the floor waiting for everything to go dark again.

It doesn't.

I look at my stomach in the light. There's a small pinprick, but no spider bite.

The spin haired black widow was a lie.

Maybe there was a spider. But that's not what got me. Richard or someone shoved a little needle into my stomach and my brain completed the illusion.

They convinced me I was about to die.

I thought I had died.

You win, Venn. You win.

I'm done here. No more.

I lean against a locker and pull myself to my feet. Something scrapes the wall. I'm still grasping the gauntlet. I walk over to a trash can to toss it. My backpack is sitting in a chair nearby.

For some reason I just shove it inside instead.

A minute later I'm out the back door and walking across the empty football field.

School isn't out yet, but I'm finished. I'll get my GED or do something online. Mom will understand. At least I hope she will.

This is all too much right now.

The wet grass makes a crunching sound as I walk toward the sidewalk and away from here. A cool breeze blows through the forest, rustling the tall trees. I can smell pine.

On any other day, this might be a pleasant afternoon.

Not today.

I walk past the bleachers overlooking the football field and track. The sound of cracking boards is coming from behind a hedge that hides the metalwork supporting the stands.

Crack!

Crack!

Something makes a scraping sound.

Clang! One of the supports is struck.

I hear a growl. Through the leaves there's a movement. Two people are moving back and forth.

I tell myself I don't care. My feet bring me closer.

Through a gap between hedges I see Richard. He's

holding a wooden shaft. Someone is swinging at him. Richard backs up then trips.

The other person leaps over him and straddles him. He shoves his shaft under Richard's neck, pinning him to the ground.

"Yield!" shouts Venn.

"I only meant..." blurts Richard.

"What? You know the rule!"

"You're not the..."

"What? I'm not the what?" says Venn as he pushes his shaft into Richard's Adam's apple.

Richard makes a gurgling sound. "It was a mistake."

"Yes. A big one."

At first it looks like Venn is going to kill him, then he relaxes and lets Richard up.

"Again!" shouts Venn.

"I've had enough," replies Richard.

"AGAIN!" barks Venn. He kicks Richard's staff over to him.

Goddamn weirdos.

I walk away before they can see me. But I'm spotted by Benny on top of the bleachers, talking to Carrie. He gazes down at me and gives me a nod. Mr. Wilson flickers in the wind, pinned to his lapel. Carrie just stares.

I ignore him and keep going.

Weirdos.

On the walk home I try to figure out how I'm going to tell Mom I'm done here. I can't mention anything that happened.

She'll just blame herself, like she does with everything else.

I could fake being sick. She'll either see right through that or panic and make me get some tests.

I'll just have to flat-out tell her that I can't do it. Night school, GED, whatever. I just can't go back to Ellison.

I get to the apartment and go to my room.

A few hours later she opens my door. I give her an angry look. I have my headphones on full volume.

"Everything okay?" she asks.

I stare back at her. I don't have the nerve to tell her. Her question was her way of asking for reassurance. She wants to know that at least this part of her life isn't screwed up. Guess what, Mom? It is screwed up.

"Yeah, fine. Close the door."

I wait for her to say something. Instead she just closes my door with a slam.

Damn. She doesn't even have the energy to argue.

Damn it.

I'm a jerk.

Guess what? That's the theme of the week.

She'll just have to get used to it, because I can't do anything right.

I put my headphones back and try to forget the world exists. At least I don't have to worry about any more stupid pranks, because I'm not going back. I'll tell Mom when she's in a better mood. In the meantime, I'm just going to skip school.

Screw it.

After I get tired of blasting out my eardrums, I turn off my music and just lie there. I can hear the wind blowing through my window. The trees in the forest creek and crickets chirp.

Mom is watching television. I don't remember hooking it up, but I can hear talking. There's a laugh. She's laughing. That's good. There's another laugh. A different laugh. A young man's laugh.

Venn's laugh.

Christ. He's in my living room talking to my mother.

Jesus. Christ.

He just crossed a boundary.

This crap stops now.

CHAPTER ELEVEN

Study Group

I slam open my door. Venn and my mother twist their heads at the sound.

"What the..." I growl.

"Hey buddy," says Venn as he leaps to his feet interrupting me. "I was just telling her about the spider."

I'm dumbfounded. Satan has marched into my house. MY house. And now he's confessing to my mom? All I can do is repeat what he said. "You told her about the spider?"

"Yeah. Embarrassing? Isn't it? But I thought she should know."

"It's funny, Marv," says Mom. "Nothing to be upset about."

"Nothing to be upset about? I thought I was going to

die." I point to Venn. "Did he tell you about the sheriff, too?"

"He laughed at me, too," says Venn.

"Sheriff?" asks my mom.

"Doing one of his classroom talks," interjects Venn. "After I thought I got bit, I ran to him. Marv tried explaining to me it was harmless. I should have listened, him being a nurse's son and all. But no, I'm too scared to listen."

I'm confused. "You got bit?"

"Of course not. I know that now. You don't have to rub it in, Marv. Last time we volunteer to clean the basement, though. Extra credit or not. No more spiders, harmless or the imaginary black widow Benny made up to get me."

So that's his story: We're the best of buds and we were cleaning up the basement and he imagines he got bit by an imaginary spider. Only it's me, level-headed Marv, who tells him to relax.

It's beyond pathological. He's like a teenage Lex Luthor.

Venn nods at me. "Marv took it kind of hard. He was real worried about me."

Mom gives me a smile.

She's falling for his bull.

I want to shout at the top of my lungs that he's a liar. I want to scream all the horrible things he's done to me. I want her to see him for what he really is.

Then what?

I didn't tell her for a reason. I can't let Venn get to me now. I just have to get him out of here.

Before I can say anything, Venn speaks. "Well, time to go. It was nice to meet you, Mrs. Whitlock."

"Are you sure you don't need me to look at the bite?" she asks.

"It was just a scrape. The school nurse put some peroxide on it." Venn lifts the side of his shirt and shows a Band-Aid over his hip. "Pathetic. I know."

He even wore a Band-Aid. I want to rip it off and expose his lie. Knowing what I do now about Venn, he's probably got a matching cut.

"Really, Venn, a spin haired black widow?" asks my mom.

"I know. I'm gullible," says Venn with a shrug. "See you soon."

Not if I can help it.

Venn walks toward the door. He looks back at me. "Well, Marv?"

"Well what?"

"Don't be back too late," says Mom.

"Study group starts in twenty minutes, Marv. Come on. Grab your bag."

"Study group?" I stumble over the words.

"That's what we call it here. You know, homework?" Venn raises an eyebrow and holds the door open.

Two minutes later I'm outside, ready to knock his lights out. Venn hops down the steps in great strides before I can say anything.

He comes to a stop in the parking lot and faces me with a

grin.

"What the hell?" I drop my bag and clench my fists.

Venn sees my anger. "Do you want to hit me?" He turns his head to the side. "Go ahead. I won't stop you."

I remain still, fuming.

"Come on, Marv. You know you've been dying to. Go ahead. I won't even retaliate. And even if I did, you might be able to take me. You cleaned Rhode's clock." Venn grins. "Poor Rhode." He points to his chin. "Go ahead."

"I'm not playing your games anymore."

"No game, Marv. Just a good tension-releasing punch."

"No." My fists unclench. "I'm tired of this."

"Come on, Marv? You're still standing. You gave to Rhode better than he gave you. Believe it or not, you got his respect now. The fake grass? Even if I hadn't stepped in, the sheriff would have let you go when he did a field test on the grass. As far as the basement, come on, we told you what was coming. In the end, you're here and that's all that matters."

I want to punch him, but he won't even put up a defense.

Venn waves his hands in the air. "This is all over. No more games. No more secrets. Well, only one. You'll like this one, though."

"I don't believe you," I reply.

"I've never lied to you," insists Venn.

"You lie all the time."

"I've lied in front of you. Yes. But only to protect you. Mostly. It's all to get to this point. It's all about character.

Like I said in the library."

"Character?" I shake my head.

"Yes. When Rhode came at you as the Ox, that was to see if you were strong. Good lord, you passed that one. You handled that awesomely. Oh God, when you threw him into the table? Priceless.

"The incident with the book was about your sense of honor."

"Incident?" I blurt out. "They almost hauled me off to jail."

Venn's eyes narrow. "I never would have let them."

"What if I'd named you or Benny?"

"You didn't. You had honor. You didn't name Benny because you weren't sure if it was his doing. You didn't name me for the same reason. You could have, but you didn't. You didn't name an innocent man. You have honor."

"Honor?"

"Honor, Marv. How many people in a hundred do you think we could do that to and not have them snitch? Do you have any idea?"

I shake my head.

"And I'm not talking a bunch of wannabe gangsters who aren't snitching because of something they heard on a rap album. I'm talking people who can keep their cool and not start running their mouth. People who'll protect a stranger. How many?"

I shake my head. "Not many."

"Exactly. But I'm going to take you to the ones you can

trust. All of this about here and now. We were testing you. Remember I told you the problem with tests?"

"They don't work when you know they're coming."

"Exactly! I couldn't tell you."

"I didn't ask to be tested."

"But I knew you'd want what you get if you passed."

"How?"

"Everyone wants it."

"What?"

"I have to take you there."

"Where?"

Venn hesitates for a moment. "Well, that's a secret..."

"Good lord. You and your secrets! I'm going back to my room."

"No you're not, Marv. This one is worth it. No Demon Oxes. No fake drugs. No spiders."

"No getting punched in the balls?"

"Uh, yeah. Richard lost control. I had a talk with him."

A talk? So that's what the stick fight was about. Venn was beating up on him because Richard sucker-punched me. These people were weird.

"So, Marv? Have it in you for one more mystery? No torture, public humiliation or physical attack this time. Just something cool."

"This better be a time machine or a UFO," I reply.

Venn lets out a laugh that echoes through the parking lot. "Oh, man. You're almost half right."

He's insane.

"Your word? No more tricks?"

"Yes, Marv. I swear it."

"All right. Show me." I'm insane.

"Excellent. There's just one little catch." Venn pulls a long piece of black fabric from his pocket. "You have to wear this."

"A thong?"

"Um, no." He holds it up and looks at it in the streetlight. "I never thought of it that way. It's a blindfold."

"Jesus Christ."

"It's the condition."

"Fine. Now?"

"Not yet. Just when we get to the edge of the woods," says Venn.

"Oh lord. Just wait until after I'm dead if you guys are going to rape me."

Venn's laugh didn't exactly reassure me.

Why did I follow him, I rationalized? If he was a man of his word then the tormenting would stop and he was being serious with me. If he wasn't, then refusing wouldn't make a difference.

CHAPTER TWELVE

Into the Woods

Rape and murder jokes are funny to a teenager until you're being led into the woods in a blindfold by the most potentially sociopathic person you've ever met.

Venn didn't make me put on the blindfold until we reached a path between the apartment complex that bordered the edge of the forest. It was already dark out. The tightly packed trees loomed in front of me like an impenetrable wall designed to keep out giants.

As he walks me through a narrow trail, grasping my elbow, he tells me to duck or to step over something. It's slow-going.

My mind keeps trying to rationalize why I've let him lead me here. He can't really be a serial killer? I mean, they're always loners.

Venn has lots of friends. More than me.

Charles Manson had friends, too. So did Jim Jones.

Crap.

This is some kind of cult thing...

"Heh," I ask, "you're not going to sacrifice me on an altar or anything?" I try to make it out to be a joke.

"Don't be stupid," says Venn.

I breathe a small sigh of relief – not that he would tell me the truth if he was going to.

"It's not a full moon," he continues. "It'd be a total waste."

"Yeah. Right. Of course." I let out a tepid laugh.

We walk a little farther. Venn grabs my shoulder and stops me. "Hold still." His voice is a whisper. "There's someone out there."

I don't move. Maybe I should? What if it's my mom and the cops coming to rescue me?

What if? Venn would probably talk his way out of that.

They could find him standing over my dead body, holding a bloody knife, and he'd convince them I killed myself – all eighteen times I stabbed myself. Venn had that kind of charisma.

That's the word – charisma.

It makes you want to believe the best. It makes you want to think it'll all turn out well.

It's what cult leaders have. It's why people follow them. It's why they get them to do stupid things – like let them blindfold them and lead them into the woods.

After a minute goes by, Venn grabs my arm again and moves us on. "We're fine."

"Great. Couldn't be more perfect," I say. "So, uh, Venn, this isn't like, um...some cannibal thing?" I make the worst attempt at sounding like a joke.

"No, Marv. And it's not a date either."

"Uh yeah..." That was a weird thought. "Good for that."

"I think Carrie likes you, though," Venn says.

"What?"

"Don't say anything to her. She'd kill me."

"Really? Carrie?" It's the first normal conversation I've had since I got here. A girl likes me?

Even though she's an Amazon, she is pretty. I try to think of what she looks like with her hair down. My stomach is filled with butterflies at the thought of talking to her.

We keep marching through the woods and I try to wrap my head around the idea of a girl having a crush on me. It makes me nervous.

My brain does a backflip. A minute ago I was worried that Venn was going to carve out my liver and eat it. Now he's got me thinking some girl likes me.

"You're very clever, Venn."

"Thank you, Marv. Um, you're very, uh, stoic," he replies, treating my comment as a compliment.

"I mean, you're good at distracting me."

"Oh. Still afraid I'm going to murder you?"

"At least my hands aren't tied," the words almost die in

my mouth as I realize I might be giving him ideas.

"You're not a prisoner, Marv. You could run away at any time. I wouldn't stop you. Although at this point, you'd be quite lost. These woods are deep and we're going somewhere very few people know about."

"That's, um, not very reassuring."

"If we wanted you dead, you'd be dead," he replies matter-of-factly. "Lots of places to hide a body out here."

"Maybe it's more convenient to get me to walk to the killing grounds."

"True. Good point."

"I've been thinking that over."

"This is interesting to me," he stops for a moment, "I have to know something."

"My blood type is AB-."

"Yum."

I feel my stomach drop.

"We're not vampires, Marv. Maybe Richard. But not me or anyone else."

"Well there's that bit of comforting knowledge."

"My pleasure. What I want to know right now is what you think this is about. I'm curious. What's your best theory?"

"Seriously?" I ask, not knowing where to look.

"Yeah. You have to think this is leading somewhere. Where do you think this is going?"

"I think it's another prank. I think you're going to stop talking and you're going to leave me all alone. Probably not murder me. But just leave me out here in the woods." The words just form themselves.

"You think I'm going to abandon you?"

"I hope not. But that's what I'm afraid is going to happen," I reply.

"So you're afraid of the worst, but hope for the best?"

"Well, the worst would be you murdering me out here. So, not that. But yeah, I still hope for the best."

Our feet hit hard stones.

"And what's the best?" asks Venn.

"That you're just having some fun. Maybe leading me back to the apartment complex."

"That's the best you can imagine?" he asks.

"The best I could hope for," I reply.

"Poor, Marv. Remember when I said this would be awesome?"

"Right now, not having my liver carved out of my stomach sounds awesome," I say.

"You need to imagine a little bigger."

Venn brings me to a stop. My footsteps echo. Through the blindfold I can see faint light.

Venn's hands reach up to the knot and untie it. "Marv, welcome home."

My eyes adjust to the lights all around me.

We aren't back at the apartment building.

I'm in the middle of a circle of people. I count at least fifty. They are faces from school. But instead of jeans and T-shirts, they're wearing armor and chain mail. Each one holds a torch.

The firelight illuminates the room around us. The walks are stone and faded into a dark ceiling. Tapestries hang from the walls. Before me stands a pedestal. On it sits a carving of a black dragon.

"This is our world," says Venn. "And we want you to be a part of it."

Holy. Crap.

I was standing in a medieval castle.

They have a castle.

They were knights.

Mind blown.

CHAPTER THIRTEEN

Dragon Rook

I look at Venn for an explanation. He just grins. I find the words eventually. "Where are we?" I almost say "when."

"Somewhere in the forest. I can't tell you where yet."

He raises his hand. He's holding a metal dagger. "There's a little matter of a blood pledge and I can tell you everything."

"Blood pledge?"

"A promise," says Venn. "Just a little nick and offer it to the Black Dragon," he points to statue. "You must promise us you won't reveal our secrets." He hands me the knife, handle first.

I don't ask what kind of secrets. I just take the knife and cut my hand. "Like this?"

"More than enough," says Venn. "Place your hand on the head of the dragon and repeat after me."

I walk over to the dragon and place my bleeding hand on its head.

"I solemnly swear," says Venn.

"I solemnly swear," I repeat.

"On my blood."

"On my blood."

"On my soul."

"On my soul."

"On my honor."

"On my honor."

"To keep these secrets."

"To keep these secrets."

"And to share them with no one outside my clan."

"And to share them with no one outside my clan."

"Amen."

"Amen."

Venn shakes my bloody hand and guides me to the circle of people. I shake each of their hands. Leather gloves and metal gauntleted hands shake back and grasp my elbow. Some are gentle on the wound. Richard is not. He squeezes my hand and looks me in the eye. "Welcome," he says in a very unwelcoming way.

When I get to Rhode he gives me a nod and shakes my hand gently. Benny gives me a big grin. Carrie nods then looks away. Okay...

When I'm finished bleeding on everyone, Venn hands me

a handkerchief. "Wrap your hand, brother. Now I'll show you what this is really about."

"There's more?"

"You didn't think we just stand around here dressed in armor? This is about something bigger."

"Bigger?"

"Treasure."

"Treasure?"

"Yes. The part where you repeat everything I say is over. Follow me to the tower."

I walk down the hall after him. They have a tower?

We reach the bottom of a staircase that winds upwards into the shadows. "We built this," says Venn. "Our clan did. Over many years." He slaps a block of stone. "It's mostly poured concrete. A lot faster than carving rocks. But we built it. Adding to it year after year. We kept adding until we had this."

"A castle," I say.

"Our castle. Now it's your castle, too. Dragon Rook." Venn grabs a torch and climbs the steps.

I follow him up, trying to gauge how big this all is.

"The castle is in the middle of a crop of redwoods that are almost 300 feet tall. The only place you can see us is directly overhead. It's really well hidden. The reason we built this is because of what's out in the forest."

"What?"

"The treasure."

"Treasure?"

"Hidden by the person who started this all. It's a kind of game. Only it's not a game in the sense that there's a referee, or that it's not real. This is very real, Marv. Real as your life."

"Who started this?" I ask.

"It kind of evolved over time. The way it's done. But it was started by someone we call the Game Maker. He put this all in motion."

I'm trying to fully understand what 'this' was.

We reach the top of the stairs and come to a landing that opens onto an open turret. The forest is all around us like a dark blanket. I can hear crickets, frogs and owls. The stars shine overhead as the wind blows at my jacket.

Venn sits on the ledge with his back to the forest and faces me. "You'll hear different versions of the story, but this is probably the most accurate. The Game Maker was young like you and me once. Only he had a condition that made him weaker as he got older. It was a muscular disease. His parents were rich, but they couldn't do much for him. He spent his time out here in the woods, walking around with a cane. The forest belonged to his family, actually his grandfather.

"His grandfather was supposed to be a real jerk. Made his money in some shady ways. But he was also the source of the family money. Nobody knew how he got it. One day the Game Maker found out. He was digging around in his grandfather's library and found a secret room. Secret room? I know, this sounds like bull, but we're here, right?"

I nod. I'm still wrapping my head around the castle.

"Inside the room he found a safe. He spent months trying to figure out the combination. He'd wait for his parents and his grandfather to leave and he'd go in and try a different combination. Finally he cracked it. He figured out the combination.

"Nobody knew where he got his money from. His grandfather traveled a lot, overseas, he knew government officials and not the good governments..."

"What was inside?"

Venn grins, "A stack of gold bars half as tall as him."

"Gold?"

"Gold, Marv. Not just any gold. The Game Maker saw where his grandfather got his wealth. Stamped into each bar was an eagle and a swastika."

"Nazi gold?"

"Nazi gold. The Game Maker found out the family secret. His grandfather had been a collaborator in World War II. He'd worked for the Nazis and fled right when the war ended.

"So the Game Maker took the bars out one by one and hid them somewhere out here. His grandfather was already senile by then. No one knew what was gone.

"The Game Maker inherited everything anyway. But he didn't want the gold. He left them for us."

"Us?"

"You, me, whoever could find them."

"Why?"

"Because he was dying. He knew he'd be in a wheelchair by the time he was 20. He couldn't play sports or do anything else. I can't imagine how hard it was to bring the gold out here. But he did, brick by brick. They're out there somewhere. It's the way for a kid who couldn't play any games to get us all to play his game. A game that's been going on for years."

I turn away from the forest and face Venn. I can't tell if he's lying again. The story is so fantastical. He sees my skepticism and reaches into his pocket and pulls out a rag to hand me. There's something heavy inside.

"Open it," he tells me.

I unwrap the cloth. Polished metal shines back at me in the torchlight. It's a gold bar. It has to weigh at least two pounds.

"It's real," says Venn. "You're holding about $50,000 in your hands right now."

The bar suddenly got heavier.

$50,000 dollars. All I can think about is new jeans and a pair of sneakers

"The Game Maker gave it to the clan as proof, so we'd know it wasn't a trick."

"Why not just spend it?"

"It's more valuable as proof and it belongs to the clan. To all of us. Even you, now that you gave us your blood promise."

The weight of that promise is sinking in.

I hold it up and see the eagle and swastika. "This is real?"

I ask, unbelieving.

"Very," says Venn. He points to the forest. "Out there is more. A lot more. The game is to find them."

"Why the castle and the armor? Why not just a metal detector and some shovels?"

"You could search for a hundred years and not make a dent out here. And because that's not the way the Game Keeper wanted it to be found. That wasn't the game. He couldn't play games, so he invented the most elaborate game imaginable. It's been going on for years without a winner."

Venn takes the bar back from me and puts it in his pocket. He dumps the torch into a bucket and everything goes dark. The trees are black against the night sky.

Venn points to something in the distance. There's a faint light far away.

"See that at the other end of the forest?"

"I think so."

"That's Demon Keep. That's the castle that belongs to the kids that go to Parker Academy."

I squint my eyes at the distant flickering lights, trying to imagine what's at the other end of the forest.

"They're after the treasure, too. Whoever gets it first wins."

"The treasure."

"Yes. And more importantly, Marv, winning the Game. You'll understand soon enough. It's about the Game. The Game is everything."

"More important than the gold?"

"To some of us it's just a trophy. I think you'll understand. But first you have to learn the rules."

"Rules?"

"It's what keeps us from killing each other. It's also why the Game has gone on so long."

"How long is that?"

Venn heads back down the steps. "Too long. I'm going to change all that. I'm going to do it with your help."

CHAPTER FOURTEEN

The Game

"The Game," Venn explains as we step back into the main hall, "is simple to understand, so far, impossible to win. So far..."

There's the sound of wood hitting wood as two people go at it with large wooden shafts, taking turns striking and blocking. Other people are working on armor made from football pads, hockey helmets, chain mail, leather and anything else. Others are just talking among themselves and hanging out.

Venn points to the rafters above us. "This used to be a barn. It barely made it through the first siege. So we rebuilt over time with concrete blocks. First we built the wall you'll see outside. Then we made the great hall, here. Finally, we added the tower. That was only finished last year. Up until then, it was just a wooden platform."

I looked around at the stone blocks and high ceilings. Behind the throne and past the entrance to the tower was a corridor blocked by heavy doors, similar to the ones I assume I was led in from.

"It looks like a lot of work," I say lamely.

"It was. We've been working on it for a long time. Close to 5,000 blocks in all. But in any given year, there's about 150 of us in the clan. After a while it adds up. It's just one part of the Game."

"Building a castle?"

"Building a defense," he replies. "Follow me." Venn heads toward the doors in back of the throne dais.

"Who sits there?" I ask.

"Anybody who wants to," replies Venn. He knocks on the doors and there's the sound of metal sliding. The doors swing open to a narrow hallway lit by two torches. A stocky teen in a leather tunic is standing on the inside. A large staff is leaning against the wall.

Venn continues to talk as we walk down the hall toward a room at the end. "The Centaurs, that's what Parker Academy calls themselves, have half a map. We have the other half. To win the Game, we need both halves and to decipher the code. They keep theirs locked up in Demon Keep. We keep ours hidden here."

"Stupid question. Why not just share the reward?"

Venn stops at the entrance and looks back at me for a

moment. "You'll understand. For one, it's not allowed. To play the Game we have to agree on one winner. Second, it's not about the treasure. Why don't teams in the Super Bowl agree to a tie? Because that's not the point."

We go through another door. Inside is a large oak table with a candle next to a map.

"This isn't the map. This is something we work on." Venn points to the dark gray sea of trees. "This is the forest. We call it the Realm. This is where the Game is played." He points to a stylized drawing of a castle with a spire. "We're here at Dragon Rook." His finger traces across the map to another castle. This one is built into a hill. "This is Demon Keep. More of a maze of tunnels. We build. They dig."

Between the two castles are thick clusters of trees, hills, ravines, streams, and several small lakes and ponds.

"To win, we need their map to match with ours. Not this map. But the one we have hidden away. Like our map, it's probably locked away somewhere in their castle. To get their map, we have to take their castle. That's the game."

"Is that all," I reply.

Venn smirks. "To do that, we have to be able to defend our castle and lay siege to theirs. That's the first complication of the Game. If we're attacking, we have to be defending. We're roughly matched in people. Part of the key is being able to mobilize them quickly. We have to get from our end of the forest to their end and then lay siege."

"Siege?" I ask.

"Tear down their doors, break down a wall, sneak in,

whatever it takes. The challenge is that it's a whole lot easier to defend than attack. To that end, we try to take territory." Venn traces a finger along a ridge near the edge of the map. "We spent the whole Summer War trying to recapture this area. The clan had lost lots of territory before I became the leader. It made it difficult to plan an offensive when we barely had any room to defend."

I still wasn't getting it. "When you say 'attack' and 'defend,' what do you mean? Is this like tag or something? How do you attack?"

"This isn't Capture the Flag, Marv. This is real violence. This isn't a game of pick-up touch football. This is war."

"War?" I ask. "Are you talking about killing each other?"

Venn shakes his head. "God, no. We're not savages, Marv. We want something. They want something. To get it, we have to use force. Same as one of your judo matches. Only we have to keep ourselves from letting things get out of hand. We use different combat methods, singlestick, full-contact fighting, and then a form of nawajutsu." Venn raises an eyebrow. "Are you familiar with that?"

"You mean with a torinawa, the capture rope?"

"Yes. We use a thick knotted rope. After you get someone into a submission hold you use the cord to tie them up. That's how you defeat them."

"Let me get this right. You go out there in armor, knock each other around with wooden swords and try to tie each other up?"

"Pretty much. If we actually killed each other, parents

would get upset and then no more game and no treasure. Hitler wins..."

"I could see that," I reply. "And nobody gets hurt?"

"We get hurt all the time. Count on it. We have fewer concussions and sprains than the football team on average. But we're getting smashed up a lot. Remember when I asked you in the library if you'd ever broken anything? I needed to know if you were willing to go all in."

Venn stabbed his finger on Demon Keep. "They want to hurt us. They will hit hard. They will tie you up and drag your ass back to their cage to ransom you back."

"Ransom?"

"Kind of like being benched."

"For how long?"

"Weeks. Months."

"Months? Sitting in their cage? Won't people wonder?"

"You go home at night if you agree not to escape or fight. You can leave the game. But if you want back in, you have to return as their prisoner."

"What if I go home then come back here instead?"

"We wouldn't let you, unless you escaped their custody."

"Sounds like touch football."

"It's called parlay. It's what they used to do in actual warfare. It's why we have things like a Geneva Convention. If we break the rules, then they break the rules. Then all hell breaks loose and we have people going for blood. They don't just tie you up. They break your arm or worse. Just because there are rules we follow doesn't mean this isn't real. Still up for this?"

"And if I say no?"

"You keep our secret and we give you something safe to do. But I know that's not what you want. You're a fighter, Marv."

"I'm in. All the way."

Venn walks over to a chest and pulls out a folder. "I need you to sign something." He hands it to me. "I made this for you."

Mom,

Things are a little too much right now for me with all that's gone on since dad passed away. I need some time to think things over. I've got some friends I'm going to go stay with for a little. I'll give you a call. I just need some space. I'm not into drugs or anything. Nobody is pregnant.

Love,

"What the hell is this?" I ask.

"Your runaway papers. In case you get held captive and can't be parlayed or ransomed," says Venn.

"She'll never fall for this," I reply.

"The police will. Especially when all your friends corroborate the story."

"What if I don't sign this?"

"Then you don't sign it. You won't be a full combatant.

You'll have to sit out the Game." Venn starts to close the folder.

"Hold on. I didn't say I wouldn't sign it. I just...I just..."

"You're not used to lying to your mother. I know. This is a worst-case scenario. We have to protect the Game. Sometimes that means little lies."

The letter gives me an uneasy feeling. "You're not going to ask me to sign a suicide note next, are you?"

"No, Marv. This isn't a death cult."

He sets a pen down on the table. I pick it up and sign the paper. "I could write you a better one, you know."

"It's more of a ceremony than anything else."

A ceremony where they could kill me, hide my body and have my mom and the cops thinking I just ran away.

"So that's it? I'm in?"

Venn puts the note back in the folder and slips it into the trunk. "Pretty much. There's one more little thing."

"Of course."

"Relax. We're short of knights around here. We have a whole long process, but given how you handled Rhode in the library, I'm not worried about you physically. We'll still need to teach you our style of combat and nawajutsu. But before I assign some people to do that, I need to know you're worth the effort."

"If I'm not?"

"We'll make you an auxiliary. You can help defend and maintain the Rook, but you won't be a main part of the campaigns."

"Or get my share of the treasure..."

"Actually, you will."

"I will?"

"Everyone who takes the pledge gets a share if we win it. That is, unless they've graduated."

"So I don't have to go out there and get beat up? I can just stay here and let you guys do the fighting? Why become a knight?"

"Well, Marv, would you rather sit in the bleachers and cheer? Or would you like to be on the field helping us win? That's the real secret to the Game. I told you, you're a fighter."

"Understood. What do I have to do?"

"I don't know yet. I'll figure something out so you can prove you're a warrior."

"Then I'm a knight?"

"You'll be on the front lines."

"Thanks?"

Venn's mind begins to race as he thinks of a suitable test. The longer he thought about it, the more worried I should have been...

CHAPTER FIFTEEN

Morning Workout

The cave is nothing more than a hole in the earth no bigger than a drainpipe. Mud-colored gnarled roots line the walls and dangle from the ceiling like the inside of a rotting pumpkin, which is exactly what it smells like in here. This is where animals go to die – either by their own volition or by being dragged here.

I try to keep close to the wall, not that there's much room to leave to the center. Jagged rocks stuck in the mud scrape and cut into my forearms as I try clinging to the sides. They're like teeth in one long, hellish mouth.

As quiet as I try to be, my feet splash in the puddles along the floor. I'm not doing a very good job of being silent. The roots wrap around my neck and I lose balance trying to pull them free. The quarterstaff isn't much help. There's barely enough room to swing it around or to use it as a walking stick.

Muddy water sloshes over the edge of my sneakers and soaks my socks. The noise echoes throughout the tunnel. I pause to listen to the sound deeper inside. I hear another splash.

It wasn't my echo.

Something is in here with me.

I hear more splashing. Loud splashing. It's the sound something heavy makes as it moves through water.

It's coming toward me fast.

This isn't some teenager dressed in bull armor.

This beast is real.

This beast can kill me.

Hours earlier, Venn showed me the way home from Dragon Rook. He took me along a path that went to the edge of the forest and worked its way back to the apartment complex.

"There are faster ways," says Venn. "But they take you through Centaur territory. You're not ready for that yet."

"I can hold my own," I insist.

"I'm sure you can, against one or two. But they patrol in packs. I don't need you getting caught on your first day. We have to show you how to evade them first. And how to fight back. Remember, this isn't some judo match where you can tap out. They'll choke you out, then put you into a restraint.

This is real fighting."

I nod my head. I'm beginning to understand there's much more to this game than I realize. In judo, after you've been choked out, had your arm twisted out of joint, and been body-slammed so hard you pass out and see stars for the rest of the day, you kind of get used to it. But there are always coaches and referees to put a stop to things.

Out here, I'm beginning to realize, things only come to a stop when one person is unconscious or physically unable to fight back.

"How often do things get out of hand? You know, before a sore loser picks up a rock and tries to crack open a skull?"

"We try to train that out of you. You're no good to us if you're facing manslaughter in juvenile court. They know that, too. That said, we wear armor for a reason. Head shots are verboten, but we wear helmets anyways. If someone misses with an arrow, you don't want to lose an eye."

"Arrows?" Oh crap!

Venn holds his fingers up a half-inch apart. "Needles on dowels, really. Think of it as involuntary acupuncture."

Jesus Christ.

"The best part," adds Venn, "is that a stinging tree sap has a habit of getting on the tips. It's not supposed to, but it does. Burns like a bee sting." He gives me a grin.

"You ever been hit by an arrow?" I ask.

"We call it getting stung, that way parental authorities are out of the loop. And yes. I've been stung a lot. It's how we defend territory. We put archers in trees and they sting anybody not on our side. You will get stung. A lot. But don't worry, the first few time will be by us, so you're prepared."

"Gee, thanks."

Venn left me at the edge of the complex. Mom was already asleep when I got back inside. I tried to sleep myself, but I couldn't take my mind off Dragon Rook, the clan and everything else I'd seen.

Part of me was afraid that this was still one of Venn's elaborate setups.

Fine. I'm in. They had a castle.

My mind was so preoccupied I'd forgotten about everything else.

I hadn't even thought about Dad for the last few hours.

Maybe that's the way it's supposed to be, but I feel guilty now that I realize it. For several hours I'd been pulled into Venn's little world in the forest. I'd forgotten about all the other things in life. I'd forgotten why life had turned to crap lately.

Did that make me a bad son?

I fell asleep with an uneasy conscience.

I wake up to a tapping sound. The sun isn't even up yet and some crazy bird is trying to peck its way into my window. I pull my pillow over my head and ignore it.

Tap. Tap. Tap.

For crying out loud. I pull back the curtain to tell the little jerk to fly somewhere else. There's no bird there.

Something hits the window.

I look down and see Benny and Rhode standing in the grass on the first floor. They wave for me to come down. Rhode is holding a spear.

I remember a weird dream about a castle in the woods and Venn not being quite the sociopath I'd feared.

It was no dream.

My fingers have trouble tying my shoes as I try to wake up. Two minutes later I'm downstairs. Mom won't be up for hours. I left an empty glass of milk on the counter so she'll know I was home.

Benny greets me with a broad smile. "Morning, buddy!"

I give him a nod and glance at Rhode and his spear.

He gives me a grin. There's an uncomfortable gleam in his eye. He hands me the spear. "This is for you."

"Um, thanks. I left your present upstairs."

"This is my present," he replies cooly.

I look at Benny and raise an eyebrow. "Should I be worried?"

Benny nods. "I hope you took a dump, because you're going to be crapping yourself shortly. Venn has decided it's time for your knight's test."

"So soon?" I ask.

"We're at war," says Rhode. "And as soon as you pass, the real fun begins."

"What's that?" I ask nervously.

"You belong to me. I get to train you."

I'm about to point out who made who submit in the library, but I'm pretty sure this is foremost on his mind. "I'm sure I have a lot to learn."

Rhode nods his head.

I hold up the wooden spear. "So, um, we going on a weenie roast?"

"There's no 'we,' " says Benny. "We're just taking you part way."

"There's someone we want you to meet," adds Rhode.

"Vlad the Impaler?" I ask.

"Sawtooth," says Rhode.

"Who's he?" I ask.

Both of them grin back at me. It's a maniacal grin for a secret they can't wait to surprise me with.

If I'd known, I probably would have stayed in bed.

CHAPTER SIXTEEN

Sawtooth

We take a different path into the forest than the one Venn lead me back on last night. At the edge of the woods Benny and Rhode retrieved shields, wooden staffs and their helmets from a hiding spot in a bush.

They kept their helmets slung over their shoulders as they walked me through the narrow trails. We were still mostly in our territory, but that didn't mean there wouldn't be Centaurs on raiding parties or their own patrols.

We stop at the edge of a clearing. "Hold on," says Rhode. He holds up his hand and makes a signal toward the trees. I can't see anyone up there.

"Come on," he says.

"What was that about?" I ask.

"It's so you don't get stung," answers Benny.

"Stung by what?"

Rhode stops us again. "Here, hold this," he hands me his shield. "Raise it above your head."

"Okay? Now what?"

There's a loud snapping sound and the shield feels like it got struck by a hammer. I lower the shield and see an arrow stuck into the wood.

"Oh," is all I can say. I look around, but can't see the archer. "I can't see him," I admit.

"That's the point," says Rhode. "Let's go. Sawtooth is waiting."

I pull the arrow out and look at the needle tip. It's no bigger than a thumbtack really, but I wince at the thought of getting hit by one. The force of the shaft alone would leave a nasty bruise.

I'm beginning to grasp that the taser shocks I got in the basement were merely an appetizer for what was to come. I decide to change the topic to the task at hand. "So tell me about Sawtooth? What am I supposed to do?"

"Avoid him," says Benny. "Avoid him at all costs. He's gored a dozen people and put more stitches on us than we've all done each other."

"I see..." Not actually seeing. "So what or who is Sawtooth?" My head is filled with the image of a deranged forest man running around with a knife, slashing at any kid who comes near – an image not that far from the truth.

"Sawtooth is a wild boar," says Rhode.

"A pig?"

"A razorback. A very, very large one. We have a lot that live in the forest. This one is special."

"How special?" I ask.

"He's a carnivore the size of a tiger. Maybe 500 to 600 pounds."

"A carnivore? I thought pigs were more the scavenger type." I try to interject some nature channel facts to ease my nerves.

Benny interjects, "Explain that to Sawtooth. He's probably part Australian razorback. They'll attack deer and lamb. Sawtooth will chase a man down. He's mean. Real mean." Benny's eyes widen as he says this.

"And none of you with all your weapons have managed to bring him down?"

Rhode turns to me, "We've tried. The arrows and the sticks have only made him meaner. He sees us as a threat." He points to my spear. "That's just so you'll feel better. The shaft will break before you pierce his skin."

I stare at my stick. "Then what the hell is it for?"

"Maybe you can pole-vault over him. He'll probably rip out your testicles with his tusks, though. They're at least two feet long."

"Bull."

I get real nervous when neither one argues with me. Rhode shoots Benny a glance that says, "Let this dumbass find out for himself."

"Crap," I mutter.

"Exactly," says Benny. "And by the way, I'm, uh, sorry for setting you up. I just want you to know. In case..."

I ignore the ominous tone. "So what do I do with this? Go tickle him?"

"We want you to shove it up his ass," says Rhode.

"What?" I blurt.

"No, dumbass," replies Rhode. "You want to avoid him at all costs."

"So why the hell did you wake me up? I was avoiding him quite well in bed. I'd say I was a master of that."

"There's a catch," says Benny.

"Of course," I grumble.

"You have to go into his lair." Rhode says "lair" with a demonic undertone.

"Lair?"

"Lair," repeats Rhode. "Inside there you'll find a sigil."

"What is that? A root?"

"No dumbass. A sigil is a pendant. A Black Dragon pendant. You have to go in there and retrieve it."

"How in hell did it get there?"

"Venn put it in there," says Benny.

"Oh, he's on friendly terms with Sawtooth? Of course."

"No. We waited until Sawtooth went to his watering hole. Then he put it in there."

"I don't suppose Sawtooth is still getting his morning drink?"

Benny shrugs. "Who knows? After we were done, we came and got you."

"So where's Venn?" I ask.

"Sleeping," replies Rhode.

"So it's just us, then?"

They shake their heads.

"Nope. Just you." Rhode points toward a narrow ravine filled with dried thorns. "He lives back in the thorns. There's a small cave. Looks like the earth's bunghole. Can't miss it."

"Wonderful." I take a step down the cliff then turn back. "Seriously. What do I do if I run into him?"

They both shout back at me, "Run, dumbass."

Still not sure if it's a lark or not, I walk down into the ravine holding the spear shaft at my side.

"Don't be a hero," shouts Benny.

I wave him off and start threading through the tangle of thorns.

The canopy of branches grows darker and the brush more claustrophobic. Sharp barbs pull at my shirt and pants and dig into my skin. It's like walking through dusty barbed wire.

I still think it's a put-on until I spot a small puddle of water. I kneel down to get a closer look at the tracks in the water. I spot a cloven hoof.

The trouble is, the hoof is as large as my splayed fingers. It's also deeper than my footprints. Much deeper.

The print is also fresh.

This pig is big. Real big.

I turn back to where I'd last seen Rhode and Benny. They're out of sight beyond a twist in the ravine. The back of my neck starts to tingle.

This isn't funny anymore.

Part of me, actually, almost all of me, wants to go back, but I pick myself up and keep going forward. The thorny brush continues its assault on my skin. I realize the leather armor and chain mail they wear isn't just for decoration.

The thick brush begins to ease up as the ravine ends in a large dirt cliff. An oak tree sits at the top with huge roots grasping the edge like a giant's knuckles. Below the tree and in the middle of the brown earth is the entrance to a cave.

Rhode described it perfectly, only he left out the hairy part.

I try to find my courage by making a joke. "Knock, knock, Mr. Sawtooth. I'm coming into your hairy bunghole of a home."

I wait at the edge of the hole for something to stir inside. Nothing does. I push away some vines and probe my spear inside. Nothing.

Praying he's not home, I step inside.

CHAPTER SEVENTEEN

Hellhole

For a moment. Only a fleeting one. When I first saw the hole in the earth and the entrance to the lair under the tree, I had an image of some kind of fairy-tale adventure. I'd take a few steps into the dark and scary cave and then see Venn and the others gathered around a candlelit table filled with tea and cookies, like some kind of Tolkien Hobbit story.

The instant the smell of decay reaches my nostrils, the image is erased and etched like acid with a darker one. The pit smells like the inside of a rotting stomach. There were dead things here.

Something hard crunches under my foot. I lift my foot and see the spine and ribs of some decaying animal. These weren't bleached bones you see in movies. These still had yellow bits of sinew attached. Blood red vessels cling to the vertebrae. Whatever it was, its head was no longer attached. Large like a dog, Sawtooth may have just dragged it here after it died.

My hands tighten up on the shaft. I push the pointy end – barely sharp enough to write my name in the mud, let alone kill something that weighed a quarter-ton – into the darkness.

I jab the end into the air and try to swat at the loops of roots that are obscuring my view. They resist. For all my effort, I manage to get a few clods of dirt to fall onto my head and break apart, sending dust into my eyes. I scratch at them and make myself sneeze.

Too afraid to fully let go of the shaft, I decide to endure the discomfort. A few paces farther in, I decide to stop trying to pull down the roots. It's like I'm a pathetic mouse trying to wield a giant crochet needle at a sweater that's trapped me inside.

I let the roots scrape past my face, further covering me in a layer of grime and dirt.

My feet make a splashing sound as I step into a puddle. In the thin light I see a small, narrow animal skull half submerged, as if it went to take a drink without its body – or something decided to munch on that before.

All my so-called knowledge about wild boar was academic now. Even if Sawtooth wasn't the carnivore Rhode had lead me to believe, he was dangerous. I was in his home.

I had no doubt now something large lived here. There

was a faint musky smell under the decay and the presence of another source of warmth.

I take a further step and hear the echo of my splash. Only this wasn't an echo, I realize. Something stirred awake by my noise is walking through another puddle.

The sound of water sloshing grows louder.

I hear a snort and a growl.

The ground beneath my feet begins to shake as something large stomps its way toward me.

There's another snort and I swear I can feel the wind of exhalation of the beast as he grows closer.

CRAP.

I see the gleam of his eyes. They're higher than my waist. Roots catch in his tusks and rip from the walls like a paper streamer.

With jet black hair that shines in the dark cave, he looks like a grizzly with a massive snout and two huge sabers jutting from his jaw.

Panicking, I throw my spear in his path.

The slightly less blunt end sticks in the mud a foot in front of him.

Sawtooth twitches his head and snaps the rod between his tusks out of spite.

I run backwards. My heel hatches on a thick root and I start to fall over.

Desperately afraid of getting trampled and gored, I grab at the roots hanging from the roof of the cave. My fingers grasp a thick knot of wood.

Water splashes me as Sawtooth stomps through a puddle. I freeze for an instant, thinking its my own blood as he rips my leg free.

I pull up on the root, lifting my body.

Something bangs my ankle. I kick it up and manage to loop it over another root.

The back of Sawtooth's head rams into my ass, sending me to the ceiling.

I then feel a sensation I'll take to my grave.

As he rushes under me his thick body pulls my shirt up and the sharp bristles of his hair claw at my back like a steel Brillo pad. The pain seers into my flesh. Both the pointy bristles and the friction burn of his speed. I understand more than I ever wanted to know about why they're called razorbacks.

The tunnel grows dark as he closes on the entrance and blocks the light. My stomach turns to ice at the thought that he's going to turn around and finish me. I can't hold myself up much longer. The roots begin to slide out of the mud.

I'm falling.

There's a loud snort and the sound of his steps grows softer.

Light returns to the tunnel.

I think he's gone.

For now.

Relieved and exhausted, I let go and fall into the puddle. I instantly regret it. It smells like stagnant piss. The dirty water seeps into the sores in my back, stinging me all over again.

All I can think about as I crawl to the back of the cave is getting to a bottle of disinfectant as fast as possible.

Then I see it hanging from a root, a silver chain with a small dark metal medallion, reflecting the distant light. It's the image of the dragon I saw in the great hall. It's the sigil of the Black Dragon.

I grasp it and march out of the cave. Sawtooth be damned. He can rip open my belly with his tusk now. I don't care. I'm triumphant. I faced my fear. I found their sigil.

I find my way back through the thorns. Sawtooth is nowhere to be seen.

When I reach the end where I'd left Rhode and Benny, they're standing there with their arms folded.

I hold the sigil up for them to see.

"What took you so long?" asks Rhode.

"Sawtooth," I shout back as I climb up the cliff.

"No, seriously."

"Your damn wild boar," I insist.

"He doesn't live here anymore. Stop lying," says Rhode. "It was all a put-on."

I face him nose to nose. "You're mistaken."

"I think you have an active imagination," he snaps back.

"Are you calling me a liar?" I ask.

"Hey guys," says Benny.

Rhode ignores him. "I think you're working too hard to prove yourself."

"Um, Rhode," interrupts Benny.

"I don't think you're cut out for this," says Rhode.

"HEY DUMBASS," shouts Benny,

I wheel around to confront him. Only he's yelling at Rhode.

"WHAT?" barks Rhode.

"Shut up and look at his back." Benny reaches behind me and pulls something out.

I let out a yell in pain.

Benny shoves the thick tuft of hair in Rhode's face. "What does that look like to you?"

Rhode inspects my back. "Holy crap."

"Looks like Marv wasn't lying," says Benny.

Rhode touches a deep scratch. "Holy crap."

He pulls away more bristles and inspects them. "Well, that doesn't mean it was Sawtooth. There are hundreds of boar out here. You probably just scared some sow and her piglets."

"Why don't you go back there and wait for her?" asks Benny.

"Um, we got class," Rhode says meekly.

"Thought so." Benny gives me a grin and clasps me on the shoulder. "Holy crap, Marv."

I hand him the dragon pendant.

He pushes it back. "No. That's yours, man. You earned it. Holy crap did you earn it."

"I'm still not convinced," grumbles Rhode.

"Whatever, man. We know your position on the matter. Let's go find Marv some hydrogen peroxide before he gets gangrene. Then you can explain that to Venn."

Halfway back, Rhode puts a hand on my shoulder. "Good work, Marv. Good work."

I could tell it was hard for him to work up the praise. He was still smarting from what happened between us in the library, but I could tell it was sincere.

"I mean," he says, "just because it was another wild boar doesn't mean it wasn't a dangerous one."

Benny gives me a wink telling me to leave it alone.

No problem. The pendant on my chest is all the validation I need. I'm so proud I barely notice the wounds on my back. Barely.

"So...are you ready to go to war?" asks Rhode.

War? I'm only beginning to understand what that means to these people. If just testing me involves a fight with a razorback before breakfast, God knows what their idea of combat is going to be.

CHAPTER EIGHTEEN

Knight Club

"Pressman is a prick," grunts Rhode as he slams his staff at my skull.

I barely block it with my own staff. There's a loud CRACK as they make contact. I flinch at the thought of mine snapping and splinters getting shoved into my brain.

I step back out of his range and hold my staff in front of my body defensively.

"Don't go to my left! You just saw that I'm right-handed. My left is my kill zone." He says the word "kill" with a certain amount of glee. "You want to retreat to my right side, where I don't have as much strength." He swings his shaft toward me and taps me hard in the ribs.

"Damn it!" I blurt out.

Carrying on the conversation as if nothing happened, he continues, "He's always pressing us for information about the Knight Club, as he calls it. The other teachers know not to ask. As long as we keep it in the Realm, they don't bother. Half the town went to school here or at Parker."

"How come they don't talk about it?"

"It's just the thing. Maybe they do with each other. But never to us. It'd be like a grownup asking one of us who was banging who or how far you got your fingers up..."

I swing the end of my shaft toward his head. He steps back and slams the butt end of his into my stomach.

"Ooof," I exhale as I fall back.

"You're too damn open! Don't be such a pansy target!"

He slams his shaft into mine again. The sound of impact echoes through the trees. Somewhere Benny is perched on a branch keeping watch with a bow and stingers.

"Anyhow, we don't talk about it to adults. They don't ask us about it."

"You'd think they'd want to know what we're up to."

"I think you kind of just move on once it's over. Like a fraternity or something. I guess that's the closest analogy. You know when you're young why you don't tell the adults about it. When you're an adult, you know not to ask." Rhode drives the staff into my chest.

I may have bested Rhode in the library, but I'm now understanding that may have been more of a fluke. He's deadly with the staff. He's also not a bad teacher.

I get in a few blows of my own, but he doesn't get mad.

When he tries to tap me on the back of the skull, I duck down and sweep one of his legs by hitting him on the back of the knee. He lets out a howl then says, "Nice!"

Today was starting off to be a great day – other than almost having my intestines ripped out by a wild boar – until Pressman's class, where he cornered me and started asking about Venn and the Black Dragons.

From the moment the morning bell rang, everything was different from the previous two days. I got friendly nods from the kids I'd seen last night at Dragon Rook. I was one of them. I was in on the secret. I was a brother.

I hardly knew any of their names yet, but I'd been accepted. Word had already gone out that I'd faced my first challenge. While Rhode wouldn't admit that it was Sawtooth, he'd described the wild boar he never saw, as a man-killer none the less.

Venn walked up to me in the hall and shook my hand. Everyone was watching. He held it above ours heads, like the winner of a prizefight. "I just want you losers to know that this man has balls bigger than all of your pathetic sacks put together."

I hadn't felt like that since I won my first judo trophy. After Venn left, Benny stopped me between classes and made me lift up the back of my shirt to show other members of our clan.

"Check out Marv's skateboarding injury," he'd say.

"Wicked," someone would reply admiring the wounds,

knowing what really happened.

"We never say exactly how an injury happened outside the Realm. So we'll call this a skateboarding injury," Benny informed me after I already picked it up.

"Got it," I replied.

"And whatever you do, don't go to the school nurse. We don't want to let on how much goes on out there. Besides, we have more experience treating this kind of stuff than she does."

"My mom's a nurse."

"She ask questions?"

"She's used to me getting judo injuries."

"Well, now field hockey injuries are going to start adding up."

I got the sense that showing off war wounds was just as much a part of being a part of the Game as anything else. They were bragging rights. Forget medals and trophies, well, except the sigil on my chest. The other kind were bullshit. Scars were real.

We stop Carrie on her way to class. She looked at the scratches and gave me a nod. "Next time, wear some armor."

"I think she likes you," Benny replied, after she walked away.

Two other girls, who I would have sworn walked right past me the first day, stopped me in the hall.

"Benny says you took a spill on your skateboard," asked a cute blonde with deep blue eyes.

"Yeah," I mumble, still not sure how to talk in their code.

"Can I see?" she asked.

"Uh, sure," I turned around and lifted the back of my shirt.

They giggled, making me self-conscious.

"Were you scared?" asked her redheaded friend.

"Very. I thought he was going to kill me."

"Who?" asked the redhead.

Oh crap.

I almost said "Dad." I had to cover. I thought they were in the clan. "Oh, the guy I almost ran over."

"Oh, yeah. I bet he was pissed," she replied.

The blond girl gave me a look and mumbled under her breath as her friend turned to say hello to someone. "Careful..."

I nodded my head.

That's how it was. Your best friend could be in the Game and never tell you about it. Strange. It seems odd. But then I had friends I never told about my judo experiences. Not out of secrecy, it just wasn't their interest. Come to think of it, I had no idea what some of my friends in band did at practice or on their trips.

I guess we're all in our own little world.

I was feeling proud of myself and strolling through the halls like a conquering hero. The sigil was under my shirt, but it felt like a blazing sun. For once in a long time I had done something right. Well, mostly right. I'd fight a wild boar for breakfast every day if it meant feeling like this.

That was until Mr. Pressman's class. After he finished

droning on until the bell rang, he asked me to stay behind. For a billionth of a second I thought it was going to be for an apology. Not a chance.

He sat on the edge of his desk and folded his arms. In his mind, I'm sure he thought the tweed jacket and the beard made him look older and less like someone only a few years out of college.

"So you've joined Venn's little gang, I hear."

"Pardon me?" I reply, feeling suddenly small and vulnerable in my desk.

He raised a finger to his lips. "I know, lots of little secrets. Can't let the grownups know what you're doing out there."

Nobody had told me yet how to handle these kinds of situations. So I just say nothing.

"You're going to have to learn how to be your own man, Marv. Following Venn Maddox around isn't how you do that. Secret handshakes and little rituals may sound like fun. Grabbing bananas in a toilet while blindfolded may be a thrill..."

"Maybe for you," I reply without thinking.

I see his face twitch. I seriously don't understand what he's talking about. Bananas in toilets? Blindfolded?

Oh...

Gross.

"Peer pressure is just that. It's making you do things you wouldn't otherwise do. Venn is a master of that. Don't be fooled."

I want to shout back and defend Venn. Which is crazy, because less than 24 hours ago he was watching me get humiliated by Richard in the basement. He made me think I was about to die. Now? Now I want to punch Pressman in his stupid head for talking about him.

I take a deep breath and bury my anger. "I'm new here, Mr. Pressman. I don't really know anyone that well. I appreciate the advice, though." It takes every ounce of willpower to make that sound sincere.

"Right. Right. Just remember, if you ever need someone to talk to, I'm right here."

Good lord. I couldn't think of anything worse. I'd rather go ask Sawtooth for advice.

"Thank you, Mr. Pressman." I stand up and head for the door.

"No problem. We'll talk again. I'll tell you a little about what I know about the Black Dragons. Maybe it'll change your mind on some things."

Hearing him say the name of the clan made me freeze for a moment. It was like he'd violated some secret place. I don't know what to say. Was he testing me? Am I supposed to pretend I don't know?

I just walk through the door, too stupid to play it off. I resolve to keep my mouth shut until Venn or someone tells me what I'm supposed to say.

That's probably how it is in most cults, I assume.

CHAPTER NINETEEN

Man at Arms

Venn wasn't at lunch. I didn't see him the whole day after he congratulated me. After school, Rhode and Benny are waiting for me. "Follow us," says Rhode.

"Last time I did that I almost got killed by a wild boar," I reply.

Benny gives me a grin. "Almost. Almost."

"Old Sawtooth is the least of your worries," says Rhode. "We're taking you to the Rook, but not the baby way we've been using."

"The baby way?"

Neither of them answers me. We go across the overgrown field next to the school to a cluster of storage buildings.

Rhode walks over to the door of a wooden shack that hasn't had a new coat of paint since the movies added color and takes out a key. "Five others have these keys. If you need to get into here, you'll have to see one of us."

"What's in here?"

Rhode ignores me and swings open the door.

It takes a moment for my eyes to adjust to the dark because there's no light or window. On either side stand rows of wooden shelves. On them sit box after box of foot lockers. The outsides are a variety of colors, covered in nicks, scratches, cartoons, drawings and stickers.

Rhode walks down into the shed and pulls a footlocker from the shelf. He gives me a look, shakes his head, then puts it back. After a moment of intense consideration, he runs his finger along the lockers and stops at another one on a high shelf and pulls it down.

He steps outside and lays the locker at my feet. "Here you go."

I eye the locker, not sure what happens next.

"Open it," says Benny.

I kneel down and look at the top. Covered in black paint, the lid has fancy letters etched into it.

<u>Property of Lord Dark Heart</u>

"Who's he?" I ask.

"A ghost," answers Rhode.

"A ghost?" I look over at Benny. My hand reflexively

pulls away from the box.

"An alumnus," explains Benny. "Still alive somewhere. He graduated. The box gets passed on. It was given to him. Now it's yours. You can put whatever name you want on it."

"Oh," I reply, pretending to understand. I undo the latch and raise the lid.

"You'll probably want to make your own at some point, but this is yours now," offers Rhode.

On top of the heap in the footlocker is a broad chest plate. A dragon, the Black Dragon, is painted in gray on the black metal. This is armor. My armor.

I raise the chest piece to have a better look. It's light and feels like aluminum. The top ends in two large shoulder pads that extend outward.

"This is forest armor," says Benny. "Designed to be lightweight and mobile. It's kind of like kendo armor, but something you'll be able to spend long hours inside. For all-out warfare we use football shoulder pads, too. It gets kind of hairy out there."

I pull out two leather arm guards. The ends extend over where my wrists would go. Underneath them is a pair of leather gloves. Thin, they're the kind a mountaineer might use.

There's also a cotton waistcoat with pieces of metal in strategic places, including a codpiece. To go over it is a broad leather belt with different straps.

Rhode points out the different parts. "We'll show you where to attach your binders – the cords we use to tie them up, your shaft and the other stuff."

I pull out a shield, almost the size of the box. It's extremely lightweight. Curved at the top, the shield forms a point at the bottom. The front is a dull black with splotches of green. There's no fancy heraldry symbol on it. This is designed for camouflage.

"Some of the them are Kevlar wrapped in canvas. Some are aluminum." He slams the shield with his fist. "This is aluminum. Arrows will bounce off."

"That's good, right?"

"Depends. With Kevlar they stick and don't make a sound. With aluminum they make a ping sound. That's how they can spot you if they're shooting stingers blindly into the trees."

"They do that? What if they hit me in the face? Poke my eye out?"

"That's what the helmet is for." Rhode reaches inside, pulls out a helmet and hands it to me. It's small and made from either plastic or fiberglass. To me, it looks kind of like a field hockey mask with a large visor. There's a piece of clear plastic that goes over the eyes. So this is my protection from blindness.

"We've never had anyone lose an eye," says Benny. "I think."

Rhode pulls out a leather collar. "You'll want to keep this on. A stinger in the neck is the worst."

At the bottom of the box is a wooden rod lying diagonally. Athletic tape is wrapped around one end. It's a club of sorts.

"We have all kinds of weapons. That's your short shaft, or 'stick,'" he says as he takes it from me and slams it on the shield, making a loud crack.

I notice the grooves cut into the wood to spread the point of impact, kind of like a kendo sword.

"The goal is pain and not to break a bone," explains Rhode.

"What's the difference?"

"Ever break a finger?" he asks.

"My toe once."

"Which hurts more? That or getting it pulled out of joint? A razor blade across the skin hurts; getting slapped really, really hard hurts more. There's not always a direct correlation between damage and pain. Our style of combat is about pain, shock and disabling you so we can capture you.

"The Mayans used to use wooden clubs with bits of sharp glass-like rock sticking out of them. They only scraped and penetrated an inch or so. Historians thought they were so much more civilized than our European steel swords that hacked off limbs and killed people instantly. What they didn't appreciate was how much more those Mayan weapons hurt than a clean cut, or the fact that a hundred tiny abrasions are harder to treat than one cut you can sew up. Maybe more combatants walked off the battlefield, but far more died of infection later on. So who was more cruel?" Rhode hands me the stick.

I slap it against my hand and feel a sting across my palm.

"Damn! So I guess we're trying to think like the Mayans?"

"In a way. But they got their asses kicked in the end. We take anything that works. We're not a bunch of medieval re-enactors playing out some romantic notion of a bygone age that never really existed. This is street fighting – only in the woods."

"You're in a gang, basically," offers Benny with a happy chirp to his voice.

"Yes," corrects Rhode. "But we leave it in the Realm. The Realm is our real world." He points to the street and neighborhood opposite of the forest. "That's make-believe-land. That's where we all try to play along and be nice. If you fight a Centaur in the woods and he clubs your brains out, when you see him on the street, you either ignore him or tell him what nice weather we're having. Got it? It's no different than a judo match where one second you're trying to choke the living crap out of some guy and break his arm and the next you're standing on a podium shaking hands and smiling."

"I get it."

"I hope so. If we take the fight out of the Realm, we lose. This isn't about sportsmanship or civility. It's practicality. You're probably looking at your dinky stick and thinking, 'Why not use a real head cracker or maybe a knife?' The answer is simple; split open someone's skull and we get the cops here. Pull a knife and you're doing hard time or they come back with a gun. Crack them with this and you leave a wicked bruise – same as they'd get playing hockey. Hit them with a stinger and it looks like a bee sting."

"No evidence."

"Sort of. It's not like the Centaurs are Nazis, not all of them at least. They're just soldiers like you and me. Killing them isn't the point – besides the whole morality thing. You just want them out of the Game."

Benny hands me the waistcoat. "Now put this on so we can take turns hitting you." There's a sadistic gleam in his eye.

"If we train you right," says Rhode, "The hardest knocks you'll take are from us."

There's a comforting thought.

"We got to hurry, though. Venn has called a meeting at the Rook." Rhode hands me my chest plate. "We'll give you the quick tour on the way. Just remember to duck when we say 'duck' and run when we say 'run.'"

"Which way do I run?"

"Away from the arrows and the people trying to hurt you. Lesson number one."

CHAPTER TWENTY

The Realm

We were hiking through the forest, or rather the Realm, in armor. Rhode had the forest version of his Ox Armor and Benny was wearing a helmet similar to mine.

My armor. I was wearing armor.

This wasn't a costume. This wasn't a dress-up game. I was wearing armor because at any minute someone could come running out of the forest and attack me. Or shoot me with stingers. Or ambush me.

It was frightening.

It was awesome.

I clench my short stick with both hands and keep my eyes on the trees, ready for anything that may come at me. This morning my biggest threat was a wild boar. Now it's my fellow man.

"We're still in our territory," explains Benny in a hushed voice. "But that doesn't mean the Centaurs aren't out here. We send patrols into their area all the time."

"Patrolling for what?" I whisper.

"Weaknesses." He points to a line of trees along a ridge. "Remember the arrow this morning? That came from a fort in the trees. We've got...well, lots of them." He hesitates to tell me the actual number. "Some of them just have one person in them. Some have more. Others are empty. We rotate people around so you can never know how many are in there. If the Centaurs try to invade, they don't know which way is the safest. Even a tree fort with three people can pin down a dozen Centaurs with stingers. Put enough of them on the ground crying out in pain and they'll call a retreat."

Our path takes us over a rocky hill. A small lake is visible through a gap in the trees. Benny stops to point it out.

"Before the Summer Wars, where we're standing was Centaur territory. They'd made it around the lake and managed to have us pinned down all the way past here."

"It was embarrassing," adds Rhode.

"We changed all that. It was a long summer." He makes air quotes, "Our Boy Scout troop took a three-week trip to Canada."

"Welcome to Canada," remarks Rhode.

"You're in a Scout troop? I don't understand."

"Troop 199," says Benny. "It doesn't exist. There's a Troop 198 we sometimes meet up with. 199 was created so we could go camping and spend our summers at war."

"Whose idea was that?"

Benny shrugs. "I don't know. It's always been a thing. There are a lot more things you'll learn. Anyway, we called up everyone we could and kept pushing back at the Centaurs. Reclaiming the territory that had been lost over the years. It was Venn's campaign, really."

"It was a lot people's idea," replies Rhode.

"But Venn made it happen."

"We lost a lot of people."

"And we got them back."

Listening to them talk about their Summer Wars makes me envious. I spent my summer in the hospital watching Dad die. But it's not just that. Between them, between all of them, they have a special memory. Most of my summers were spent watching television. I went to a few judo camps and tournaments, but they pale in comparison. These guys fought a war. Not an all-out war where people died, yet something real close. It was the ultimate game.

"Goddamn Canada," growls Rhode. "I spent my summer sleeping in a tree over there. I don't think I took one piss in a real bathroom."

"And we got back the territory."

"Damn straight," replies Rhode. "Damn straight." He turns to the woods across the lake. "Up yours, you Centards!"

A "Shhhh!" comes from somewhere in the trees.

I look around, but can't tell where it came from. Rhode

and Benny move us along. After we're out of earshot, Benny explains.

"One of our hiding spots. He was following Centaurs. They probably spotted some inside our territory and were planning an ambush."

I turn back the way we came. "Should we go help?"

Rhode shakes his head. "If they needed it, they'd ask. Probably just an aerial assault. We're no good on the ground unless they want captives."

We come to the edge of the ridge. The lake wraps around the front and ends in a meadow where another lake winds around the trees. Rhode leads us away from the meadow and toward a cluster of trees at the far end.

"Across the field is Centaur territory. They've got their own forts all along there. You can bet they see us right now. To get to either side you have to either march through here, go around the ridge and through our forts, or swim."

"What about entering the forest from behind? Is that not allowed?"

"Everything is possible. We built our castles in areas where it's almost impossible to get to from behind. There are one or two paths, but they're watched all the time." He points to the center of the meadow. "This is the main area of conflict. You can get more people through here than anyone else."

We reach a cluster of tall redwoods. One stands taller than all the others. I strain my neck looking at the top. Odd clusters of leaves are in sporadic places along the trunk. I spot netting and camouflage.

"This is Skyperch," says Benny. "It's our largest fort outside Dragon Rook."

After he points that out I notice the circular decks around the trunk. There are several levels, including walled-in areas. It looks like some kind of multilevel house you'd see in one of my dad's old architectural magazines.

"We can house 50 people up there," comments Rhode.

"50?"

"Archers, mostly. They protect the area in shifts. You can hit someone in any part of the meadow with a stinger from here."

I try to gauge the distance from Skyperch to the meadow. The thought of an arrow hitting me with that much force makes me shudder.

"Never, ever try to cross the meadow without a helmet on," Rhode admonishes me. "We may hold Skyperch, but they're on the other side. Waiting."

As we walk on, I take a look back at the towering fortress in the sky. It has to be fifty feet from the ground to the first level!

"That's what the Summer Wars were really about," says Benny. "Taking Skyperch."

"How the hell did you do that?" I can't even wrap my head around trying to climb to the first level, let alone launching an assault on it.

"It wasn't easy," Benny remarks. "Lots of climbing. Lots of waiting. Lots of stingers. I got shot so many times my arm blew up like a balloon. We waited them out and kept them cut off from their friends. One by one they gave up until there were just a few left and then we made our assault."

"Climbing up underneath?"

"Free climbing. Venn had us practice for weeks. The Centaurs thought the only way up was with ropes lowered from above."

"They were wrong," adds Rhode.

I can't imagine anything more suicidal than trying to take a fortress several hundred feet in the air. It seems like something only a fool with a death wish would attempt.

When we get to Dragon Rook and find out what Venn's next campaign involves, I realize I'm a fool with a death wish.

CHAPTER TWENTY-ONE

Venn's War

"Black Tree," says Venn as he stabs a finger at a dark line of graphite on the map. "That's our target. That's how we'll take Demon Keep."

We're gathered in the main hall. The large round oak table has been dragged from the back and placed in the center so we can all see what he's describing.

"Black tree?" asks Jason. He's a senior and the tallest one here. Normally quiet, he tends to watch and observe. "Is it critical? It's useless for a frontal assault."

His finger traces out the lake that wraps around the ridge Black Tree is located on. The thinnest part of the lake is still a hundred feet across. I can understand what he's saying. You can't use Black Tree to make a forward assault. The

Centaurs hold it and the patch of land on the south end of the lake. We hold everything else except that area.

Jason points to the end of the ridge and the area below. "We hold this area with two forts. The ravine and thorn alley are too hard to move anyone through without difficulty. It's not worth it."

I recognize the ravine as the place where I was this morning. The ridge where Black Tree was located was several hundred yards north of there. Trying to get through would be almost impossible. You had to either go to the end where Rhode and Benny waited for me, or you had to go to the far end where the oak tree was. From what I could understand, we had fortifications near there, making any kind of passage by the Centaurs difficult.

"It's the last patch of territory we need to reclaim before we take Demon Keep," replies Venn.

Jason is having trouble with Venn's plan. "But is it worth it? They're already pinned down pretty well. They have to sneak in reinforcements one at a time in the middle of the night. It seems like more of a disadvantage to them now."

"All the more easy to take it. Strategically, it's critical." Venn locks eyes with Jason.

"Okay, but how? We can't launch an assault from there. It's taking them resources to defend it. Resources that will be freed up if they lose Black Tree."

Benny and Rhode are silent. Carrie has her hands on her hips and is watching the exchange between Venn and Jason. I get the feeling that Jason is pretty well respected by them all and is making valid points.

Venn is far too calm for this to sound like an argument. I still don't know what the hierarchy is here. Venn is clearly the leader, but half the clan is older than him. Jason looks to be the oldest.

"This war has gone on for years," explains Venn. "We take some territory. They take some territory back. We try to siege them. They do the same to us."

"My first year we held Demon Keep for two days," Jason points out. "That was the longest anyone can remember."

"And did you get their shard?" Venn's voice is sharp.

"We couldn't find it. If we had it longer...I'm sure we could have."

"You had their fortress for two days and you didn't get it."

Jason's eyes narrow. "You've never been in there. It's a maze. They dug hundreds of tunnels. They're like rats."

"I've seen the maps."

"It's not the same. There are dead ends. Traps. Only a few Centaurs even know what's back in there." He waves his hand at the hall. "It's not like here. They designed Demon Keep to defend itself when you're trapped inside. Centaurs spend their first weeks learning how to get around in there blindfolded."

Holy crap. They built an actual labyrinth.

Jason continues, "We hold our prisoners in a stockade at the edge of our wall. They bring theirs inside the Keep, because they know there's no way out unless they show you."

"I understand this. That's why we need to take Black Tree." Venn sounds exasperated. "Black Tree is the one place this side of the meadow that gives us a full view of the Keep. You can see further than Skyperch. You can see the back of the Keep."

"See what?" asks Jason, raising his voice. "A pile of dirt? A small mountain? A few turrets we already know are there? They built their fortress into the earth, not stone by stone like we did."

"And that was their mistake," Venn replies. He lowers his voice. "You're our most experienced fighter. You've seen more than all of us. But this is your last year. Do you want to leave here a ghost? Or do you want to graduate knowing you were here the year we won?"

"The year you won, you mean."

"I thought we all win," Venn forces a smile.

"It's about you being the youngest to run the clan. The youngest to reclaim territory. Now you want to be the youngest to win the Game."

Venn holds up a finger. "Correction. The only one to win the Game. And I don't plan on waiting until my senior year. That's what they're expecting, a long campaign over the next two-and-a-half years. They're not counting on me, or rather us, going all in now. I want this for you, Jason, just as much for me." Venn turns to face us all. "All of us." He stabs a finger back at Black Tree. "Not everything is evident at first. We can't play the Game the way it's been played before.

That will only repeat past failures. Black Tree may look like it's got minimal value. Trust me, it's far more than that." He turns back to Jason. "Did we take Skyperch?"

Jason reluctantly nods.

"Did we reclaim the land we'd lost over the last three years?" There's a dig in his voice as he points out that during Jason's period they'd lost to the Centaurs. "We won those battles through unconventional tactics. We'll win this war the same way. We're going to hit them so hard, the Summer Wars will seem like a school dance." Venn pauses for a moment and makes eye contact with as many of us as possible. "We don't have fancy titles here. It's not like the Centaurs. The only 'Lords' are those of us not in the auxiliary. I lead by the will of the group. I only have that will as long as you think I'm the right leader. Jason has made some important points. He's pointed out his concerns, as is his job. Now I need to know if you trust me. If you trust the plan. The plan starts by taking Black Tree. Are you in?"

There are nods around the table.

"I said, are you in?" Venn's voice is far more loud and booming than his age implies.

"Dragons!" screams someone from the back.

"Hooah!" the crowd shouts back as they shake their fists in the air.

"DRAGONS HOOAH!" we all yell.

Jason raises a fist but his mouth is silent.

It's like we're going to war.

No, I realize, it was war.

CHAPTER TWENTY-TWO

Fight School

Benny dragged me out of bed the next day. "Your real training begins," he explains as we walk to school before the sun is up.

I'm still half-asleep, but relieved that only people will be trying to kill me today and not grizzly, bear-sized wild boars.

He takes me to the shed by the field on the edge of the school property and we dig out the armor we'd packed there the night before.

"Rhode will teach you mostly weapons. I'll show you the other stuff."

"Is this how it's done? You guys pair up?"

"We switch out partners so we don't get too complacent.

We also have our own mini-tournaments." He takes a wide stance and faces me. "I want you to take me."

Benny is shorter and skinnier than me. I'm sure he's tough enough, but this is ridiculous. "Benny, I'll kill you."

"Sure. Maybe. But this isn't judo, is it?"

"Physics is physics." His hands are open and our fighting sticks are sitting in the grass.

"Sure," he says. "Pretend I'm a Centaur you have to get past."

In judo you use your opponent's inertia against them. That's why you let them to attack first. But there are ways to launch an assault that have the same effect.

I reach a hand out and grab the back of his leather collar.

"Okay," says Benny. "Now what?"

I push his head down and wait for him to resist. As soon as he does, I step toward his side and sweep his leg.

Benny falls backward into the grass. I land on top of him and raise my other hand to grab his arm in a pin – except my hand is caught on something.

I turn my head to look and find myself off-balanced to the side. Benny is holding onto one end of a cord wrapped around my wrist. He gives it a jerk and I go sideways.

Benny pulls the cord around my back, yanks my other wrist and binds them together. He jumps back and watches me writhe on the ground, trying to untie the ropes.

"Physics," he mocks.

"I didn't know we were using weapons," I grumble as I try to free my hands.

"I don't remember saying we weren't." Benny kneels down and unfastens the rope. He hands it to me.

Much shorter than the torinawa fighting rope, this is a simple knotted cord designed to tie someone up. This was the style of nawajutsu they'd developed.

"There's no tapping out in the Realm, unless it's to let them tie you up," says Benny. "You can't just pin someone and wait for a ref to do a thirty count. You have to incapacitate them. That's why we use the cord."

"What about handcuffs?"

"Anything goes. This is faster. We've tried zip ties, too. The problem with handcuffs and zip ties is they're meant to be used by someone holding a gun. The cord is the weapon."

I pull on the rope. There's a thick knot on one end and a loop on the other. Benny must have had it on his wrist, waiting for me.

"We also practice getting out of them." He tosses a piece of metal the size of a bottle opener at my feet. One end is a sharp edge. The other has a point like a small letter opener. "That's yours. It'll get you out of rope, locks and handcuffs."

I remember Venn unfastening my handcuffs in the school office. So that's how he did it...

"The real secret," Benny confides, "is not getting taken captive. I figured I'd rope you before you knew what I was trying."

"Care to try it again?" I gently threaten.

"Yup. That's why I'm here."

Benny traps me three more times before I understand the

basic moves. I manage to get him, only after pinning an arm over his head and physically overpowering him. It wasn't elegant, but it worked.

After our session with the cord, he pulls out a small bow and arrow for me to handle.

"We all specialize in something, but everyone knows how to use the bow. It's our main source of defense." He hands me an arrow to nock.

I walk toward a tree and take aim. A sharp pain shoots into my back. "AAAAHHH!" I scream.

I turn to face the source of the pain. Benny is standing twenty feet away holding a bow. My hand claws at my back and pulls out the arrow. The shaft is light, like the wood you'd use on a kite. The needlepoint has my blood.

"What the hell?"

Benny grins. "You got to know what it feels like. That's not even a stinger tip."

"No warning?" I complain.

"No more than what the Centaurs will give you." He points to the tree. "Now try to hit it."

I aim the bow again. A sharp pain hits my leg. "DAMN IT!" I yell. An arrow is sticking out of my calf.

Benny is grinning even more. I'm about to yell at him when I notice a burning sensation in my leg. It feels like an insect bite.

"That's what a stinger feels like," he grins.

I yank the arrow out. My skin feels like it's been hit by a bullet. When I lift the leg of my pants I can only see a tiny prick. It hurts like hell. I want to itch like crazy.

"What is that?"

"Honey and pepper spray, basically. We have all kinds of tips."

"Jesus Christ."

"Non-toxic, I should point out. Low chance of infection. I'd still treat it. Can't be too sure."

"Not with you around," I glare at him.

Benny raises his shirt and shows me his stomach. There are a dozen red welts across his chest. "I went on a recon three days ago without my full armor. We call it 'going ninja.' I got spotted. Twelve stingers. A dozen more on my back."

"Yikes. I hope it was worth it."

"I was counting archers at Black Tree. Now I know how many. Boy, do I know."

After the pain lowers to a dull roar, I take some shots with the bow. The first few go wild. The arrow is so much lighter than I expected. Since it's intended not to kill, I understand why. I try to be thankful I won't be on the other end of a normal arrow.

"What's the deal with Jason and Venn?" I ask as I go pull my arrows from the tree and nearby grass.

"Jason was going to be our next leader. Venn had other plans."

"So Jason is pissed, I take it."

"Maybe, but I don't think he really wanted it. Venn is the best man for the job. Sometimes I think he feels like he deserves more respect from Venn. Jason is a great warrior. One of our toughest. He's a good guy, too. All the girls like him. He's just not the tactician Venn is."

"He doesn't think much about Venn's plan for Black Tree," I reply.

"No. No, he does not. None of us really understand it fully. Then again, none of us really understand Venn. Don't take this the wrong way, but we can't understand his obsession with you."

"Me?"

"I think your judo and all is a great asset. I'm sure you'll make a great knight. It's just that we don't normally rush people through so quick. Venn must think you're special."

I'm not sure how I feel about that. Benny said it in a polite manner. It was hard to take offense to it. If someone showed up at my dojo, even if he was the toughest one around, we wouldn't rush him through his belt tests. It's about so much more than that. Part of it is patience. You have to earn people's respect.

"Yeah," I say, "I don't want to get in anyone's way. I just want to do my part."

"I'm sure you're going to be fine. I'm looking forward to having someone to talk to besides Rhode on patrol."

The bell rings. "Oh crap!" I exclaim as I look at all the arrows I have to pick up.

"What's the hurry?" asks Benny.

"Did you hear the bell? First period!"

"Relax." Benny reaches into his pocket and hands me a

slip of paper.

"You guys steal a pack of hallway passes?"

"Something like it..."

I open the paper. It's a class schedule. My name is at the top, but it's not the schedule I was given three days ago. "I don't understand. These aren't my classes."

"They are now. Read them."

I scan the list of classes:

Period	Class
1	Conservation Club
2	Study Hall
3	Lunch Group 1
4	History
5	Calculus
6	Economics
7	English - Individual study

"What's Conversation Club? Debate?"

Benny shakes his head. "Conservation Club. That's the class where we go around the forest and examine mushrooms and crap. It's your science class now."

"Who's the teacher?"

"There is none. It's self-guided, like your English class. Just get A's and B's, stay out of trouble and nobody bothers you."

I reread the schedule. "You mean I don't have a real class until 4th period?"

"Yup, and then Calculus."

"Is this...legal?"

"Yeah. Thank the hippies that started Ellison. They have some very...liberal policies about education."

I still can't wrap my head around the schedule. "You mean I only have to be here for three hours?"

"Pretty much. We only do this for full-timers. Auxiliary have more normal schedules."

"And all I have to do is let people club me over the head and shoot me full of arrows?"

"Yup, and spend every day in mortal terror that you're going to die out there and get eaten by a razorback that thinks he's a grizzly bear."

"THIS. IS. AWESOME." I'm grinning from ear to ear.

"This is how we defend Dragon Rook. Attacks can happen at any time. Oh, and then there's the fire alarm and the PA System."

"What?"

"Let's say the Centaurs decided to lay siege on us. Most of us are in school. How do we defend?" Benny answers his own question. "Fire alarm. Ellison has a very buggy fire system."

"Isn't that illegal?"

"Let's not go there. We've also hacked the PA system. If you're in history class and we need you, there'll be an announcement calling you to the office."

"What does the office say?"

"They don't. The announcement is only in your room. One of the girls sounds a lot like the secretary. We've recorded her already."

"Holy. Crap."

"Welcome to the Black Dragons. Welcome to the war. Ready at a moment's notice."

CHAPTER TWENTY-THREE

First Blood

The war hammer slams into my chest so hard, I'm knocked backwards off my heels. I fall on the Centaur behind me still trying to pick himself up off the ground. Under my weight, he falls to the dirt in a crumple of leather and bent metal plates.

My lungs still can't pull in air when the wielder of the hammer stands over me, ready to bring the mallet on my skull. He seems oblivious to the fact that I don't have a helmet on – or doesn't care. A minute ago I'd never even seen a Centaur. Now the impossibly tall teenager with the horse mane jutting out from the top of his red helmet may be the last thing I'll ever see.

Ever since Benny told me about the PA system and the fire drill, the few hours I was in school were spent staring at the classroom loudspeaker, waiting to hear the bell go off. Most of my time was spent at the Rook. That's where I learned more fighting skills and the intricacies of the Game.

Bookshelves in one corner of the hall held textbooks for all the classes offered at Ellison. There were also cheat sheets and notes taken by previous students. They pointed out to me that if you flunk out of Ellison, you're out of the Game.

Time not spent learning how to crack skulls or navigate the secret trails was spent making sure I didn't blow my classes. I even studied for the ones that quasi-existed. Anyone paying close attention to the Conservation Club syllabus might notice it bore an uncanny resemblance to a forest survivalist guide.

Venn admonished me to make sure I had "balance." This was code for making sure your parents weren't freaking out that you were never home. I tried to catch dinner as often as I could with Mom.

Sometimes Venn or Benny would join us and we'd tell her heavily redacted stories about the Conservation Club or our field hockey matches. Mom was thrilled when I told her I was signing up for Scouts. Venn even gave me a realistic permission form for her to sign. Just for show, I had her drop me off in front of a Troop 198 meeting where the church parking lot was filled with other parents.

I felt bad about lying to her. I tried not to weave too

elaborate of a story – most of it was true. We spent a lot of time in the woods – just what the Conservation Club or any good Scout would be expected to do. What we did there was a different matter...

To make it easier to stay out late on weeknights, some of us had cover jobs. Venn got me a job at the local movie theater. The assistant manager was a junior at Ellison and an auxiliary. I worked two nights a week cleaning up the theaters and bathrooms.

It was a flexible job. I either did it right after the shows let out or before the afternoon matinees.

Benny worked with me. I asked him if the owners suspected anything was up. He explained the theater was owned by an alumnus who never asked questions. We just had to make sure the theaters were kept clean. Worst-case scenario, we could get some freshman kid to come do our work.

I was getting into the routine of things when the fire alarm finally rang. Mr. Pressman looked agitated as the bell interrupted his lesson.

"All right. Outside in an orderly fashion," he commanded as he held open the door.

His job was to see us outside then send us to our counting stations. This was where they did the headcount to make sure we were all out of the building.

Carrie grabbed my elbow in the hallway. It felt like a vise.

"The Rook is under attack. Parker had a half-day today.

They managed to keep it offline. We just found out."

I start to run. She pulls at my sleeve. "Walk calmly to the shed. Then we run."

There were twenty more of us. It took us a quarter of an hour to get to the Rook. When we arrived, at least thirty Centaurs were inside the compound and battling it out with our day shift guards.

Combat wasn't anything like I'd imagined. We didn't fight in orderly ranks or break out into one-on-one sparring matches. You ganged up in pairs or squads and tried to pick them off one or two at a time and bind them.

The closest I could describe this is the police busting a riot and trying to handcuff everyone. The difference was that the rioters were also cops with billy clubs and handcuffs trying to bust a riot.

Carrie and several others split off to go climb the wall and help out the archers. Benny and Rhode charged at a group of Centaurs trying to use a ladder to climb the side of the Rook.

I was left alone on the ridge.

At the side of our hall, almost out of view of the main battle, I spot three Centaurs with pickaxes, trying to smash a hole in the wall. Six more stand around them with shields and weapons, defending them.

Nobody told me what I was supposed to do.

I let out a yell and run right toward them.

I build up a lot of speed going down the hill. The defenders see me. Two of them kneel down and brace their shields.

There's no plan to my attack.

I keep going. I land one foot on a shield and another on the shoulder of a Centaur. My foot clips off one of the wooden wings he's decorated his helmet with. It flies over his head along with me.

My knees hit one of the pickaxe crew and he goes sprawling. The other two turn from their work and face me. I'm still kneeling on the first axeman. One of them raises their pickaxe over my body. Crap.

A loud voice shouts, "Holdfast!"

I turn to face my savior, only to realize it's one of the Centaurs telling the other not to commit homicide. That's when the red-helmed devil with the horsetail slams me with his war hammer and I go flying.

Three of the defenders lunge toward me. I shove the shield in the face of the one to my left. When he grasps it, I let go and give it a kick. He stumbles backward.

Someone hits me in the back of the knee with a stick. I buckle to the ground. I feel his hands yanking at my boot to drag me away and bind me.

I grab the leg of the nearest Centaur and transfer the force. He falls to the ground. I keep climbing up his body.

My spine is smashed by a staff. I grab the chest plate of the Centaur under me and roll him over me before the second strike. The eyes that look back at me from the helmet are the eyes of a scared kid.

He lets out a scream as he's accidentally pounded by his

companions. There's a stomping sound as the legs of other knights come running by. My clansmen are attacking the Centaurs near me. Before he has the sense to struggle, I use my cord to bind the kid I used as a shield.

As I stand, one of the pickaxe wielders is coming at me with just the handle. I catch the shaft near his hands and throw him over my shoulder.

The extra foot of distance between my hands and the center of gravity makes his body hit the ground like a bullwhip.

"AAAAAAAAHHHHH", he screams.

I flip him over and bind him with another cord.

"Can you feel your toes?" I ask.

"What?" he says under his grasping breath.

"Feel this?" I slap him on the thigh.

"AAAAHHH!!! I'm down, prick!"

I leave him be, satisfied I didn't snap his spine.

The other Black Dragons have swarmed into the compound and are cleaning things up. The red devil with the war hammer runs when he sees he's outnumbered.

Beyond the entrance I see a cluster of Centaurs on the hill. Two of them stand in the center. One is taller than the other. He has his helmet tilted as he leans in to listen to the other.

"That's Lone Wolf," says Benny as he drags a Centaur by the leg next to the two I've tied up. "He's the leader."

"Who's the other one?"

"Cutter. His lieutenant. We think. We're still not sure

how the power changed after the Summer Wars."

"Do we go after them?" I ask.

"No. They'll just pull us into an ambush. Hey, get him!"

"What?" I turn and see one of my captives has slipped my cord. I chase after him before he can get over the ridge.

I tackle him to the ground and bind him again. This time I search his waistcoat for the blade he used to free himself and toss it aside. I drag him back to the row of other captives, all lying on their backs.

There are at least four of them. The others managed to escape.

I'm about to ask Benny what we're supposed to do now when I notice he's bleeding from the neck.

CHAPTER TWENTY-FOUR

The Centaurs

"You're bleeding," I tell Benny.

"We're all bleeding," he points to my forehead. I touch it and see a splatter of blood on my fingertips. "Yeah, but not like you."

Benny's neck guard is stained red. Venn walks over and has a look. "Hold on," he says as he pulls something out from the leather.

Venn hold up the tip of an arrow. It's a needle. A really long needle.

His face fills with fury. He kicks the nearest Centaur. "Who shot this?"

"I didn't do it!" pleads the kid.

Someone had taken their helmets off and stacked them

like skulls in a pile.

The Centaur is younger than me. All of the captured ones are. There are three boys and a girl. Her dark hair is pulled back, revealing an innocent face.

She's watching Venn intensely as he moves on to the next Centaur. Venn kneels down, pressing his knee into his back. He shoves the needlepoint near his face.

"Who shot this?!"

Benny has taken his neckpiece off. Carrie and a dark-skinned girl named Myra are holding a square of gauze over the wound.

"Take it easy, Venn," says Benny, swatting away a hand with a bandage. "It's just a prick."

Venn pushes his knee further into the back of the boy on the ground. "What's next? Metal tips? Bladed weapons? We haul you out of here in a helicopter to the hospital? We have rules for a reason!" Venn shouts the last words into the boy's ear.

The kids eyes begin to well up. "I'm sorry! I'm sorry!"

Venn pulls an arrow from a quiver at the boy's waist and holds it up. It has a long tip like the one from Benny's neck. He jabs it in the ground in front of the kid's face.

"I didn't know! I didn't know! I just grabbed the arrows."

"Then whose quiver is it?" asks Venn.

"I don't know!" the kid pleads.

Venn yanks the arrow out of the ground and holds it over his head. He nods to someone I didn't notice before standing by the gate. A heavy-set boy with glasses is holding a yellow banner on a pole.

Venn hands the arrow to me. "Go show him."

I take the arrow and run to the boy by the gate. I don't know who he is, but I don't question. He looks down at the arrow then pulls out a ruler from a pocket. He measures the length of the needle and nods his head.

Venn watches us from the compound. The boy with the banner nods his head to Venn.

"We have two," the boy tells me.

I run back with the arrow, still unsure what transpired. The boy wasn't any Black Dragon I'd seen. His armor looked like the Centaurs'.

I hand the arrow to Venn. "He says they have two."

Venn snaps the arrow over his knee and throws it at the ground by the archer. "Your watchman agrees. That was illegal."

"I...I...didn't know," the kid pleads.

"The rules are the same with you guys, last I checked. Your weapon. Your fault."

The kid begins to sob. Venn turns to Carrie. "Who are we missing?"

"Eric and Ross," she replies. "They were at the outer gate."

"Figures." Venn turns to the girl captive. "You're the one they call Sparrow?"

"Yes," she replies.

"Kind of odd they'd send you out on a berserker raid," he says.

Sparrow says nothing. She just looks Venn back in the eyes as if she's studying him.

"I guess you were a spy." He looks over at the ring of gathered people. "Who caught her?"

"I did," says Myra. "Over on the south ridge."

"What was she doing?"

"Watching us. She got off a few stingers, too."

Venn looks back down at Sparrow. "Interesting... Rhode?"

"Yes, sir!" Rhode shouts in a loud voice. "Prisoners, we are going to the meadow to parlay. Do all of you agree to conduct yourselves properly? Or do we require more restraints?"

They all agree to cooperate.

"Your watchman is observing. Should any of you break rank, there will be repercussions. Understood?"

They agree.

"Escort squad, form up!"

Twelve knights gather around the prisoners. Each one holds a length of rope and a quarterstaff. They begin marching them toward the front of the compound.

Venn nods to me. "Follow close."

The kid with the arrow starts to cry out. "NO! NO!"

Venn motions to Rhode. "Hold up."

"Hold!" shouts Rhode.

Venn walks over to the crying kid. "You broke the rules. You're out."

"NOOOO! I'm sorry. I'm sorry. I don't want out! Don't

kick me out of here. I'll take the finger! I'll take it!"

Venn looks the kid over, "What's your name?"

"Reed. Reed Claremont, sir."

Venn shoots a glance at the watchman at the gate. He nods back at Venn.

"All right, Reed. The easy way out is to just surrender and leave the Game."

"I don't want to leave. Take the finger!" Reed falls to the ground. "Please."

Venn looks a little uneasy. Sparrow is staring at him, waiting to see what he does.

"Richard!" shouts Venn.

Richard comes running. There's a fiendish grin on his face.

"Reed says he wants the finger," says Venn.

"First or second offense?" asks Richard.

"First," replies Venn. "Just the first. Be careful or it'll be yours next."

"With pleasure," says Richard. He walks over to Reed. "Kneel!"

Reed falls to his knees.

"Hands!"

Reed holds his hands out and stares at the ground.

"Which hand are you?"

"Left."

Richard grabs his left hand.

"Richard!" shouts Venn.

"I'm just kidding." He lets go and grabs Reed's right hand

and spreads his fingers.

Sparrow looks away from Reed and watches Venn. I feel a pit in my stomach.

Reed buries his head in his shoulder.

"Watch!" shouts Richard.

"He doesn't have to watch," says Venn. "Just get it done."

"Do you have to take the fun out of everything?" growls Richard as he pulls Reed's finger out of socket.

"AAAAAAAAAAHHHHH!" screams Reed as he stares at his finger twisted off to the side.

"My work here is done," says Richard as he walks away smiling. "Don't forget to see the nurse about the bill."

I run over to Reed. He's tucked his hand under his arm. "Show me your hand!" I yell at him.

He pulls away from me. I recognize him as the Centaur I used as a shield.

"SHOW ME YOUR HAND!" I yell.

Reluctantly, he holds his twisted finger forward. Tears are streaming down his face. I grab his wrist and his pinky.

I don't look at Venn or anyone else. I can't let the kid suffer. "I'm going to fix it. On the count of three? Ready?"

Reed nods.

"3..."

I yank the finger back into place.

"AAAAAAAAHHHH," he screams. Between breaths he complains. "You...you...said on three!"

"Sorry," I reply.

"Would you rather wait for it?" interjects Benny.

"Besides, he did do it on three..."

"Oh," says the still shocked Reed. "Th...thanks." He looks over at Venn and climbs to his feet. "Thank you, Lord Venn. Thank you!"

Venn gives him a nod then heads toward the gate. "Don't mention it."

Jesus Christ. What a world. The poor little bastard would rather have his finger pulled out of socket than get permanently kicked out of the Game.

I'd think him a fool, but I'd do the same. And I've only been at it for a week.

The Game is a drug. I still feel a rush of adrenaline from my first battle.

As we march to the meadow, two things go through my mind: the glee that Richard took in hurting Reed and how Sparrow never took her eyes off Venn – or his eyes off her.

CHAPTER TWENTY-FIVE

The Yellow Banner

Across the meadow is a row of Centaurs standing shoulder to shoulder. I count at least fifty of them. Three of them stand apart from the rest in the front. One of them is holding a tall banner with the logo of the Centaurus constellation on a field of red.

I recognize the tallest one as the red-helmed one with the war hammer. Next to him is Lone Wolf in dark leather armor; Lord Cutter in his polished metal armor and full-face visor is standing in the middle. I can't see any of their faces.

It's an intimidating sight. There are fewer than twenty people in our party. We're outnumbered two-to-one. Neither Venn nor anyone else seems worried, though. The Centaurs' watchman is marching out in front of us with his yellow banner.

"He's a Quaker," Benny whispers to me.

We're both in the rear walking in formation behind the escort squad. I'm trying my best not to look out of place. I just do what Benny does.

"The Quakers are pretty trustworthy. We chose their watchman. They chose ours."

"Where's ours?" I ask.

"Watching," replies Benny, as if it were obvious.

Rhode brings the march to a stop at our end of the meadow. Our prisoners are brought to the front and made to kneel down. The Centaurs split and two of our captive people are brought forward and made to kneel as well. Venn walks to the center of the meadow. Jason is at his side.

"How do we trade if we have more than them?"

"We can ask for territory, take a raincheck if they'll offer one. Lots of ways. Or not at all."

Venn and his party meet Lone Wolf and Cutter and speak. I can't make out what they're saying. Venn points to Reed. Lone Wolf turns to the watchman. He nods his head. Lone Wolf seems to understand. Jason and Cutter are silent.

"Lord Cutter came up in the Summer Wars. I've seen him leading raids. We're not sure, but he and Lone Wolf may have a shared power arrangement. This is Lone Wolf's last year."

"Who is Cutter?"

"I don't know. The Centaurs like to trade armor and hide their identities. Lone Wolf is hard to miss."

Lone Wolf motions for our two Black Dragons to be released. They're untied and come walking across the meadow rubbing their wrists. Both of them have been stripped of their armor. Back in Dragon Rook there's a trophy room of Centaur helmets. I imagine they have the same.

Reed and the two other boys are pushed forward toward the Centaurs. Sparrow is left behind. Venn and Lone Wolf seem to be arguing over something. Cutter is shaking his head.

"That's odd," says Benny. "You'd think they'd want Sparrow back first. She's a second-year and a good archer. The others are just freshmen."

"How is that bad for us?" I ask.

"If she won't parlay out of the Game, it means we have to watch her. Hold on."

Venn walks over to Sparrow. "Your friends don't want to ransom you back yet. They've decided to take the other three. You understand what this means?"

"Yes," says Sparrow in a firm voice.

"Are you going to be our captive or our guest?"

Benny explains it to me again. "Being captive means she has to be bound all the time or confined so she can't escape. In some cases we don't even have to let you go home. Being a guest means she can't run away or be rescued outside the compound. If they raid us and free her, that's fine."

"And people are okay with this?"

"Last time it got out of hand, we had people chained to

trees for days. Nobody wants to go back to that. Your word is the honor of your clan."

Sparrow looks over at the Centaurs. They're already retreating across the meadow. "I'll be your guest," she tells Venn.

Venn turns to the watchman. "You hear that?"

"Yes." He speaks in an official voice. "Sparrow may only be ransomed or rescued from the Black Dragon compound. Agreed." He follows after his clan.

Our party returns to Dragon Rook with Rhode in the lead. Sparrow is flanked by the escorts. Jason takes up the rear guard.

Venn walks over to Benny and me. "That's weird."

"What's that?" asks Benny.

"That they don't take Sparrow."

"Spy?" asks Benny.

"Got to be."

"Spy?" I ask.

"She's probably going to ask to stay at the compound," explains Venn. "As a ransom, she can stay home and watch television and just wait for them to ransom her or raid us. My guess is that they want her there watching us. Since she parlayed, they can't free her when we escort her to the Rook. It's the only thing that makes sense."

"Not the only thing," says Carrie as she walks over.

"What else?" asks Venn.

"Maybe she pissed someone off over there. Maybe she's being punished."

"For what?"

"Not letting Lord Cutter take her to the dance. Who knows."

"Huh," replies Venn. "That sounds so...uncivil."

"I'd break your neck if you tried that with me," says Carrie.

"Noted. Let it be known that I will not now nor ever ask you to escort me anywhere both here in the Realm or outside in the minor universe."

"That's not what I mean," Carrie replies.

"I don't understand then," says Venn.

"For a smart guy, there's a lot about women you don't understand."

This makes me grin.

Carrie turns to me. "You either."

"I think it's a ruse," says Venn, rapidly changing the topic to something he understands. "Lord Cutter and Lone Wolf were watching the whole attack."

"Counting bodies?" asks Carrie.

"More than that. I think they wanted to see our response time. Next time it will be different. Strategically, it was a wash for them."

"Except losing Sparrow," I point out.

"Yes. This my suspicion. But there are other ways to turn her over to us. We could just put her in the stockade...or..." Venn was lost in deep thought.

I wasn't sure if another attack was imminent, not understanding fully parlay, so I keep my eyes on the trees.

"It's worth the risk. We'll have to be careful around her. Perhaps try some misinformation to see if that makes its way back to them. Curious. Very curious."

Venn continued to stare at the ground as he thought this over all the way back to Dragon Rook.

A hundred feet in back of us, Sparrow quietly kept her plans to herself.

CHAPTER TWENTY-SIX

Night Watch

Tonight is my first overnight patrol. It's my turn to stand guard at the front line and protect the boundary for the Black Dragons. Benny met me at the apartment after dinner with Mom. I told her I would be staying over at Benny's and we'd be walking to school from his house.

She was cool with it because all my friends were courteous and respectful when they came over. We had a game night with Rhode, Benny and Carrie. Mom played a few rounds of Trivial Pursuit with us then pulled me aside to tell me she thought the move was a good idea and how much she liked my new friends.

I liked my new friends. Sure, we spent most of our time bashing each other with quarterstaffs and the other half trying not to get struck with arrows, but this was the most fun I could remember having.

We left the apartment and changed into our armor just outside the forest. Once we set foot inside, we were fair game. Nighttime was the most dangerous period. You could get hit by friendly fire almost as easily as unfriendly.

I made the mistake of forgetting the day's pass phrase once and fell under a hail of stingers. I didn't make that mistake again. I spent two hours in the bathtub trying to get all the venom out.

Benny called out the pass phrase to the lookout on Skyperch. He responded with the second part and we answered back. It was a complicated code that changed often. Listening to us or guessing wouldn't help. The wrong word and you fell under a hail of arrows.

The bottom platform of Skyperch was a dark disk around the base of the tree. I could make out the faint light of a lantern, but nothing else.

"Stand back," Benny says.

A heavy knotted rope ladder falls from the sky.

"You first," he pushes me to the ladder.

I swing the bag of supplies we brought over my shoulder and place a foot on the narrow step. When I'm twenty feet off the ground, the ladder begins to swing in the breeze. The weight of my pack makes it even worse.

"Just keep climbing," Benny tells me.

Fifty feet. That's five stories. Parts of Skyperch go even higher. The tallest section is 200 feet off the ground! That's higher than most office buildings.

I try to ignore the height and keep climbing. Benny is ten feet below me. I try not to think about how much weight the ladder can hold.

"You free-climbed this tree?" I ask hesitantly.

"Yup. It's not like they were going to throw us a rope."

"Free-climb? As in, no rope?"

"That's the kind. We used climbing cleats and claws. If you look close you'll see some of the spikes we hammered into the trunk. We pulled most of them out after we took back Skyperch."

I look up and keep my attention off the ground. "And they just sat there?"

"Hell no! They dropped everything on us. Rocks, arrows, piss."

"And you kept climbing?"

"We used a shield. Actually a shield on the end of a long rod. That way the guy highest up could hammer in the spikes and not worry about getting pelted. The guy below him held up the shield."

"Clever."

"It was Venn's idea."

"Makes sense."

"It took days. Long days."

"Nobody fell?"

"Nobody was permanently injured. I fell from 30 feet."

"What?"

"That's the other part. We took a bunch of refrigerator

boxes and put them at the base – in case we fell. Which some of us did."

"Hurt?"

"Oh lord. My back was bruised for weeks. But not broken."

When we reach the top of the ladder there are two knights waiting to help us through the hatch. I climb through and take my first look over the rail. Somehow, it doesn't seem as high up from the safety of solid planking.

Benny walks me around the deck, showing me the vantage points. We have a clear view of the ground beneath the tree line. He takes me up a ladder that goes up another thirty feet.

From here I can see the meadow, the top of Dragon Rook and a small part of Demon Keep. We then go up another twenty feet and climb into a walled-in room.

"This is where we sleep, unless you want to go even higher. We have mats on the top deck and netting so you don't fall off."

"That's a good idea." I'm scared by the idea of rolling off.

"Come on." Benny leads me up a ladder to the upper deck.

I take a seat close to the edge and look through the net. My stomach does a jump as I realize we're swaying. "We're moving," I realize.

"Of course. The way nature intended. In high winds it's even more intense. Try it up here in a rainstorm, too." He sees the hesitant look on my face. "Afraid of heights?"

"Terrified."

"Great time to tell me."

"I'm trying to overcome them."

"Don't worry, you evolved from tree climbers. It's second nature."

"Tree climbers that decided to leave the trees."

"Here," Benny points to a small orange light in a distant tree. "See that?"

"Yeah?"

He points to one on the other side. "And that?"

"Yeah."

"Those are our other forts. Right now we've got people in a half-dozen of them. It's been that way for a long time. Every night for years. They're up here, too. Not as high, but out on platforms like us."

That brings up a question I'd been dying to ask. "How long has it been going on?"

"The Game? Years."

"How many years?"

"I don't know. I'm not sure if anyone knows exactly. We kind of make it a point not to know. You could ask Venn, though."

"More than ten years?"

"Probably."

"For over a decade? This war has been going on for that long? Most real wars don't last that long."

"Most real wars aren't this fun. Some of us don't want to see it end."

I hadn't thought about that. What would I do if tomorrow this was over? I'd feel cheated.

"What if it did end?" I ask

"Well, there's the treasure."

"Yeah, that." I realize my thoughts of using my share to help Mom out had been selfishly forgotten.

"Between you and me," Benny says, "I'm not worried."

"You don't think Venn can win it?"

"Oh, I know he can. I'd never bet against him. He's a long-term thinker. If he wins the Game, that doesn't mean it'll be the end of it."

"He'll keep it going?"

"As long as I've known Venn, he's really only looked up to two people, his older brother and the Game Maker."

I remember Venn beating his brother's record in the chess championship. "So if he beats the Game?"

"He'll probably try to figure out an even better one. Maybe solve the problems with this one. That's just my guess."

Before he can explain the problems, someone pokes their head through the hatch and whispers, "Centaur patrol. At least five of them. When you hear me shout 'volley,' give them everything you got. Arrows first, then there's some rocks over there and a bucket of water."

"What about Mr. Freely?" asks Benny.

"Just don't hit us," the boy replies then goes back down.

Benny and I go to opposite sides of the deck and aim our arrows down. "Who's Mr. Freely?" I whisper.

"First name Ignatius. Second name Peter. Likes to go by his first two initials."

I think it over for a moment: I.P. Freely.

Good lord.

I hear someone shout "Volley!" I begin shooting arrows blindly into the dark.

Benny fires a few off then stands on the edge, balancing himself on the rail. "I think it's going to rain!"

Far down below, someone screams. I'm not sure if it's from an arrow or what Benny is doing.

"Screw you, assholes!" shouts someone from below.

Benny starts to laugh and falls backwards off the rail. His canteen rolls across the deck.

The Centaurs decided to leave us alone the rest of the night.

After it quiets down and there is only the sound of the wind, Benny and I lie out on the deck at opposite ends and stare up at the stars. There's a light rain, but it doesn't bother me.

"This is my favorite place in the world. I like it even more than Dragon Rook," he explains.

In the distance a lantern flickers. Benny turns to watch it. He lies back down with a smile. "That was Myra, telling me goodnight."

"She's out there?"

"Back at the castle. Morse code relay. It's our social network."

"It's not very private."

"We have a code."

"I'm still trying to understand how long the Game has been going on."

"I don't think that's as important as how long there's something like this. I think that's what Venn wants. The only way he can make sure of that is by winning."

"I'm not sure I understand."

"I'm not sure I do either. You read much science fiction?"

"A little."

"Ever read Dune?"

"No."

"How about Asimov's Foundation series?" he asks.

"No."

"You have to check them out. Start with Foundation. It's about a scientist who sees that civilization is coming to an end. So he tries to save the universe by creating a society to prevent us from falling back into the Dark Ages."

"Huh. So Venn sees himself as that guy? Isn't that kind of ironic?"

"What do you mean?" asks Benny.

"Aren't we in the Dark Ages out here? Clobbering each other with sticks? Shooting arrows?"

"No. Not at all. I know Venn likes to say this isn't some romantic medieval kind of game. But it is. The Dark Ages were a period between the fall of the Roman Empire and the rise of the medieval period when we rediscovered civilization and chivalry. Soon after that we had the Enlightenment. I think Enlightenment Era thinkers understood us better than we do ourselves. They understood the difference between being a savage and having virtue."

"Deep."

"Go read Foundation, then Dune. Start thinking on a different scale. All of this will make a different kind of sense. You'll really appreciate what we have out here."

"I think I do."

"Sure, sure, but you'll appreciate where it's taking you. Who you'll be when it's over."

Over? I was still adjusting to this new life. Graduation seems like a million years away. So does Dad's death, in a weird way.

After our watch, I fall asleep under the stars wishing I could tell Dad about this. I think he'd understand.

CHAPTER TWENTY-SEVEN

The Ko Rule

After spending every day for two weeks straight in the forest, I stopped in the Rook and found Venn on top of the spire. He was sitting next to a gridded board with white and black disks.

"Playing checkers in the dark?" I ask

Venn lets out a laugh, then looks through a pair of binoculars at tiny lights in the distance. He picks up a white piece and places it on the board. I step closer for a better look. The pieces are laid out in weird patterns.

"Do you play Go, Marv?"

"Once, I think. I don't really remember."

"Great game. Some say it's better than chess. There's really only one or two rules, but the combinations are endless. If we met another intelligent species, chances are, they'd have a game just like it. Maybe not 19 squares across, but something close."

"You working on another championship?" I ask.

"God, no. Go geeks are even worse than chess nerds. I like the game because it helps me think. Have a look. See how my opponent is trying to capture that row over there, little by little? He's hoping I don't realize that. He loses a piece here and there and makes his play seem unplanned, but it's not."

I try to see the pattern in the game. I remember the basic rules. You win by surrounding their pieces.

Venn looks up from the board. "See the lanterns out there?"

"Our forts?"

"Our forts, their forts. In a way, the Game is like Go. We're out there trying to surround positions and swallow them up." Venn puts a black piece down on the board then flashes the lantern.

"Who are you playing with?" I ask.

Venn grins. "I don't know. There's a light out in the forest that's not one of our forts and it's not one of the Centaurs'. I was up here one night and saw the lantern flickering. It wasn't our code. It was just Morse code. I've gone out to where the lantern light was coming from, but never found anyone."

"You thought about putting a patrol near there to ambush them?"

Venn tilts his head, "And take the fun out of it? I like not knowing. It could be anyone."

"Are they good?" I ask.

"Better than me," replies Venn. "I win a few, but they have the edge. I'm getting better. I think I'm learning the way they think. Sometimes, though, I think they play games just to show things to me."

"Like what?"

Venn points to the board. "See how this space is empty here? I can't move here. It would return the game to the previous state. It's called the Ko rule – it keeps you from going in a loop. It makes the game move forward." Venn points to the forest. "That's the problem with the game we're playing. Every few years, everything resets. There's no Ko rule. It makes it impossible to win."

"Maybe that's what the Game Maker planned?"

"Maybe. Or it was a flaw."

"A flaw?"

"Nobody is perfect. Maybe it's something he couldn't have foreseen."

"Are you sure he didn't just want the Game to continue forever?"

"Possibly...but there's another theory about that."

"About what?"

"This game, Marv. The Game Maker didn't die after he created this. He set up a trust for these woods. He moved away. He went on to do other things. I think he may have created other games."

"Other games? You mean there are more kids out there fighting in woods like ours?"

"Maybe," replies Venn. "There could also be a whole level beyond all this. Maybe if you win this game, you go up against the winners of the other games." He shrugs. "I know, it's a crazy thought. I probably spend too much time up here."

Venn picks up his binoculars and watches the flashing lantern. He sets them down and puts a white piece on the board. It closed off a line of his black ones. "I didn't see that coming. Well played."

I watch him as he studies the board. "You think it might be him?"

Venn doesn't look up. "The Game Maker? I think he's long gone by now. But that would be a nice thought."

The idea of other Realms besides ours blows my mind. I like the idea that we're not the only ones out there fighting our battles in the shadows. Venn's notion of a greater game beyond this one is something I can't even comprehend. What would that be like?

"You doing great here, Marv. Better than I hoped."

"Thanks, Venn."

"There's just one thing. I have a special mission for you," he looks up from the Go board.

"What's that?" I ask.

"I want you to spend a day somewhere outside the Realm. You've got to practice being normal. Go see some movies at the theater. Ask out one of the girls here. Just spend some time outside."

"Did I do something wrong?" I suddenly feel guilty.

"No. Not at all. It's just that we all get obsessive our first month or so. You need to get out and pretend to be a normal kid for a while."

"My mom doesn't suspect anything is up."

"It's not about her. It's about you. Trust me. Just go be normal for a few days. You don't need to be up here going slowly insane like me. It's okay to step out from time to time. Even sailors get shore leave."

"All right." I leave him to play his game of Go with his mystery opponent.

CHAPTER TWENTY-EIGHT

The Enemy

Walking along the row of posters in front of the movie theater, nothing grabs me. The action films all seem so silly and small. I had tried taking Venn's suggestion to heart. The problem was my life was centered around the Realm. Even when I wasn't in there, I was doing things to maintain my life there. I'd hurry up and clean the movie theater so I could get back to Skyperch or go on a patrol. I never thought about actually sitting in a seat and watching a movie.

Nightlife in Ellison, beyond the board games we'd play at one of our houses to maintain the illusion of normalcy to our parents, was a mystery to me.

I give up on seeing a movie and keep walking. Beyond the asphalt of the movie theater parking lot is a walk-up fast-food counter that's serving burgers and shakes. The light from the faded Burger Shaker sign illuminates a crowd of teens gathered inside and out at benches.

I walk over, hoping to see some faces I recognize. Kids from Ellison are scattered around in conversation with people who were also Ellison students, but not in the Black Dragons. I get a couple nods and friendly waves.

This looks about as normal as I can handle. I get in line and put in an order for a chili dog and fries, paying for it with my movie cleanup money. The girl behind the counter hands me a plastic number.

I walk around the tables trying to find an empty spot near someone I know. Over at the edge, Carrie and Jason are talking over a large plate of fries.

"Hey guys!" I say as I walk over.

Carrie gives me her version of a smile.

"Hey, Marv," says Jason with minimal enthusiasm.

"Cool place," I say as I look around.

"It's all right," he replies.

"So? Uh, what are you up to?"

Jason gives Carrie a look. "Talking about stuff."

"Oh," I realize an invitation to sit down isn't coming.

I suddenly feel like the biggest ass in the universe. "Cool. Well I got to run," I lie.

"See ya," says Carrie.

I give them a nod they don't see and make a beeline for the other end of the patio. I toss my plastic number in the trash and keep walking.

The strip mall gives way to a street that runs up a small hill and is lined with old houses that have been converted into small restaurants, coffee shops and an antique shop. It looks dark and far away from my embarrassment. The stores appear closed, except one at the end of the street. A light over the porch illuminates a chalkboard sign in the middle of the sidewalk.

Used Books & Collectibles

Someone had drawn a chalk sword and shield in one corner and a rocket ship in the other. For some reason the rocket calls to me. I think mostly because I want to take my mind off what just happened.

They weren't rude to me. They were just into talking to each other. Like really into each other. I'd never picked up on that before.

And I thought Venn said Carrie liked me.

Oh, I realize.

I'm an idiot.

A girl's crush is as fleeting as an ice cream cone.

Venn told me she liked me. I did nothing about it. Apparently she wasn't waiting around.

I enter the bookshop to explore mysteries more comprehensible than girls.

The counter is empty as I walk inside. Ellison is the kind of town where people will wait patiently for the clerk to come back. Not like back home at all.

The shop is broken up into several rooms, each one housing different sections. There's an entire room filled with cookbooks. Another is stacked with shelves of romance novels.

As I walk past rows of books, I see a girl about my age sitting on a stool reading a novel. She glances up and gives me a smile. With dark hair, pulled back in a ponytail, she's wearing a pair of fashion glasses only a pretty girl feels confident to wear. She's wearing a skirt above her knee and tall leather boots. She's dressed like the popular girls at my old school.

I try to return the smile, but I think I scowl instead. My eyes go to my feet and I shuffle on.

I keep wandering until I find the science fiction and fantasy books. The shopkeepers separated them in two sections. For some reason, this makes me feel good to know that the soft world of magic and dragons is kept apart from the hard science world of rockets and interplanetary intrigue.

Most of the books are dogeared paperbacks. This seems more valuable to me than a brand-new hardcover book. Someone cared enough to make sure the books stood the test of time. Their worn covers are proof that other people found them worthy of reading.

I start pulling books at random and reading their covers, then remember Benny's suggestion. I find a few of the sequels to Dune, but not the original. I move on to the Foundation books and slip one from the shelf and stare at the cover. An old guy is sitting on a futuristic throne.

Interesting.

"An Asimov?" says a voice from behind me.

I turn around and see the dark-haired girl leaning on the bookshelf. Her book is at her side with a thumb holding her page open.

"A what?" I glance at the author. "Oh, yeah. Asimov."

"You know, they say that's the Catcher in the Rye for sociopathic nerds with power fantasies."

I barely know what Catcher in the Rye is, let alone what the hell she's talking about. "Well, if I went by what other people said, who would I be?" I want to pat myself on the back for saying something that sounded almost like an intelligent comeback, but know I sounded stupid.

"So you're not planning to start a terrorist group or a cult?" she jokes.

"Not start one per se..."

"A joiner, then?"

"It depends on the cause." I search my brain trying to think if I've seen her around Dragon Rook or at Ellison. The truth is I don't really see the girls in the Black Dragons outside of their armor and Realm-wear. Most of the kids at Ellison are faceless; I'm usually staring at the clock.

"Do you have a cause yet?" she asks.

"I think so." Nervous that I'll spill my guts, I change the topic back to the book I'm holding. "So...not a fan?"

"It's all right, I guess. Kind of dry for me. I'm not all into science fiction, but I like Heinlein." She runs a finger through the books and pulls out a book. "This is one of my father's favorites."

I glance at the cover: Methuselah's Children. "What's it about?"

"A bit Randian. I won't spoil the plot. But it's about a group of people who think they're better than humanity and decide to leave society."

"What happens?"

"Read the book." She lifts the inside cover. "It's only $3.00. I'll even give you a discount."

"Oh, thanks," my heart crashes at the realization she works here and was only being nice because it's her job.

She gives me a smile then walks to the front of the shop. I spend the next ten minutes pretending I wasn't hugely devastated by looking at more books. I have trouble reading the descriptions on the backs as I keep stealing glances at her sitting at the counter.

After I've faked interest in a military space opera saga that spans more books than the Bible, I decide to leave.

I take Foundation and Methuselah's Children to the front.

She picks up Foundation and checks the price. "$2.00."

I dig inside my pockets for my leftover money. "What about the other one?"

She smiles at me and picks up the book and a pen. "On the house."

"Won't you get in trouble?"

"Mom won't miss it."

"Oh."

She hands me back the book. "You have homework."

"Huh?" I think she's talking about school and wonder what class we share.

"After you read the book, text me what you thought about it. No points for just saying you liked it."

I open the book to the inside cover. She's written her name, Jesse Buell, and her phone number...

I give her my best non-scowl and walk out the door, almost tripping over the chalkboard sign. My stomach feels tingly.

I make my way down the street and the sight of the Burger Shaker doesn't even make me feel bad. Throwing the plastic number away like a whiny little bitch does, but Carrie and Jason don't bother me. They could be face-locker right now for all I care.

I pass the theater and walk back toward the apartment, thinking about the encounter. In the streetlight I check the name and number in the book to make sure it wasn't an illusion. It's still there.

I wrap my mind about this reality.

A girl just gave me her phone number. A hot girl. A hot smart girl.

She gave me her phone number.

My heart skips a beat when the realization hits me.

This isn't just any girl. This is a girl who goes to Parker Academy.

Oh crap.

I hide the books in my jacket as if they're contraband.

CHAPTER TWENTY-NINE

Shadow Woods

Tall burnt trees, the color of gray ash, stick out of the ground like skeletal fingers clawing at the darkening sky. Benny, myself, and two juniors named Kevin and Mike are escorting Sparrow from the edge of the forest to Dragon Rook.

As a captive, she had to wait for a patrol to pick her up and walk her to the paddock. Technically, she could walk herself because she wasn't allowed to escape under the terms of parlay. The escort was more of a formality and a way for us to drill. The path we took was well within our territory.

The Shadow Woods were so far back in there was only one fort within a half-mile, located near the rear entrance to the woods. The fort was designed to watch the outer edge of the forest and let us know if there was an assault coming from behind.

Sparrow walked along in front of me about five paces. Dressed in blue jeans, hiking boots and a sweater, she looked like any other kid after school. A year younger than me, she was small for her age, but possessed a kind of steely nerve.

I'd been trying to find the opportunity, or rather the courage, over the last half-hour to ask her if she knew Jesse. I could never get her out of earshot where it wouldn't look awkward to the others. Even if that happened, I wasn't sure what I'd ask.

I finished the book, Methuselah's Children, the same night Jesse gave it to me. I read it on top of Skyperch. Although I'd rotated to other forts when I was given a duty roster, it was my favorite and I came back in my spare time. It was the tallest and largest tree. You could climb up on the top deck and feel like you were the only person in all the forest.

The swaying of the other trees in the wind made the top of the trees feel like a vast evergreen ocean. Watching the sun go down and listening to the breeze was my favorite part of the day. The frogs by the lakes would start their croaking, then the crickets would join in the chorus. In the distance, the small orange glow of lanterns in the other forts would light up, like ships far out at sea.

Even the lanterns of the Centaur forts across the meadow were somehow comforting. The thought that each one of their inhabitants would like nothing more than to shoot me full of arrows until I was paralyzed didn't diminish the thought.

After I finished the book I tried to think of something clever to say when I texted Jesse. My mind was a blank. Everything I could think of sounded like either I was trying to kiss up to her by saying something I thought she would like, or something to make myself sound smart.

I realized the problem was I'd read the book with trying to impress her in mind. I sat down and read it a second time, trying to think of how it struck me. Finally I had my answer. I thought.

I texted her back:

What I like about this book isn't the idea of living forever – it's the idea of never losing the people you love.

I stared at my phone in my bedroom for an hour waiting for her reply. Every minute tore at my heart a little piece at a time. She could have been working at the bookstore for all I knew or in a movie. Or doing some girl thing and not replying right away to mess with my head.

Thankfully she texted me back after an anguishing few hours:

Good answer. Have you ever lost someone close?

The reply was like a knife to my soul. I couldn't begin to

think how to reply without getting far more heavy than I wanted to start this off.

Start what off?

It really wasn't even a flirtation yet. For all I knew, she could do this with every person who walks into the shop. Although part of me was certain that really wasn't the case.

Watching Sparrow as she walked along, an innocent-enough-sounding question began to form in my mind. I could just ask her if she knew the girl who worked at the bookstore in town. It would sound casual enough to Benny and the others. If I didn't say her name, it made it different.

"Hold!" says Benny in a terse whisper.

Everyone freezes except Sparrow. She keeps walking. Because she was a Centaur, technically she didn't have to stop. I guess we could bind her if we wanted. Benny doesn't seem concerned with her.

He motions to Kevin and Mike to keep moving. They start going forward again, keeping pace with Sparrow. Benny falls back in step with me.

"Did you hear something back there?" he asks.

I'm too embarrassed to admit I was lost in thought about a Parker girl. "Uh, I'm not sure."

We let them get farther ahead of us as we take careful steps to not make as much noise. I hear a cracking sound in back of us. I know better than to turn around. We don't want them knowing we know.

"Rescue?" I whisper.

"Parlay," reminds Benny. He nods to the trees up ahead.

The others are taking the turn toward Dragon Rook, which goes behind a cluster of tall shadow trees.

As we make the turn, we walk toward separate trees and stop when their trunks are at our backs. To anyone watching, it looks like we kept walking.

There's another crack as someone steps on one of the dry branches from the dead trees. Benny and I grip our staffs, ready to strike. I wait for his signal.

The footsteps grow closer and more hurried. The rest of our party is out of sight, so our pursuer is trying to close the gap. It sounds like one person.

I hold up one finger. Benny nods. I'll follow him and he'll wait to see if there are others coming.

A figure in a dark green cloak comes running past us. He's so fast, he doesn't see us in our hiding place. Benny peers around the trunk of his tree then nods to me.

I chase after the person. He reaches the incline that goes up to the ridge and looks over his shoulder when I get closer. His feet come to a skid and he runs away at a diagonal.

I'm hot on his heels. If he kept going in the other direction he'd run straight into Dragon Rook. This path takes him to one of our natural barriers, a ravine filled with thorns. He doesn't seem to know this.

He keeps running along the top edge of the ravine. At the last moment he runs down into it toward a cluster of berry bushes – bushes that end in the painful thorns.

I watch as his forward momentum comes to a halt and he gets stuck in the thorns. His cloak begins to make ripping noises as he tries to pull away from them. He only gets more tangled.

I know the way through. You have to go under. Close to the ground, the thorns are more scarce. The shrubs they grow from fan out after a foot. The bottom of this ravine is a dried-out stream bed that had a mud bottom.

It's not a pleasure to crawl down it on your belly, but it's better than having sharp rocks stick into your stomach or having thorns rip at your skin.

The trapped figure is still struggling. I see his helmet turn as he tries to see where I went. He keeps looking at the top of the shrubs and the ravine, not realizing I'm like a shark underwater.

His ankle is a foot in front of me. I reach out and grab it. I give it a yank and he falls to the ground. His tattered cloak hangs above him in the thorns like a battle flag frozen in the wind.

Before he knows what hit him, I grab him by the belt and wrap his hands in a cord.

"AAAAAHHHH! MY FINGER!"

I look down and see his finger is in a splint.

"Reed?" I ask.

"Yes..." he answers in a halting breath.

"Hold on. I'm going to drag you out by your feet. Don't squirm or it'll only be worse."

"Pppplease don't hit me...."

"I meant the thorns, Reed."

"Ssssorry."

"Resist and I will hit you."

"I won't."

Dragging him backwards, I pull him from under the thorns and back into the clearing below the ridge. Benny is squatting down, looking at the trees.

"Anyone else?" I ask.

"Just me," says Reed, face-down in the dirt.

"I was talking to...never mind."

"None that I can see. Mike and Kevin will send some people back to look."

I pull Reed up by the collar so he can sit with his hands behind his back. "What are you doing out here?"

He looks at the ground, afraid to answer.

"Seriously, what kind of stupid mission did they send you on?" Benny asks.

"They didn't send me. I came on my own."

"Why?" I want know.

Reed struggles with the answer for a moment then looks at the ground as he speaks. "Sparrow."

"Sparrow?" I ask. Then it hits me when I see the resemblance. "Is she your sister?"

"Yes. I'm supposed to look out for her."

"Good job on that one. You know you can't rescue her outside of the Rook, right?" asks Benny.

"I know."

I notice the rope at his waist. "Were you going to try to capture one of us to ransom her back with?"

"Maybe."

I let out a laugh.

"The kid has balls," says Benny.

"Not necessarily, you guys," explains Reed. "I just knew there'd be Dragons coming to get her."

"You little highwayman," says Benny. "Ready to tackle us in our own territory."

"I was doing fine until Sawtooth started chasing me."

"Sawtooth?"

"Yeah," Reed tilts his head back toward where we came from. "He chased me down the path."

"He doesn't normally do that out here," replies Benny. "In the thicket or near his cave. Not out here. Are you sure it was him and not one of the mangy dogs you have tied up over at Demon Keep?"

Wild dogs at Demon Keep?

"Yes. It was him. He was bleeding. I thought maybe one of you shot him."

Benny gives me a look. "We only use stingers. The only one out here with arrows big enough is you, Reed."

"That wasn't my fault," his voice trails off. "You have to tell Venn that. It wasn't my fault."

"Tell him yourself," I reply.

"Whose arrows were they?" asks Benny.

Reed is silent.

"It's just you and us Reed," I tell him.

His eyes widen in fear. He thinks I'm going to hurt him. Although Richard pulled his finger out of joint, Reed still connects me to the pain.

"I don't mean it like that. I'm not going to hurt you. I mean there are no Centaurs here. If someone made you break the rules, you can tell us."

"He'll get mad," says Reed.

"I won't tell him you said anything."

"Red Fang. He's a prick. He had me carry his quiver."

I turn to Benny. "Red Fang?"

"Guy with the war hammer who knocked you on your ass."

"Oh, him," I mumble.

"He is an ass. Makes Richard look like a saint," adds Benny.

"Wow. That bad?"

"I hear stories. Real sadomasochist. His neighbors won't let him babysit after something happened with their kids. I heard he got kicked out of a church youth group."

"Delightful." As much as Reed's innocent nature makes we want to go soft on the Centaurs, hearing about Red Fang only makes me more angry.

"And he hates you," says Reed as he looks at me. "I mean really hates you."

"What'd I do?"

"Breathe," replies Benny. "Let's go see your sister and then find out what Lone Wolf will give us for a matching pair. Or is Lord Cutter in charge now?"

Reed shakes his head. "They're all the boss of me."

CHAPTER THIRTY

War Wounds

My hand itched toward the pocket holding my phone as I walked across the field between the armor shed and school. I was growing anxious for each new text from Jesse. When I was out in the woods trying to dodge stingers and making sure the Centaurs didn't cross our front lines, it was a little more easy to bear. It was our practice to leave our phones locked away in the shed. A ringtone could give away your position and both the Centaurs and us had handheld EMF scanners we periodically used to look for people who may have brought their phones into the Realm.

Like the night-vision goggles in the tree fortresses, they were things that reminded you this wasn't role-playing some medieval game. This was covert combat. I heard Venn call it a shadow war.

The other reason for not bringing cell phones into the Realm was the confiscation policy. If you got caught by the other side, they were entitled to take your weapons, your armor and anything else you had on you. The last thing any of us wanted was to explain to our parents what happened to our phone or having the enemy intercepting phone calls.

The lanterns worked well at night most of the time for sending codes. In the day we used shiners, small pocket mirrors, to send codes. I learned the basic codes for reporting ambushes, patrol movements and other important things you wanted to communicate from one end of the forest to the next. I was still working on our Morse code system. Some kids could send and receive faster than I could type.

I once sat with Venn on top of the turret, carrying on a conversation in the middle of the night. Without taking his eyes off me or breaking his train of thought, he flashed a code back to one of the tree fortresses using a lantern. There were lots of stories about how scary smart he was.

Outside the Realm, the only codes I cared about were from someone living in the heart of the enemy. Texts from Jesse were the one dash of color I looked forward to in the dull black-and-white outside world. Up in Skyperch or back in Dragon Rook, they made the end of a shift bearable. Walking back to class now, I stared at the screen hoping for a message to come through. Even an answer to my lame "What's up?" I sent before escorting Sparrow would lift my spirits.

I put the phone in silent mode and gave it one last look. A voice cut through the air like a rusty razor blade, intruding on my thoughts.

"Personal electronic devices aren't allowed during school hours."

Mr. Pressman is standing in the field in front of me as I look up. Arms folded, he gazes in the distance toward the forest and takes a deep breath through his sharp nose, as if he's trying to smell what's out there.

My hand holding the phone falls slack at my side as I try to think of an excuse.

"Don't worry, Marv. You can put your phone away. You're not in trouble." He looks past my shoulder at the wooden shed where we store the armor. "So, how is Conservation Club going? Do much conserving?" He gives me a smirk.

"Um, yes, sir." Venn and the others had repeatedly drilled into me that we needed to treat adults with respect at all times. "Sir" and "Mam" should be in every sentence. Words like my ever present "um" needed to be avoided. I was getting better, but I still didn't speak like Venn or the other senior members of the Black Dragons who spoke with almost military-like elocution. Using the word "elocution" was a good start, though.

"It looks like you're adjusting quite well."

"Thank you, Sir."

He folds his hands behind his back and turns to face me.

"I'm not sure if that's a good thing. Tell me, Marv, has Venn showed it to you?"

"Pardon me, Sir?" I wasn't sure what "it" was. Whatever it was, I was certain I shouldn't be talking to Pressman about it.

He gives me a wink. "Secrets. I know. I've been trusted with a few myself. 'It,' the gold bar. The so-called Nazi plunder he parades around as proof of the treasure that's out there. Has he shown it to you?"

"I'm not sure I understand," I reply. How much does Pressman know?

"Of course you do. Do you think it's real? I saw something once in a catalog of movie props that looked remarkably like that gold bar. Could be a coincidence. Or it could be a piece of electroplated junk metal."

Pressman knows about the gold bar? How could he? As far as I know he was never in the Black Dragons. Someone would have told me. Wouldn't they?

"I don't mean to confuse you, Marv. Students like to talk. I know a lot about what goes on out there. Maybe more than you. As I said, people talk. I don't want any of you getting hurt out there, so I listen."

I try to give a blank expression, yet I know my face is an open book.

"I'm not asking you to tell me anything. Unless there's something you want to tell me... Or perhaps, more importantly, something you want to ask. Is there?"

I shake my head and try to think of a way out of this

situation.

"Hmmm. Well maybe I can help. If I were you I'd want to ask someone like me several things..."

I had lots of questions still, so I take the bait. "Like what?"

"Like why Venn has taken a special interest in you? Why did you get made a knight faster than anyone else? Does he have something else in mind? Nothing is ever a straight line with that boy. Another question, the question, is if this is all real... Do you think that somewhere out in the woods there's really a buried treasure? Or is this some sadistic game invented by a bunch of unpopular students who wanted a way to inflict pain on others." He raises an eyebrow and gives me an expectant look. "Have you thought of that?"

I can't think of anything to say that wouldn't reveal more than I should. "Um, I'm going to be late for class."

"Yes, of course. Well, I'll leave you with this thought: What if the treasure was already found? Some say it was dug up years ago. But they kept it a secret. Boys like Venn decided not to let the others know." Pressman pauses and waits for me to ask why.

I keep my mouth shut, but my eyes ask.

"Because without the Game, they have nothing. If it didn't exist, Venn would be a lonely boy sitting in the library waiting for someone to play chess with. He wouldn't have any friends. He certainly wouldn't be a leader of a gang like he is. And yes, that's what you are in, a gang. Without the fiction of the treasure he'd just be one more nerd no one pays attention to. Think about that. Maybe the real game is the one being played on you."

I turn back to look at the forest, half expecting to see the trees are just cardboard cutouts from a kindergarten play. Was the Game really just that? The treasure didn't matter to me as it did when I started. But it still mattered in an important way; it made the Game real.

If there wasn't a treasure out there, we weren't really at war. We were just playing...

Pressman gives me a cold smile then walks back toward the school. My feet are frozen to the ground. Was the Game a lie?

I try to convince myself it didn't matter, but it did. Whatever the treasure was supposed to be wasn't as important as there actually being a real treasure. Something. Anything. Even a cardboard box filled with Playboys and Scrooge McDuck comics would be something real. But what if it was a lie? What if Venn had been lying to me?

It's more than I want to think about. Everything up until now felt real. Pressman was just being a prick. He sees us having fun, bending the rules, and he can't stand it. That has to be it.

My phone vibrates in my numb hand. It takes me a moment to realize I was getting a text. Jesse had replied to me: **"Hey! I have to ask...you're not one of those weirdos who hangs out in the woods? R U?"**

I type my response, **"A Boy Scout? Yes."**

It was our stock answer. A weirdo? I guess so. Coming

from her that could be a compliment. Telling her I was in Scouts deflected the whole matter.

"Which troop?"

"199."

"So u r."

Oh man. She knows. Now she thinks I am a weirdo. A few minutes ago I could have handled that. Now, with Pressman's words rolling around in my head, I feel a little more ridiculous.

"Okay, weirdo. Have fun slaying dragons!"

Crap. Is she writing me off? I didn't think I could feel any worse than I already did. Well damn.

Another text comes through:

;)

A wink. Thank God. I hope it's a good wink. I mean, nobody uses the wink to write you off, right?

Before going to class I look longingly back at the forest and the simplicity of only worrying about getting your head smashed in and trying not to fall out of a tree while you slept. The complex world of girls and nosey teachers was way more stressful.

As Pressman grows smaller in the distance, I hold up a finger to the wind and calculate how high I'd have to aim a stinger to hit him from here.

CHAPTER THIRTY-ONE

Roll the Bones

Two of the younger members of the clan drag a termite-ridden log covered in brown moss and toss it onto the bonfire. Flames shoot up above the heads of those standing and sparks flitter through the dark smoke like drunk fireflies.

Benny growls as his marshmallow liquifies and falls into the dirt. "Watch where you throw that thing!" They scatter as he walks toward the baskets of food to grab another marshmallow.

Rhode gives one of the kids a kick in the pants. "What'd I tell you about moss-covered logs?"

Venn watches this with a smile. He's standing on a large rock that sits close to the fire. The orange flames give his face a theatrical glow.

"Who's next?" he calls out, raising the wooden polygon over his head.

"Your turn, again," says Carrie. "We heard your stupid chess story before."

"You did? When?" he asks, mocking anguish.

Venn had just regaled us with his account of how he'd won the chess tournament that made him a minor celebrity. He confessed that in his last game his opponent was far more prepared for him. In desperation, Venn had used a chess move he remembered seeing the other boy studying hours before when he was poring through a manual. The only catch was, Venn had unknowingly memorized the pattern upside down. When he used it in the final match, the other player was totally confused by the strategy. Something seemed familiar, but off. It was Venn's version of humility to admit how he blundered his way to a win.

"Summer War. July," replies Carrie. "You told us the story."

"Well, not all of you," Venn insists.

"Rules are rules," says Myra.

"Why didn't you stop me?"

"Secret!" shouts Benny.

"Tell us another secret! One we don't know," echoes another boy.

"Seriously?"

"You rolled the bone. You have to tell us a secret. Your other story isn't a secret if we already know it."

"Fine. Fine." Venn drops the wooden die into the dirt.

"Or we can choose," adds Carrie.

Jason whispers something into her ear. They both laugh. Watching the two of them makes me wish Jesse could be here with me. That of course would be complicated. Although Sparrow is here. Sitting on the log near Venn, she hasn't taken her eyes off him all night. More than once he's passed her a look. In the great hall they occasionally sit near each other working on homework.

It's all in plain sight, and from what I understand, within the bounds of parlay. I get the feeling there's something more between them.

"You want a secret?" says Venn. "A real secret. Something none of you know. Something I've never even dared to say until now?"

"Get on with it!" shouts Rhode as he tosses a marshmallow at Venn's head.

Venn snatches it out of the air and swallows it. "Did any of you ever know I've been to Demon Keep?"

"Bullcrap!" yells Jason.

Venn turns toward him. "No. Not bull. You're not the only one. A week after your little raid into the Keep, I decided I had to have a look for myself." Venn pauses as we all take this in.

"Why didn't you say anything?" asks Jason with a serious tone.

"Because no one would have believed me. I still hadn't proven myself. So I kept it a secret. Until now."

"Bullcrap. Bullcrap. Bullcrap." Jason starts a chant. A

few others begin to join in.

A grin spreads across Venn's face. "Would you like to know the story? Would you like my proof?"

Jason waves a hand. "Whatever. Lie on."

"Remember the rainstorms we had the weeks after? Remember the Centaur who went by the name of Green Fire? Have you seen him around anymore? No? That's because his family moved away over the summer. Actually, his mother left his father and took him with her. I was at the supermarket and saw her buying travel toothpaste and talking on the phone to her sister. I overheard the whole conversation.

"Green Fire, Mark was his name, had black armor with a helmet with green flames that were actually just decals you could buy at the hobby shop. Hearing that he would be out of the Game the next morning, I made a helmet like his that night.

"With the rainstorms and most everyone still recovering from the first battle, we were all off a bit. The Centaurs were sending out fewer patrols. Demon Keep only had half as many people standing guard.

"At the crack of dawn, I marched to the meadow in my gear and then took the creek pass. There I put on my Green Fire helmet and marched straight into Demon Keep. The wind was howling and the rain pouring down in sheets. If they called to me from the forts to give them the code, I couldn't hear them, and they couldn't hear me. It was the perfect scenario.

"I walked straight down the main path, through the rock gate and waved to the watchman standing guard, trying not to drown in the downpour. A group returning from patrol were already knocking at the door. I just followed them inside."

Venn taps his head. "The green helmet. I knew in a few hours they'd find out poor Mark was already across state lines. But for now, they had no idea. There were maybe a dozen other people in the Keep. I kept the helmet on and nobody said anything. I was too afraid to go further in. I was sure I'd get caught."

"This is bull," Jason replies.

Everyone else is silent. We're watching the exchange between the two, trying to decide if Venn is really telling the truth.

"Ask me a question about the inside," says Venn.

"I've already described the inside."

"Not everything. What about the throne?"

"I told you about the throne and the pedestal."

"The statue of the centaur? Taller than a man, that sits behind the throne?"

"Yes. I told you. I told you all of this, Venn," Jason answers.

"What about the color of the throne? The cushion? Do you remember?"

Jason thinks for a moment. "I'm not sure."

Venn's face lights up. "Something you don't know! Purple. The cushions are purple."

"Maybe. But that doesn't mean you were there."

Venn turns to Sparrow. "Without giving away any state secrets, are the cushions purple?"

She hesitates and looks around before answering. "Yes..."

"You see?" Venn says to Jason. "I was there."

"That's it? That's your proof?" Jason glances at Sparrow. I get the feeling he's about to accuse her of telling Venn. He thinks better of it and keeps his mouth shut.

"I have one more bit of proof. I was alone in the room for a few minutes. Lone Wolf called a meeting and I stayed behind. And that was when..." Venn waits for us all to lean in and hear the revelation. "That was when I pissed all over the throne!"

There's a split second as we try to figure out if this is all a joke. Suddenly, Sparrow cries out, "THAT WAS YOU????" Her voice was like a shriek. Her reaction was so natural we all burst into laughter.

Venn gives us a wink. "Now you know why it couldn't be told until now. Man, did I ever take a piss. I think it was the sound of the rain."

"YOU ASS!" shouts Sparrow. "The hall smelled like piss for weeks. Everyone blamed everyone else! Lone Wolf swore it was Red Fang. The two fought over it. That was when Cutter..." Sparrow's voice trails off as she realizes she's talking more than she should. It's the most I've ever heard her say.

"That would be me." Venn's face is beaming. He takes a bow.

We're still laughing. Sparrow is sitting on the log fuming. She gives Venn the evil eye. Even Jason's face has slackened a bit. Somewhere a girl mocks Sparrow's voice, "That was you!"

We start laughing again.

"I hate you guys," says Sparrow.

"It was nothing personal," says Venn. "How else was I going to prove I was there."

She shakes her head. "And I thought..."

I pick up where that was going. The attraction was real. Or at least it was until Venn's confession.

Venn walks over to the wooden block and picks it up. He hold it out and spins in a circle. "Hmmm. Who's next?"

When you roll the bones, or rather the bone, since it's just one large wooden block, it can come up on one of ten sides. Each one involves a task or confession you have to make. It could be a secret, like Venn's, a talent you have to display, something embarrassing, telling a joke or the girl's favorite – telling something sexy.

I couldn't decide which one frightened me more. When Venn's back turns, I breathe a sigh of relief.

I was too loud.

Venn spins around and faces me with a devilish grin. "Your turn, Marv."

Crap. I hesitate for a moment. He pushes it under my nose. Reluctantly, I take the block from him and stand on the rock. To roll the bone, I'm supposed to toss it high over my head, but not into the fire. Carved symbols glare back at me in the flickering light. There's a heart for sexy, a frowning face for bad, a note for music and other runes that aren't too hard to figure out.

I give the block a toss over my head behind me. Venn runs over to look. "Very interesting, Marv..."

I crane my neck. The side with the lock is face-up: secrets.

It had to be secrets.

I have too many damn secrets.

This has to be one they don't know about. My mind goes to Jesse. No. I can't tell them that.

The doubts I have about Venn? No, I can't go there either. I don't know what I think.

My anxiety builds as everyone stares at me. I want to shrink away and go back to being invisible.

Secrets...

My fear that the Game may be make-believe?

Right now it's not a fear. The bonfire is real. The Black Dragons are real. I convince myself that's all that matters. And my fear is very real.

A secret...

I'm sweating bullets. I just blurt out the first thing that comes to my mind that doesn't involve the Game.

"Oh my God," says Carrie.

"Christ, man," replies Venn as he shakes his head.

I feel his hand on my shoulder and everyone's eyes on me.

I try to will the words back into my mouth.

I can't.

I said it.

They all heard it.

The secret. The one I'd been holding deep down since before the Game. The one Mom doesn't know. That only I know.

I've tried to deny it, but the truth just forced itself free. I confessed it.

I walk over to the log and sit down. They're all staring at me. They want me to explain what I meant.

"Was he a bad guy?" asks Benny.

"No!" I scream. I feel my fist ball up. I want to hit him with all my rage. "He was the best." My voice halts. "The best." The light of the fire grows blurry as tears form in my eyes.

No one says a thing.

They're trying to understand why I said what I said.

I'd told them my darkest secret.

I told them I wanted my father to die.

CHAPTER THIRTY-TWO

Patricide

Venn sits down next to me. His voice is low and soothing. "Tell us about him."

"He was a great dad," I tell him, then repeat for everyone around the fire. Their faces look like a hellish jury in the firelight. "Anything I know that's worth knowing, he taught me. He and Mom had problems. But they weren't about me. I never blamed him."

I wipe my nose on my sleeve. "I'm sorry. Forget I said anything."

"We're your friends, Marv," says Venn. "We're your family."

Myra reaches a hand out and pats me on the shoulder. "This is what the fire is about. Tell us."

I'm embarrassed to talk, but the words burst forth like a flood. "He was always strong. He'd even come close to the Olympic team for judo. Then I came along. You wouldn't know it at first, how tough he was. He was the nicest guy. The best. He was just good at everything. It's just...It's just when he got sick. I thought he'd be able to fight it off. He's my dad. He could do anything. But it got worse."

My hand reflexively grabs my arm where I'd donated blood over and over. "He got thin. He didn't look like himself. The drugs, I could tell he was in pain. Sometimes, sometimes I wanted to blame him for not being tough enough. Stupid? Then I thought he was going to get better. But he didn't. He just couldn't keep on any weight. He laid there in bed, so thin. It was like he was a puppet. My dad was fading away in front of me.

"I went to see him because I knew it made him feel better. We'd listen to audiobooks. Sometimes he'd keep coughing and I had to use headphones. I don't know. I just started to resent him for not being himself. My dad. My own dad! He would have done anything for me.

"One day he's coughing and he sees the look in my eye. I know what he saw. It wasn't sympathy. It wasn't pity. It was contempt. I hated what he'd become. I wanted my old dad. Not my sick dad.

"My old dad was still in there somewhere and he knew what I felt. Like I said, he'd do anything for me. Since he couldn't get better, he did the only thing he could. He died. That night, my father died." I wipe at my eyes. "He died because he couldn't stand the look of his own son. He died because I wanted him to go."

"It's not..." Venn starts to say.

I shrug his hand off my shoulder and storm away from the fire.

Someone else calls out my name. I ignore them and go into the trees beyond the ring of stones.

I feel so ashamed.

Ashamed for crying in front of them.

Ashamed for how I feel.

I can't stop. The tears keep pouring.

I hate myself for being so weak.

I hate myself for feeling sorry for myself.

I hate myself for wanting the one person who loved me more than life to die.

I cheated him out of a few more weeks. Maybe even a recovery. But he couldn't go on with a pathetic son like me.

I killed him.

I killed my father.

I lean against a tree as my body begins to shudder. My knees weaken and I fall to the ground.

Somewhere behind me a branch breaks.

"Go away, Venn." I bark.

"It's me, Carrie."

Christ. All I need is a girl to see me like this.

"You're not a bad person, Marv."

"Um, yeah." I rub my hand across my face and feel disgusted when I see the snot trail in the moonlight.

"Whatever."

"We're teenagers. We don't know how to deal with this crap. If we handled things the right way we'd go from twelve to college."

"Is Marv all right?" calls another female voice.

At the edge of the woods I can see Sparrow standing there. She's crying, too.

Oh crap. Now I've made her cry, too. Jesus Christ. I'm a contagious whiny bitch.

"Marv is fine," says Carrie.

"Peachy," I reply.

"My dad is an ass," says Carrie. "I sometimes wish he was dead."

"My dad wasn't an ass," I reply.

"I know. I can tell you love him. It was hard to see him that way. But that's not how you feel now, is it?"

"No. God no. I love my dad."

"I don't love mine. I just feel sorry for my mom. She's too stupid to hate. I wish," Carrie's voice trails off. "I wish I felt half the way you do now about your dad about any of my parents. I mean, I wish they were worth it."

I'd heard stories about Carrie's family. Her mother had drug problems. There were innuendos that she used to be a hooker. I can't imagine what her father is like.

I stare up at her. The moonlight has softened her features. She looks angelic. "I just wish I could take back that moment. The look."

"Marv, you didn't kill your father."

"You weren't there. You didn't see the look in his eyes."

"No. But if what you say happened, happened, it was still your dad's choice. He knew you loved him. Maybe he saw the look. Maybe he decided he wanted to go before it got worse. Maybe he let go so you could. So you could move on. Maybe he needed your permission."

"I gave it to him in a horrible way."

"We're teenagers. It's how we communicate."

I can't remember Carrie stringing more than two sentences together. Sometimes I see her whispering to Jason and wonder what it'd be like to be around her.

"We all care about you," Carrie says.

"Whatever."

"No, Marv. If you were Richard, we'd have let you storm off. But we like you. You're one of us. I don't just mean a Black Dragon. You're part of the heart of this group. For a few of us, this is all we have."

"I think you and Jason can get along fine without me," I say with spite.

"Oh..." says Carrie.

Why did I say that? "I'm sorry. Jason is a good guy."

"He is. Anyway, I hear you've met someone..."

I don't even want to ask. Girls have either ESP or a secret telegraph. "She's just a friend."

"You have a lot of friends, Marv. You're a good guy."

Her words sound sincere. "I wish you could have met him. You guys would have liked him."

"I bet we would. But I think we've already met the best

part of him."

"You're going to make me cry more," I reply, trying to make a joke.

"Crap, everyone is in tears back by the fire."

"Even Venn?"

"Well, he's experiencing his closest version of human emotions. He feels real bad for giving you the bone."

"That sounds so wrong."

"You want to come back? Want me to leave you for a while?"

"I'll come back." I pull myself up and try to wipe away the tears and snot. I feel like a gross mess.

Carrie tussles my hair as we're face to face. "We're all a wreck."

I don't see any tears in her eyes. "Some more than others."

She looks down at the ground. "I can't cry, Marv."

"Oh."

"I feel, though. Trust me." Her pale blue eyes reflect back at me. There's something deep behind them. An ocean of feelings hidden by her glacial mask.

I give her a faint smile.

Without warning, she kisses me.

Not on the cheek.

On the lips.

Full on.

My face turns bright red as she turns and walks out of the woods. Sparrow is still standing on the edge, watching.

Carrie passes her by without looking. As I leave my hiding spot, Sparrow squeezes my arm in compassion.

I'm still too numb to say anything. Carrie sits down next to Jason by the fire. I glance away guiltily when he looks toward me.

Venn is sitting on the rock with his arms folded, staring at the wooden block near his feet. He's lost in thought. The almost permanent elation is gone from his face. When he sees me he gives me a concerned look. "You all right, buddy?"

I pick up the bone. "Who's ready to tell us their deepest, darkest secret?" I shout. "I've got dibs on patricide!"

Everyone cheers. Instead of waiting to be picked, they all leap to their feet and rush me. I'm hugged by more people than I can count. I'm suffocated by the attention.

It's a good feeling.

At this point, I don't care if the Game is all bull. I'm feeling love I've never known. I've been kissed by one of the prettiest girls I've ever seen. And for the first time in a long time, I feel kind of good about myself.

We were never much into religion and an afterlife in my family, but I'm damn sure Dad would feel good about my friends. I take their hugs as a kind of forgiveness from him.

"Please stop," I finally say. "Or I'm going to make you all cry again. Now let me give the bone to Benny so we humiliate him now."

CHAPTER THIRTY-THREE

Dead Things

"Want to see something cool?" Benny asks after waking me up for our pre-dawn patrol.

Our mission was to scout the perimeter near Demon Keep in a wild area of overgrowth where there were few or no forts and limited strategic value. Venn wanted a better idea of all the Centaur fortifications before we launched our assault on Black Tree.

"Sure," I tell him, wiping the sleep from my eyes and stumbling across the parking lot. "As long as it's not too far from where we're headed."

"It's practically on the way." Practically, in Benny's mind, means not quite Seattle.

We reach the woods and strap on our forest armor so we

can be stealthy. It was still dark out, so we both had small lanterns to light the way. Once we reached the edge of our territory we blew them out to prevent the Centaurs from spotting us. The lanterns gave off less light than a flashlight, but they could still be seen from a hundred yards or so.

Benny leads us down a narrow pass between two boulders into a dried-up creek bed. Leafy branches from trees on either side blot out the sky.

"I never knew this was here." I look around the enclosed passage. It's like a long tunnel.

"It's almost invisible from back there. The hills and trees cover up the pass," Benny says.

"Cool."

"This isn't what I wanted to show you. We have a ways to go."

Benny threads through boulders that reach up to our shoulders and leads me through more overgrown brush. Hundreds of fallen logs form a barrier, like a dried-up damn.

As we climb over the logs, I start to whisper. "So..." I stretch out the syllables as I think up the right words to ask my question. It had been several days since the bonfire and my confession. No one had mentioned what was said. Which was all well and good for me. Carrie's kiss was just a memory as she went back with Jason and shared their secret jokes. The feeling tore at me a little.

My texts back and forth with Jesse were just that – texts. A little flirty, nothing else. I knew I had to make a move. Carrie had made it clear to me I'd blown my chances with her. The kiss was just a reminder. What a reminder.

"No need to whisper," Benny replies. "No one comes out here."

"Oh...so...um...what's the policy on dating?" The words sound stupid coming out of my mouth.

"I'm flattered, Marv. But I don't think it'll work out. Myra is the jealous type."

My cheeks flush. "Not you, retard."

"Now I'm hurt," Benny quips.

"I mean um...between..."

"The clans?" asks Benny.

I was about to say schools, but I guess that's sort of the same thing.

He turns around and raises an eyebrow. "I was wondering when you were going to ask."

Oh, crap. Does everyone know?

"Venn could date Sparrow if he wanted. Lots of kids have friends at Parker, some of us even with members of the Centaurs."

He thought I was talking about Venn and Sparrow. Man, that's a relief. "Friends with the Centaurs?"

"Sometimes. But what happens in the Realm is separate. You sure as hell don't talk about it out there."

"Really? I thought that would be frowned upon."

"It can't be helped. Ellison is a small town. Some of us have cousins and family at Parker."

I stop walking and consider this. "Really?"

"Yeah," says Benny matter-of-factly. "You know, like

Venn."

"Venn?"

"Yeah, Venn. His brother goes to Parker, obviously."

"He does?"

Benny turns around, shocked, "You didn't know?"

I shake my head. "Is he a Centaur?"

"A Centaur? He's the Centaur, or was at least. We don't know what's going on there."

"Cutter???"

"No, Lone Wolf."

"Holy crap! Lone Wolf and Venn are brothers?" My head feels like it's going to explode. "Brothers? Full brothers?"

"Yep. Lone Wolf is Venn's older brother by two years."

I remember the article about Venn winning the chess tournament. The last winner was his brother...

"I think that's why Venn wants to win this year. He wants to beat his brother before he graduates. A lot of tension between those two."

"How come Venn doesn't go to Parker?"

"He demanded he go to Ellison. Specifically so he could go to war against his brother."

"Wow. That's insane. Do they fight a lot?"

"Only here. Lone Wolf is a pretty mellow guy. He's smart. Real smart. But he knows Venn is smarter. It's more Venn trying to prove that to himself."

"Weird."

"I know. And the Game is different at Parker."

"What do you mean?"

"Here, you're popular when you're good at the Game. Over at Parker, it's kind of feudal. The popular kids get to call the shots, decide who does what. It's the total reverse. Legacy is everything. Venn may never have gotten a shot at leading there."

"How come his brother did?"

"It took him four years to get there and even still he's not the de facto ruler. He's more of a general."

We continue on and I try to wrap my head around the fact that the two clans are headed up by brothers at war with each other. And that Venn gave up going to Parker, just so he could compete against his brother.

The pass opens up into a flat area that looks like a dried-up mouth of a lake. More of the chest-high boulders are strewn about. In the center is a pile of rocks with flat edges, lying in a tall mound. Weeds and grass grow through the cracks.

Benny strides over to the mound and starts to climb. I follow after him. The pile sits awkwardly in the middle of the basin. I can't imagine what forces would have collected them all here. He points something out to me and I have my answer.

Carved into one of the rocks is a coiled snake. Nearby I see the head of a stone statue with a serpent's head. Broken under the rocks, it looks like it was intentionally buried.

"Welcome to Serpent's Lair," says Benny, pointing to the crumbling stone blocks.

I look to my feet, half expecting snakes to start squirming

out from the cracks. "Was this a fort?"

"A long time ago. Back when the Game began. The Serpents were another clan. I think there were four or five back then. Each school had more than one."

This comes as another shock to me. I'd always imagined the struggle had just been between the Centaurs and the Black Dragons. Other clans?

"What happened?" I ask.

Benny shrugs. "You'll hear different stories. Somewhere in the Rook there's a journal. It's kind of spotty and not well-kept. But it says that they cheated. They broke the rules. The other clans, us and the Centaurs, maybe others, we tore their castle down and banished them from the Game."

I take a step back on the rock, afraid for what might be underneath my feet.

Benny lets out a laugh. "I don't think they were inside at the time."

"Well that's a relief. What did they do?"

"I don't know. It had to be something severe."

"No kidding. This place is a heap. It's like the Romans sacked it."

"Or they just weren't good at building things."

Sunlight had begun to creep out over the horizon. On the far ridge, a dry twig snaps. Something whizzes past my ear. A stinger bounces off the rocks.

"Let's split up," Benny whispers.

We take off in opposite directions to confuse the Centaur patrols. Benny heads back across the rock bed, and I run down the side of the rubble mountain opposite of the noise and direction of the arrow.

I pick up a lot of speed as I reach the bed. Without looking back, I charge toward a low part of the riverbank closest to me, hoping a thick cluster of trees will help shield my retreat from the Centaur patrol.

Rocks scatter behind me as heavy boots stomp across the dry lake. I grab a clump of tall weeds and pull myself over the bank. On the opposite side, I roll for a few yards then pick myself up and run behind trunks. Every fifty feet I change direction, hiding my path.

I keep running for another ten minutes then stop to catch my breath. I have no idea where I am. In my escape, I got totally lost. After the trees ended, I found myself in sparsely covered ground. To one side of me are tall clay cliffs. To the other, a brown brush of the thorns.

Staying close to the cliff, I keep walking, looking for something familiar. I scan the far treetops, hoping to see a fort or a tall pine I recognize.

A rock falls from above. Something hard hits my elbow, sending a flash of pain. I turn and see three Centaurs on an adjacent cliff pelting me with rocks. A stone smashes into my helmet and dirt flies into my mouth. The impact sends me backwards into the clay.

Out of the corner of my eye I see two of them nocking their bows. Screw this. I break out into a run again and head straight into the brush. They have the advantage of higher ground. The cuts and scrapes I'll get crawling on my belly are probably worse than any damage they'll be able to do from that far away, but my pride won't stand for it.

I scurry across the underbrush and keep moving away from the Centaurs. Behind me is the scuffling sound of their boots as they reach the bottom of the cliff. The dry brush shakes from the heavy stones they throw after me. One of them bounces its way down to the ground through the branches. It's as big as my head.

Crap.

If I'd been out in the open and hit by that, I'd be unconscious or worse.

I keep crawling away from them. Sharp thorns try to tear at my leather tunic, but only manage to claw into my exposed neck. The ground gets muddier and I find myself half submerged in a stagnant puddle.

The area looks similar to Sawtooth's cave and where I found Reed. I pray I've managed to double back into slightly familiar territory. I also pray he's not home.

The sun is fully up and I'm still on my stomach trying to find a way out of here. No stones have been tossed in my direction for what feels like a half-hour. Now I'm just trying to find my way out.

At the end of the muddy puddle I come to a dry spot. I pull myself together and wipe away the sharp rocks clinging to my palms. My fingernails are black and bleeding from crawling through the muck. To clear my head, I decide to take a rest and roll onto my back.

At first my eyes can't make out what I'm seeing in front

of my face. My brain fills in the connection. It takes all my effort not to scream.

A hand.

A skeleton's hand.

Inches from my nose, the hand looks as if it's frozen in place, trying to claw at me.

I jerk back and get to my knees, ignoring the thorns shoving into my back.

Part of a forearm is sticking out of the ground. Two long bones end in a wrist. The wrist splays out into fingers and a pointy thumb.

This isn't a hoof from a deer or a wild pig.

Something is buried here. Someone?

Bits of flesh and sinew are still attached at points. The bones haven't been here too long. Maybe a few years? Maybe less?

It can't be a person?

My gut tells me the hand looks too human. My brain tells me I know jack about anatomy.

What would a large dog's paw look like?

I wouldn't know.

I calm down by reminding myself I don't know anything.

The hand stares back, taunting me.

Maybe it is a human body? So what?

It could be an Indian burial that got unearthed in a rainstorm. It only looked new. I'm sure lots of people have died out here over in the olden days.

It doesn't mean...

I try to put the thought out of my head.

I don't want to think about it.

Benny just showed me the Serpent's Lair. I saw the size of the stone the Centaurs threw at me.

What if someone did die out here?

What if someone had gotten killed playing the Game?

Would anyone tell?

Or would they keep it a secret?

CHAPTER THIRTY-FOUR

Raid on Black Tree

Black Tree was a coal black spire that erupted out of the stoney ground like a splinter out of hell. The farthest reaches of the lifeless tree faded into the low-hanging fog. Dead of leaves and spindly branches like the other obsidian-colored trees on the ridge, its only signs of life were the shapes moving behind the thick oak shields bound in metal bands and impaled to the tree by massive iron spikes.

To my eyes, Black Tree resembled a massive medieval siege weapon to attack heaven. With its huge black armor scales, making up for the loss of foliage to conceal and deflect arrows, this was no children's tree fort.

Eyes peered down at us from narrow gaps and arrows aimed at our vulnerable spots. The tension was all around –

a drawstring ready to be pulled back and released.

We held our shields tightly in place. As we climbed up, the Centaurs would be firing arrows down at us. This was going to be a bloody day no matter who came out on top.

I was a mixture of emotions, ready to throw myself up the tree on adrenaline. The skeleton had receded from my mind after several days. I didn't bother telling anyone about it, because I didn't know what I saw. It could have been an animal, an old body. I just didn't know. And honestly, I reasoned with myself, I don't even remember exactly where I'd found it. Not that I went back to look.

I spent a day online reading stories of found skeletons; the vast majority of them were misidentified animal skeletons and the occasional derelict that had gone off to die somewhere alone.

At some point I promised myself I would tell someone. Before then, I'd go back and make certain what I saw. Until then, there were a lot of other things to keep me occupied...

Today was Black Tree.

Tomorrow, if I lived, I was going to ask Jesse out on a date.

It was a big week for me. I wasn't about to let some dead dog or an Indian scout who'd preferred to be left alone to die in the woods ruin things for me.

I'm sure in the light of day, the skeleton would look different. Calling the cops or bringing Venn and the others over to find something mundane would only make me embarrassed.

Somewhere, a little voice asked if that's the only reason I didn't want to tell Venn and the others.

I shut the voice down and looked around me. There were fourteen of us in the trees below Black Tree. The rest of our party was scattered around waiting to ambush the Centaurs when they came to help defend their comrades.

We'd started hours ago by sending small parties of three and four people to different places in the forest. Quietly sneaking out in the dark, we waited in the places Venn decided were least defended by the Centaurs' lookouts.

We'd managed to get fifty of us behind their lines before they knew what was going on. The Centaurs' immediate reaction was to call in the reserves to defend their Keep, thinking that was the target.

Venn knew this would happen. The rest of our forces were now in a thin line waiting to attack the Centaurs when they ventured out to reinforce the tree forts. They would hold them off while we tried to take Black Tree.

"There's only seven or eight up there," whispers Rhode.

I don't point out that I've heard it said that it only takes one or two to defend Black Tree. The lowest platform is thirty feet off the ground. That's taller than the roof of the gym. It's the height of an Olympic high-diving platform – which would be a comfort if there were a pool below.

When the Black Dragons took Skyperch over the summer, Venn's innovation was cardboard boxes for the attackers to fall back onto. They had dozens of large refrigerator boxes to drop onto.

We managed to bring only twelve. Benny and three others were assembling the boxes and taping them shut. One by one, they carried them out over their heads and dropped them at the base of the tree, then retreated under their shields.

The Centaurs saved their arrows for more open targets. They knew the siege could go on a long time and only end when they had nothing left to fling at us.

Benny places the last box and runs over to Rhode and me. The crash pad of boxes looks tiny next to the tall tree.

"That's it?" cries Rhode, in disbelief

"According to Venn, we won't need the pad," says Jason, his voice half-mocking.

"I think the ladder will work," I reply, trying to convince myself.

"I wish Venn was here to show us how," Jason grumbles.

Venn was off leading one of the deflecting raids. He'd explained how we should take Black Tree. It made sense as he stood over his map and drawings. Out here, the crash pad looked minuscule and the untested ladder flimsy.

The problem with trying to make an ascent as you sieged was defending yourself from above. Holding a shield over your head kept one hand tied up and it grew tiresome very fast. Trying to climb like that was almost impossible.

When they took Skyperch, they used shields like umbrellas, with the man below holding onto the shaft. Venn had a better idea this time.

In our Great Hall, standing over the oak table, he

announced the complete plan to take Black Tree then made a dramatic gesture to the doors where some younger members assigned to his secret project marched in carrying the "new weapon."

It was a ladder. Two of them, each forty feet long. We were unconvinced until Venn pointed out what was different about them: the underside was covered.

"Are we supposed to slide up them?" asked Rhode.

"No," Venn explained, "we climb up them. Like monkey bars. Underneath."

Thus the monkey ladders were born.

Six breathless Dragons carried the ladders all the way to the burnt-out part of the forest near Black Tree. In a moment, we were about to put them to the test.

Jason was leading the raid. All eyes were on him as he surveyed the scene. Despite the animosity between him and Venn, he could see for himself if the plan would work. He'd already committed to it – maybe just to prove himself.

"It'll work," he remarks. "Just don't fall," he adds.

Rhode takes a step out from our hiding spot to begin the assault. Jason pulls him back by the shoulder. "You lead the ladder men. I'll take the first climb."

Rhode doesn't argue. He shouts to the people holding the ladders. "NOW!"

They burst forth from their hiding spots and snake through the trees with the ladders over their heads. Centaur archers try to take shots at them before they get too far below them to shoot under the ladder.

Arrows bounce off the top of the ladders. One of them sticks deep into the wood.

Benny gives me a look. That shouldn't happen. Someone up there is using a stronger bow than is allowed.

"Throw down the illegal bow or we'll break your fingers!" shouts Jason as he sees this.

A defiant arrow sticks into the trunk near his head.

"Crap," mutters Benny.

Jason pulls the arrow from the tree and takes a brazen step outside of the hiding spot. "I said I'll break all your fingers!"

Black Tree is quiet for a moment. Somewhere we hear angry whispers. Suddenly, Jason lurches back.

A thick arrow is sticking out of his shoulder pad. He regains his balance and stands defiantly. With his right hand he yanks the arrow free. It's bloody! The arrow had gone through the leather and into his shoulder.

"Call it off?" whispers Rhode from under the ladder by the tree.

"Hell no," replies Jason. He looks up at the armored shields around the tree. "Now you're screwed. ATTACK!"

Filled with rage, ready to settle the score, we flood from the trees to the underside of the ladder. Our archers begin shooting arrows into the tiny gaps, trying to hit anyone behind them.

Someone lets out a cry from above as they get hit.

"Surrender!" shouts Jason.

"Eat my balls!" yells someone in return.

I brace the bottom of the ladder as Jason begins to climb. He's halfway up before I get both hands on it to keep it steady. A trickle of blood splashes down on my face shield. He's bleeding a lot.

On the opposite ladder, Benny has started climbing. Jason reaches the top and starts hammering a piton into the dark trunk. He ties himself on and motions for the next man to climb the ladder. The next man is me.

Another knight holds the ladder as I start climbing hand over hand. I use my feet to carry some of the weight. The ladder buckles as I grab each rung. It feels like it's going to bounce off the tree.

Ahead of me, supported by a harness, Jason is holding the ladder steady. Blood is still dripping down his arm.

The crash pad looks the size of a napkin from where I'm at. If I fall, I'd have to make sure to fall on the right side. A sharp black trunk sticks out of the ground on the other side like a bayonet. Invisible from where we were hiding, it makes the potential drop all that more treacherous.

I reach the last rung. Jason grabs my shoulder. "I hammered in your piton." He points to a hook stuck into the tree near his own.

I take the loop from my belt and attach it to the hook, taking my weight off the ladder. He hammers in more spikes above our heads to hold onto. Across from us, Benny is doing the same.

There's a loud creak just above us as the Centaurs pull open a trap door. Arrows shoot down. Jason takes the staff hanging from his waist and jabs it up at them through the gap. They slam the door in our face.

"That was stupid," says Jason. "Hand it to me."

I stare at him.

"The crowbar. You brought it?" he asks.

"Oh yeah." I unsling the bar from my back. It's a three-foot-long pry bar. Jason takes it and shoves the end into the gap between the planks on the trapdoor.

The plan was to make our own hole and rip apart the lower level plank by plank. The Centaurs just made that easier for us by showing us where to start.

He starts at the boards with a mad fury. Through the gaps in the planks I can see the feet of Centaurs as they shuffle around trying to figure out what to do.

Boards begin to splinter and fall. I swat way debris as the next man on the ladder takes up position beside me.

Jason starts to work on the area near the hinges. A centaur manages to shoot an arrow between a space. It hits Jason's forearm, but bounces off the leather armor.

"Now!" shouts Benny.

The whole world shakes as the platform begins to tilt. We all hug the tree. Above us, the Centaurs let out a collective scream.

"Again!" shouts Benny.

The tree shakes again followed by a loud crack. Half of the shield wall comes falling to the ground just beyond the crash boxes.

The Dragons holding the end of the rope attached to the

wall let out a cheer. Benny had hooked the shield while Jason worked on the platform below. The goal was to tear it away one way or the other.

Benny and his crew on the ground managed to rip away half of the shields on the lower deck.

"Cover!" shouts Jason as our archers fire a barrage into the open space.

The Centaurs let out screams and curses as they get hit by our stingers. Some of them scramble up the ladder to next levels.

"Throw down your arms and yield!" commands Jason.

There's no response.

"Fine." He nods to the rest of us. "Let's take it!"

Jason unhooks, pulls himself up to the farthest piton and reaches over the wide gap. He pulls his body half up over the edge. Benny is right behind him. I'm after him, ready to fight hand to hand in the fortress.

Out of nowhere, a foot kicks out and hits Jason square in the face as he tries to climb over the platform. There's a loud crack as the plastic shatters. Jason lurches backwards.

Blood trickles down to his wrist and he loses his grip.

He falls.

CHAPTER THIRTY-FIVE

Man Down

Jason falls in slow motion. Mentally, I try to figure out the trajectory. The crash pads look too far away – too small. His body grows small as he hurtles toward the ground.

He hits the edge of the pads, just barely. His body bounces and he hits the ground hard. There's a snapping sound that sickens my stomach.

I turn away and face the Centaurs on the platform. All I see is red. I unhook myself from my harness and push past Benny.

Below the rush of my blood, I hear Benny telling me to wait. I'm over the edge of the platform in a heartbeat. Three Centaurs are scurrying up the ladder to the next level. One of them, the last man, the one who threw the kick, is standing there. He takes up a fighting stance. It's Red Fang.

I run at him. He throws a kick at my head. I duck, grab his foot, then sweep his other leg. He lands on his ass, shaking the platform.

I don't bind him or make him tap out. I step back. I let him pick himself up again.

"That trick won't work twice, prick," he growls.

"No. It won't."

He throws a punch at my head. I grab his arm and twist. This is what I wanted him to do in the first place. His momentum takes us to the open edge. I roll him across my back and throw him. Over.

He lets out a scream as he falls from the platform.

I grab the ankle of someone trying to make it up the ladder. They fall back to the deck. I put the stunned kid in a fireman's hold and walk to the edge. He claws at my face and armor, but I have him too tightly.

I throw him over the edge toward Red Fang, still crawling off the pad, then turn back to the ladder to the next level. Wooden shafts stab at my face as they try to defend themselves. I grab one and shove it back at its wielder. The top slams into his unguarded chin. He falls back with a cry and a split lip.

I pull myself through the hatch. Three of them are standing in the corner holding their short sticks at me. Someone fires an arrow. It sticks into my chest. It stings. I don't care.

I lunge at them and grab one by the throat. The others

start hammering me with their fists. I elbow and head-butt them. Someone grabs my waist. I put them into a headlock and twist away, tearing them from the group. I run toward the edge and let him go, sending him over.

I hope that was the right side...

I turn back to the others.

"We surrender!" shouts one of them.

They all get on their knees.

"How many more?"

They say nothing. Something slams into my back. I reel toward the edge. Hands grab my feet and begin to tip me over. Only they're not dropping me onto the boxes; I'm being pushed onto the spike.

I try to grab the rail and slip. My head passes the lower edge. I grab the floor of the platform and hold myself up. A boot comes stomping toward my hand.

I let go and barely make it onto the lower level. Benny is climbing onto the edge. He sees the rage in my eyes.

"Marv..." he tries to caution me.

I reach the ladder. The boot stomper is standing above me. He's holding a bow aimed at my face and a thick arrow.

"Eye for an eye?" he snarls. "You kill my friends, I kill you."

"Your friends aren't dead, dumbass. They landed on our pad."

His eyes flicker. I push myself up and reach for the arrow. He releases it.

Pain rips through my cheek. I grab his ankles and pull

him down hard through the hatch. His head hits the edge and makes a crack as the helmet slams into the planks.

The arrow sticks next to my foot, lodged into the floor. Deep.

My cheek burns, but I don't look. I drag the shooter by the feet and swing him over the edge of the platform.

His arms flail and he screams.

"Yield!" I shout.

"I yield!" he yells.

"Promise to quit the Game!" I scream.

"I....I...."

"Promise!!!"

"I quit! I quit! Forever!"

By the edge of a tree I see Jason leaning with his arm in a sling. He's watching, waiting to see what I do next.

The crash pad is crumpled and has gaps between the boxes. If I drop the cheater he might break his neck. Pulling him up is too hard.

"Benny! Rope!"

Benny leans over the edge and ties off the cheater's leg. We lower him to the ground screaming and crying. Jason stands over him and puts a foot on his chest then spits in his face.

The other captured Centaurs on the ground cower under Rhode's glare. Red Fang managed to escape.

"Holy crap!" shouts Benny.

I turn to see where he's looking.

Through a gap in the trees we can see far into Demon

Keep. Black Tree is on a rise across the narrow lake from the ridge that forms the outer perimeter of the Keep. You could almost shoot arrows into there from here.

Centaurs and Dragons are fighting in the gates of the Keep. I didn't realize we were going to take the assault that far.

"Should we help?" I ask.

"No. It'll be over in another minute or so," says a voice behind me.

Venn climbs onto the platform and takes a spot between us. On cue, the Dragons begin running back toward the edge of Demon Keep. They scatter in different directions. It's an organized retreat.

"That seemed futile," I mumble, not understanding what just happened.

"Oh, no. Wait a moment." Venn looks over the edge at the smashed boxes and the captured Centaurs. "Good work. So, did you know you were throwing the others onto the pad?"

I don't answer. I'm just glad Jason is okay. "Why the attack on Demon Keep? I thought we were just going to keep them pinned down."

"We did. I figured the more real the attack felt, the less likely they'd send out reinforcement. Notice that nobody has come out to help these poor bastards?"

"How many people did we lose?" I ask.

"Not as many as we captured. Nobody important. We'll get them back."

"I guess it's worth it..." I think of what could have happened to Jason.

"It's the best view. Isn't it? You'll understand." He faces Demon Keep, searching. The fighting has stopped, yet he's waiting for something.

The guard dogs begin to bark. At first it's just a trickle, like blood from a wound, then great streams of red smoke begin to pour from holes in the earthen fortress.

"Nice," says Venn as he studies the streams of smoke emerging from the Keep.

"All this for a prank?" replies Jason.

I turn to see him standing on the platform. He's obviously in great pain. I have no idea how he made it up here.

"Not a prank. It's part of the Game," says Venn.

"Smoke bombs in Demon Keep?" mutters Jason. "That's why I broke my arm?" He's holding back the pain. Beads of sweat are all over his forehead.

"No. You broke your arm because you fell. We captured Black Tree so we could see the smoke bombs from here. It's quite a view."

"A view, yeah. Now that it's safe..."

Venn reels around. "Who do you think put the smoke bombs there? Did they walk in there by themselves?"

"You did?" I blurt out.

Venn gives me a grin and lowers his backpack. "Have a look."

There's something heavy inside. I pull out a stone head. The ears are pointy. It's the Centaurs' mascot.

"Look familiar?" Venn asks Jason. "Didn't believe my piss story? Thought maybe I got Sparrow to collaborate? Charmed her into the lie?"

"Sneaking around in other people's armor isn't warfare," growls Jason.

"Neither is falling and breaking your arm. What good are you now?"

Jason takes a step toward him. Venn doesn't flinch.

I step between them. "Relax. We got Black Tree. You got Black Tree," I tell Jason.

He shakes his head. "No. You did. I was stupid." He gives a wary look to Venn. "And for what..."

"To win."

Benny and Rhode take over defending Black Tree while Venn and I escort Jason back to the Rook with the captives. While Myra helps set Jason's arm, Venn leads me into his war room.

He unfurls a map on the large oak table. "Jason is good. Real good. He's not a tactician. We're stuck in Ko in the game of Go. All of this is about getting one thing: their shard. We have to do things differently."

"You've been in the Keep twice, I'd think you would have found it by now," I joke.

"It's not that easy. Do you know where ours is hidden?"

I shake my head.

"Exactly. Only a few people in each clan know where the shard is hidden. It could be under your nose and you would never know. Why...it could even be in this room."

I gaze around the almost barren walls. The only things in the room are the map and the table. I pick up the map and hold it to the candlelight.

Venn shakes his head. "I wasn't trying to make this into a guessing game. My point is that the shards are well-hidden. We know very little about Demon Keep. Dragon Rook, on the other hand, is out in the open. You can bet they have their own maps and blueprints of what goes on inside here, while they dig away and create new tunnels at the Keep. Black Tree lets us see more of what they're doing. It's kind of a satellite."

"What about the smoke? Another way to piss on their throne?"

"It's meant to feel that way. When it all clears and they see their mascot is missing his head, they're going to be pissed. Real pissed."

"Why couldn't you have told us what you were up to?"

Venn leans in and whispers, "Because we have a spy."

"A spy? You mean Sparrow?"

"No. She only sees what we want her to see. I mean one of us..."

My stomach sinks at the thought of one of our friends betraying us. "Who?"

"I can't get into that. But it happens. Sometimes people get confused about their loyalties. Sometimes they keep talking when they should shut up. Sometimes they just want to impress someone."

I shake my head. Who would possibly do that?

"The problem with this game, Marv, is that in chess you can count on doing what the player wants. Not in the Game. Unfortunately, these pawns have minds of their own."

CHAPTER THIRTY-SIX

Fear Itself

I've risked my life facing down a half-dozen armed Centaurs, had a close encounter with a razorback that wanted to gut me and maybe came face to face with a real live dead body; so why can't I muster the courage to close the one-inch gap between my hand and Jesse's?

Maybe it's because in those other situations, the only other outcome was death. That somehow seems preferable to living with the embarrassment of being rejected. High on the capture of Black Tree, I came home that night and sent her a simple "You want to hang this weekend?" text.

An anxiety-ridden hour later, she said "Yes." The movie theater, an art house in a nearby town, was her suggestion. I was too afraid to be seen with her to worry if it was because she was embarrassed to be seen with me at my theater. I just assumed that was the case.

Sitting there in the dark, I keep watching her out of the corner of my eye. She's just as pretty as when I saw her in the bookstore. Her hand is on the armrest near me. I try to plot out different scenarios to capture it.

Should I gently brush her hand?

Make a bold dash and grab it?

I know asking her would be stupid.

Girls like alpha.

So I just sit here and think about the hand. Occasionally she turns and looks at me. I look away.

I'm a coward.

I think she likes me. But I can't tell if it's in a friend way or not. This part is easy for girls. They say it's not, but it is. Want to know if a boy likes you? Are you really cute? The answer is "yes." It's always "yes," unless he's gay.

Something scary apparently just happened in the movie. I wasn't paying attention. Jesse puts her hand on mine and squeezes.

I'm pretty sure it's a sign.

I hold her hand back.

She gives me a smile. "Are you enjoying this?"

"Uh, sure." Wait! She's talking about the movie, dumbass. "Yeah. I never saw it before." Smooth talker.

"I thought you'd like it." Her gaze lingers on my face.

I'm real self-conscious about the red streak from the arrow. I tried putting a bandage on it. That just looked stupid.

Her hand reaches toward my face. I flinch. Oh, lord, I'm a coward.

Jesse laughs. "I wasn't going to touch it. I just wanted to see it."

I turn the cheek toward her. She runs a finger below the edge. "A branch hit you?"

Technically speaking, yes. The arrow was a branch at one point in its life. "All right, a dueling scar," I whisper. "Pirates."

"Hmmm. Pirates. Throw any overboard?"

My face goes flush. How could she know? I try to think of something clever. How does she know?

Because I said "pirates."

She doesn't know. I'm just assuming.

Or maybe there was talk at her school...

Her eyes go back to the screen. I relax and try to enjoy the moment. Right now her hand inside mine is the entire world. Her fingers are mine. Her soft skin is touching my calloused hands.

My heart races in fear of taking it any further. The hand is everything right now. Her smiles out of the corner of my eye are like waves knocking me flat.

Maybe I'm gay. Maybe that's why she likes me. The thought makes absolutely no logical sense at all. But that's the kind of thing that races through your head when you try to understand why a pretty girl likes you.

I'm stupid.

I'm a coward.

I'm holding her hand.

Relax. Enjoy it.

My mind goes back to Skyperch and sleeping under the stars in the swaying breeze. This feels kind of like that. The fear of falling is like rejection. Or something.

I'd spent one night in Black Tree already. It's not the same as Skyperch. But it's interesting in its own way. From the platform you can see all of Demon Keep. We watch them night and day.

Since the raid, they've been adding to their fortifications. They know we're watching them. Sometimes they raise large green nets to block the view. Venn thinks that's more for show.

They've been raising the wall along their side of the lake. I could almost piss on it from Black Tree. There are also more dogs. They've been taking in every stray in town and feeding them.

Dozens of dogs roam around Demon Keep. At night they chain them to nearby trees to act as sentries. I'm not sure if it's cruel or humane.

They've also been marching in precision and working on new tactics. It looks like there are more of them. A quarter of Parker Academy must be a Centaur now.

Jesse has to know people in the Centaurs. I never ask. She jokes with me about my forest activities, making me feel a little silly. Some girls treat the Game seriously, but many in our clan are there because that's where the boys are.

The Game could be something else. I think they have different instincts. It's probably a good thing.

I'm glad not all girls are Amazon queens like Carrie. Carrie is perfect in her own way, but I'm just glad some girls are like Jesse.

This is a good balance for me, I decide. I've spent the days since we captured Black Tree rebuilding the reinforcements to make sure they can't take it back. Venn had some good ideas for how to defend it.

He showed me pictures of bird feeders. "Squirrels are the smartest creatures in nature when it comes to getting into high spaces. Trying to design something a bird can eat out of and a squirrel can't is almost impossible. But there are some clever designs."

We settled on making an inverted cone below the lower platform. We hammered spikes into the surface and filed them into sharp points. An assault from below wouldn't be as quick as it was for us. Also, pulling away at the spikes would rain heavy shrapnel down on the people below.

When we finished rebuilding Black Tree, we held a party on top of it and made plenty of noise for Demon Keep to hear. At the celebration, Benny and Rhode dropped a bundle with a bow on it at my feet.

"What's this?" I asked.

"Open it," replied Benny.

I unwrapped the cloth. It was an old parachute.

"Just in case," laughed Benny.

"Maybe we should test it on you," I replied.

We ended the party by seeing who could throw a streamer of toilet paper the farthest into Demon Keep. They returned the favor by sending a group of archers to fire at us from the ridge. We ducked behind our walls and called out taunts to them.

The Centaurs tried to ambush us several times as we changed shifts. We never took the same path twice. This gave rise to another one of Venn's crazy plans.

He'd laid out a network of rope bridges that would allow us to move from tree to tree all the way back to the Rook. The problem was defending them and keeping them from being a highway straight into our castle. Even Venn wasn't sure how to prevent that.

The first bridge was going to be from Black Tree. All the parts were still in the Rook. Until then, defending Black Tree was time consuming. The Centaurs know that we can't stay up there too long. Eventually we all have to go to school or let our parents know we're alive.

As an intermediary step to the rope bridge, we set up a zip line that goes from the top of Black Tree to a cluster of trees a hundred yards away. As luck would have it, I was the first to test it.

It was almost as scary as holding Jesse's hand. Almost.

The sensation was amazing. The line went right over treetops. It felt like flying. Centaurs would try to shoot at us, but the arrows rarely made it. I think they were more jealous than anything else. After my test, the others were eager to give it a try – now that they knew it wouldn't kill or cripple them.

The credits come up and Jesse lets go of my hand. I'm trying to think of what to say and drawing blanks.

"Will you wait with me?" she asks.

"Yeah, sure."

"What time is your mom picking you up?" she asks.

"Uh, soon. I guess." Actually, I took the bus here. Now that it was late, I was going to have to walk the five miles back home in the dark.

We went outside and sat on a bench. I managed to make some intelligent conversation. She sat close to me. Real close. Our knees were touching.

Jesse pulls out her phone and looks at the screen. "My mom is running a little late. It'll be another twenty minutes."

"Oh," I reply. I think there's a hint there.

I look at her face. It's perfect. Her eyes are smart. I can tell there's a lot going on there.

She reaches out and touches my face again. "A branch?"

I grin.

She leans in and kisses my cheek. It burns. But it feels good. I still let out a howl.

"Then kiss me where it doesn't hurt," she replies.

Oh my.

I lean in and kiss her on the lips. Her hands grab the collar of my jacket and hold me for a moment.

We sit back and stare at each other.

"I was afraid you didn't like me," she says.

Seriously? "I was afraid I didn't like me."

She punches me in the arm and manages to hit a bruise. "Oh come one. Big tough knight like you can't take a little punch?"

How much does she know?

She puts a finger to my lips. "Keep your secrets." Her eyes widen as headlights flash. "My mom's here."

I pull back as if I've been caught doing something wrong. Two teenagers kissing isn't hardly anyone's idea of wrong. It's innocent, yet feels guilty.

Jesse stands up and looks down at me. "She won't shoot you if you give me a hug."

I get up and embrace her. Her mother is invisible behind the headlights, but I feel her watching.

"Sure you don't need a ride?"

"I'm good," I reply. Mom was still working and can't come get me.

She gets in and they drive off. I can't wait until I'm sixteen and able to drive. Although, I'd need a car for that to be a reality. And a distant reality at that.

I start back toward Ellison and take the path by the highway. It's a cold night and I can see my breath. It doesn't really matter. I've got a gooey warm feeling inside me.

Lost in thoughts, I almost didn't hear the car horn. Jesse rolls down the passenger window as her mom pulls up next to me. "You big liar. Get in."

Jesse's mother, who looks a lot like Jesse, calls out to me, "Come inside, hun."

I climb into the backseat without an argument.

"Your mother working late tonight at the hospital?" asks Jesse's mom.

"Yeah." I didn't realize she knew where my mom worked.

The car is brand new. As we head toward my neighborhood, I realize why I resisted the offer for the ride. Jesse was from Parker. Her parents had money. I went to Ellison and lived in a small apartment. I felt shame.

Now I feel shame for my shame. Mom works hard. So did my father. Both of them were educated. We weren't poor. We just weren't rich.

Jesse turns back to look at me. "You live off of Grey Oak?"

"Yes," I reply. That was the street at the end of the apartment complex.

Jesse's mom pulls off the highway and takes me to my neighborhood. The apartments look dull and squalid. I'd never thought about them until now. Beat-up pickup trucks are parked all over. A group of people wearing T-shirts, drinking beers and smoking cigarettes lean over the bed of a truck and watch us pass.

It looks like a white-trash neighborhood. It is. It's where I live.

That's what I am in her mom's eyes.

The car comes to a stop. I try to think of something to say, like I can't wait until we move into the house we bought. I know it will sound false.

"Thank you, Mam. Goodnight, Jesse." I hop out of the

Jeep and wave them off.

It had been such a good night until now. Their car drives away and I sulk back to my building. Across the street, a man takes a drag from a cigarette and watches me as I walk back to my apartment with my head down low.

CHAPTER THIRTY-SEVEN

Secrets

Venn is fuming as he leans over the map on the old oak table. All the senior knights are gathered around. I'm getting pulled into more meetings since we took Black Tree. It was Venn's plan and Jason's leadership that got us the fort. I just went berserk and threw a few Centaurs overboard. Apparently that was enough to earn me my battle stripes.

Jason is standing in the corner. His arm is out of the sling, but he still wears a brace under his armor. He's been quiet since Black Tree. Now it's Richard's turn to needle Venn. At least with Jason I felt that there was something more sincere there than Richard's selfishness.

"It wasn't my fault," grumbles Richard.

Venn was laying into him for two people getting

kidnapped. One of them was a high-level fighter. They were on their way to a fort and got ambushed.

Venn stabs his knife into the fort on the map. "And who was supposed to be escorting them?"

"I got pulled into a skirmish," replies Richard.

"Yeah, a skirmish out your ass. Now I've got to trade back two of theirs, probably more to get Donovan back. If this keeps up, they're going to get the fort."

"We'll take it back," replies Richard.

"Is that all it takes? Just saying the words?"

"That's how you do it," sneers Richard, his face somehow even more sour.

"Every play is a gamble." Venn points to Jason. "Sometimes there are serious consequences. Sometimes it's not worth it."

"Uh, thanks," mutters Jason, not sure if Venn was saying that it was sometimes worth it to get his arm broken.

"And that gets to my other point." Venn pulls the knife from the table and regards it for a moment before making eye contact with each of us. "We have a problem with secrets. Maybe you were just off taking a dump, Richard. But there have been other things going on here that make any coincidence feel suspicious."

"What are you saying?" asks Jason.

"I think we have a leak. Maybe not a full-on spy. Maybe someone letting the other side know more than they should. Someone who doesn't understand the full risk of fraternizing with the enemy..."

Venn gives a sharp look in my direction...

"You mean like cooing with Sparrow?" asks Richard. "Boy, what does it take to get the all-knowing Venn to help me with my homework? Do I have to show you my tits?"

Without a blink, Venn shoots a sidekick to Richard's chest, sending him backwards into Rhode and two others. Venn leaps onto his chest before he hits the ground.

"Say that again," shouts Venn into Richard's face.

I've never seen Venn that angry.

Richard looks around for someone to help him. We all stay back.

Venn puts his face into Richard's, nose to nose. Venn is half a head shorter than him and forty pounds lighter, yet Richard looks scared.

"It was nothing," he whimpers.

"SAY IT!"

"I...."

Venn grabs Richard under the exposed bicep and squeezes a pressure point. "SAY IT!"

Richard howls. "Do...do...do I have to show you my tits?"

"Yes!" says Venn as he leaps to his feat and grins. "But I doubt I'll like them."

We're too stunned to react. Venn walks back over to the map and points to the tree. "Oh, come on. Richard likes it when you play rough." He calls over his shoulder, "Don't you?"

Richard slowly gets to his feet. "I'm...I'm sorry."

"I didn't ask for an apology," replies Venn. "Just more respect."

Like a wounded wolf that just had the alpha snap him back into line, Richard nods his head. "Yes." There's a glare in his eyes and ice on his tongue, but he says nothing else.

"The Centaurs are plotting," says Venn. "They've expanded their moat. They're preparing for a siege." He points to a line of our forts. "I think they're going to try to make a new path into our woods. They gave up on Black Tree too easily."

"Too easily?" I blurt.

Venn glances up from the map. His face looks like it did right before he struck Richard. After his innuendo about me and Jesse, I half wish he'd try it. The last person to try to kick me got dropped thirty feet.

"No one is saying you and Jason didn't fight hard. I'm just saying they've given up on it too easily. They're up to something else."

"What?" asks Jason.

Venn glances back at him. "To get our shard, of course."

I couldn't help but notice the way Venn's fingers point to the table as he made his point. Not the map, but the oak table.

I wonder who in the room knows the actual location of the shard? Jason, probably. Rhode? Rich would be too risky.

Venn is smart, probably the smartest person I've ever met. But we all have our tells. I say nothing and watch.

"We're still vulnerable here in the Rook. It's much more

easy to take than they realize. Last time they tried weakening the walls on the west end. All it takes is one good rainstorm and the earth wall will be loosened enough for them to penetrate."

"They don't know that," says Rhode.

"I'm sure they do. And more. Like I said, we have a spy problem."

"Who?" asks Carrie.

Venn shakes his head. "I have my suspicions."

He doesn't look at me this time, but I know what he's thinking. Someone saw me at the theater the other night. Going all the way out of town made things more suspicious than they needed to be.

Jesse was just a normal girl who happened to go to Parker. Venn's own brother was leader of the Centaurs. And Richard was right, Venn did spend a lot of time around Sparrow. Maybe he was deflecting guilt? Maybe Venn has said more than he should?

"If anyone here wants to understand the severity of betrayal, go take a walk over to the Serpent's Lair," says Venn.

Instead of the fallen stones, I think about the skeleton in the ground. Was there some darker threat here? Venn's eyes are filled with cold fury.

The meeting ends on that dark note. I go back to Black Tree taking a random path and climb up to the tallest part of the platform. I try to put the meeting behind me.

At night you can see why Demon Keep has earned its

name. The glow from the fires inside illuminate the eye sockets, nose and mouth carved out of the hill, like a skull. From certain angles, it really looks like a demon.

The Keep doesn't get any less frightening the closer you get. Their sentries walk along the ridge below us with their torches. Beyond them, archers lie hidden in the trees, waiting for an attack. Deep inside the bowels of Demon Keep, they plot our capture and the destruction of Dragon Rook.

Their Keep looks like something out of the Dark Ages. Sinister. Evil. Nothing about this feels like a game right now. Part of me wants to cut out early and go home. Only that would mean staring at my phone, and since I haven't heard from Jesse since the night she and her mother dropped me off, that would only make me more depressed.

I was probably supposed to text her, but I couldn't bring myself to do it. I couldn't face up to the idea that some big lie had been revealed to her.

What lie? I never told her we were well-off. I never told her we weren't, either.

Did she care?

Maybe she didn't, but I'm sure her mom did.

That world now worried me just as much as this one. With Venn implying that I might be talking, that just combined them all in a horrible way. Was I reading too much into what Venn said?

He'd just told me earlier his concerns about a spy. Was the look meant to be more of an affirmation about our earlier discussion?

My attention is pulled back to the present when I hear something rustling in the trees below.

Somebody is trying to sneak up on Black Tree.

CHAPTER THIRTY-EIGHT

Night Raiders

A hundred yards away from me I see a white beam cutting into the night. Our backup defenders are late, so I'm all alone in Black Tree.

I wait a moment before calling out a challenge. For now, my position is concealed. I'd blown out the lantern an hour ago, not wanting to give the Centaur archers something to shoot at.

The light goes behind a tree. I make out a low voice talking to another and then the sound of metal hitting rock and dirt. Are they setting up an ambush? I can't remember seeing a flashlight out here. In some of the forts we use night-vision goggles to see, but there are none here.

I grab a bow and nock an arrow. "Who goes there?" I call

out.

The flashlight aims up at the trees. I hide behind the shields. The light goes up the black trunk and passes me.

A voice calls out to me. A deep voice. A voice older than any I'd heard out here before. "Stay in your fort, kid, and you won't get hurt."

The air is punctuated by the unmistakable sound of a shotgun being pumped. A shiver runs down my spine as I cower and move around the trunk so it's between me and the interlopers

The light flashes away and the tree goes dark. I stay frozen. Below me I hear the sound again of metal on rocks and dirt.

It continues for several minutes. Somewhere I find the courage to crawl on my belly toward the edge of the platform and peer through a slit at the men below.

I see two men wearing thick jackets with hoods pulled down. They're digging a hole near a tree. At first I have an image of them burying a body, but they're obviously looking for something. The digging continues until one of them throws down the shovel. They argue in hushed tones.

One of them picks something up and they move to some other point. The air is punctuated by a high-pitched beep beep sound. It reminds me of a metal detector.

Their light fades into the black. The forest grows quiet again. A strange smell wafts through the air. It's the licorice scent of a clove cigarette.

I keep my eyes focused on the direction they departed,

while listening to the sounds of the forest and any sign of a Centaur ambush. Who were they? Treasure hunters out for our hidden gold?

Using the lantern, I send a coded message to a distant fort. No reply returns. Hours past when the relief was due, I fall asleep. I'm awoken with a startle when something in my pocket buzzes. My phone. I forgot I brought it out here.

Crap. I broke the rule. I'm about to shut it off and hide it when I see a text message.

It's from Jesse. **"Hey stranger!"**

This somehow makes me relax from the panic brought on by the shotgun wielders. I text her back then shut off my phone. A little while later, Benny calls out to me. I drop the rope down so he can climb up.

He pulls himself through the hatch. "Sorry about the relief. There are others out in the woods tonight."

"I saw." I explain to him the two men with the shotgun and metal detector.

"Ghosts," says Benny.

"Ghosts? They looked real to me. Especially the gun."

"Ghosts, as in they're dead to us. Alumni coming back here to find the treasure. They obviously don't play by the same rules. Did you see their faces?"

I shake my head. "One of them was smoking cloves, though."

"Zach Becker. He went to Ellison awhile ago. Still lingers around. I wonder who the other one was. Sure you didn't get a look?"

"I was too scared. The shotgun."

"Yeah."

"Keep an eye out for me," I say as I climb over the edge.

I light the lantern and walk over to where they had been digging. There's a deep hole, maybe four feet, a few yards from the tree. There's nothing at the bottom. It didn't seem like they found anything either.

The hole seems so random. I raise the lantern and look around. A few feet away from the tree a rock sits out of the ground like a gray egg. I'd passed it dozens of times, never paying any attention to it.

In the flickering light I see a shadow from a carving on the rock. It's a cross in a circle, facing the tree. I walk over to the trunk and notice the same symbol carved into the bark. I climb back up and tell Benny.

"You've never noticed the runes before?" he asks.

"No. Not that I realize."

"They're everywhere. They're part of the Game. The Game Maker left them behind."

"What for?" I ask.

"Clues. False clues. I don't know. I'm not sure if we've ever figured them out. The ghosts were obviously hoping to find a buried fortune there. There are so many of markers, it doesn't make much sense to dig near them all."

"I guess that's why they brought the metal detector."

"Good luck with that. There's so many buried nails and bits of metal out here, they'll have to dig the whole forest up."

I let out a yawn, "Excuse me."

Benny reaches into his backpack and hands me a thermos. "Sorry about that."

"About what?"

"Taking so long to get out here. Venn wanted to cut back the manpower up here. He held us back while we waited for the ghosts to pass. I argued with him. It wasn't right leaving you up here."

"It's okay. Don't tell him I fell asleep, though. Does he always get like this?"

"What do you mean?"

"I don't know. It just seems like he's mad at me about something." I don't mention Jesse.

"That's just Venn. He's stressing out about capturing Demon Keep."

"We still have half a year left."

"I think he's moving by a different time table."

"I wish he'd tell us what it is."

"I think he's still figuring out what it is."

"Whatever his plan, leaving one person at a time to defend Black Tree isn't going to help us keep it."

"Well..." Benny starts to say.

"What?"

"I'm not supposed to say anything, but in case you haven't noticed, we're not at full attendance. We don't have enough for every patrol. Morale has been a little down. People have been coming up with excuses. We're spread thin." He nods toward Demon Keep. "Meanwhile, they look like they've recruited half the state."

"What's the problem?" I realize he's right. There have been fewer people in the halls.

"Maybe it was the Summer Wars. I don't know."

"It's Venn," I reply.

"It's not so much him as the way he keeps to himself. We used to be a bigger part of the strategy. Now it's all him all the time. Every raid, every mission is something he planned."

"They seem to work."

"Yeah, for sure. That's why people are still around. It's not that he isn't good, brilliant actually, it's just that we kind of feel left out of it."

"Has anyone told him this?"

"Lots of times. Every way you can imagine."

"And what does he say?"

"He says is doesn't matter. He could win the Game with three people and a cardboard sword."

"That sounds like Venn."

"Yeah. But the crazy thing? I think he's kind of right. We all feel that way. Venn doesn't need us."

"That's ridiculous. He'd never be able to keep the Rook."

"He'd give it up if it meant getting their shard. Venn will try to win this thing at all costs." Benny looks me in the eye. "We're just his pawns."

I think about Venn's observation that chess pieces have the obedience to do what the player wants. That's really what Venn wants – pawns to do his bidding without question.

"Yeah, but here's the thing," I try to frame the words. "Venn is smart. Real smart. He's not one in a thousand. He's one in a hundred thousand, maybe a million."

"So?"

"I guess what I'm trying to say is, what do you think it would have been like to be around Alexander or Caesar or Napoleon?"

"They were great leaders."

"Not when they were fifteen."

"Point. Listen, I like the guy. I'll follow him to hell and back. Even being a puppet is still better than nothing for me. But just don't be shocked if one day he decides to cut the strings."

"On me?"

"On any of us. It's what a general has to do sometimes."

CHAPTER THIRTY-NINE

Sheriff of Ellison

After spending three hours in classes, I went home to take a shower before heading to the forest. When I walked past the sheriff's car in the parking lot I didn't think twice about it. The police showed up in this apartment complex a lot.

When I walk up the stairs to the apartment and see him sitting at the top, waiting for me, I have to resist every urge to run. The last time I saw him, I was put into cuffs and about to be dragged away from school for drug trafficking. Somehow, that seemed like happy days compared with right now.

"Headed out to the forest?" asks the sheriff.

"Headed to my apartment," I reply.

"Smartass."

I take a breath. "Sorry, Sir. I didn't mean to be. When I'm nervous, I'm blunt."

"Why are you nervous?"

Seriously. "Um, just am?" I look past him. He sits still, not about to get out of my way.

"So what do you do out there in the woods?"

Telling him about Scouts or Conservation Club didn't feel like the logical thing to do. "I just like the outdoors."

"Me too. So what do you do out there?"

Part of me wants to tell him to ask my lawyer. I'm sure that will go over great. He's just making conversation.

"I don't know. Stupid games and stuff."

"Is that how you got that mark?"

The red burn still hasn't faded away. Mom bought the branch story. I'm not sure if the sheriff will. "Branch."

"Uh, huh," he says. "You know how many kids we get with branch injuries and broken fingers from field hockey? You'd think we'd have a world-class team of botanists and field hockey players. I doubt any of you could play field hockey worth anything."

"It's the ice. The cubes keep melting when we try to spread them on the grass."

The sheriff stares at me for a moment after my lame joke. "Funny," he says without a trace of laughter. "Why don't you go tell Amy Davidson's mom your joke. I'm sure she'll think it's a barrel of laughs."

"Amy who?" I don't remember a girl by that name.

"Davidson. Oh? You don't know who she is?" His eyes narrow on this piece of information.

"No, Sir."

"Her friends never brought her name up?"

I shake my head.

"Odd. We don't get too many missing persons around here. You'd think when a fourteen-year-old girl vanishes, the other kids might be a little concerned. Apparently not. Either they forgot, or they don't want to talk about her."

"Vanished?"

"I can tell by your reaction this is news to you. Amy used to be in your little club. She went missing right before the school year. Nobody has seen her since. Last ones that did were your friends. They all have the same story. Word for word. I was hoping maybe you have a little more sense than they do. Maybe you were a little more honest. Your teachers tell me you're a better kid than them. Maybe they're wrong."

"I don't know anything about her." The words don't sound so sure as I say them. I think of the skeleton in the woods. That had to be a lot older than a few months. Right? Unless that's what happens when it's left out in the open...

I hold back a shudder. I feel like telling the sheriff about the skeleton. I shouldn't keep it a secret. Something holds me back. It's not fear. Something doesn't seem right. He should be talking to me in front of my mom. He's obviously trying to manipulate me.

"Something you want to say?" he asks.

"No, Sir. If I hear anything, I'll tell you. Honest truth." I look toward the direction of the forest. "That's just a game to me. Nothing more. Nobody is supposed to get hurt."

"Kids get hurt all the time."

"They get hurt out on the football field. A kid got paralyzed two years ago trying to run a touchdown. You going to shut them down?"

The sheriff holds his fingers a fraction apart. "You were this close to sounding like a reasonable young man. Now you sound like your leader, Venn."

"I take that as a compliment." I try to sound as earnest as possible.

"Sure, you look up to him. Because you don't know any better. I see his type all the time. Thinks he's too smart for the world. Then he starts into something. Cooking meth, LSD, whatever."

"Venn?" I almost laugh out loud. "Hardly. He'll be the CEO of some billion-dollar company before I finish college."

"Let's hope so. Let's hope I'm wrong about him. Let's hope that Amy Davidson is somewhere waiting for her boyfriend to strike it rich and come rescue her from wherever she is."

Venn dated Amy?

The sheriff sees me taking the bait. "Yep. Amy was your pal's little girlfriend. Some say they had a falling-out. No one saw Amy again. Venn is the real cool type most of the time. But when he cracks... Ever see him angry?"

Venn kicking Richard in the chest comes to mind. It was

so quick and it would have been lethal if Richard hadn't been wearing armor. I couldn't say Venn would never hit a girl because we don't know who's behind the armor when we go to war.

Venn just doesn't seem like the type. I've only seen him get physical with Richard. He's never done that to anyone else. And Venn was right – Richard almost begged to get beat down. It was like he had to be put into his place. It was the only way he could accept orders from him. I see it all the time on sports team. Even our dojo was like that. My dad could kick anyone's ass in there. Some guys had to be politely reminded of that. I watched him put pro boxers and SWAT team cops into submission holds. They respected him for it.

"I don't think Venn would ever harm a girl out of anger," I reply. It felt like the truth.

"I didn't say anything about Venn harming her," replies the sheriff.

I'm about to point out that was his obvious insinuation but don't. "Then why are we talking about Venn and Amy?"

The sheriff looks in the air past my head. "Maybe something else happened." His eyes fall on my mark. "Maybe an accident everyone wanted to cover up. I noticed Jason Mann walking around with a sling. Know how that happened?"

"Fell out of a tree," I reply, which happened to be the truth – more or less.

"Fell or shoved?"

"Jason could tell you."

"No, he wouldn't. None of you will. Which is fine when it's your own sorry necks. But not when it's someone else. I should haul all of you in for questioning."

"I didn't even live here then!" I protest.

"People talk," he replies.

"No. They don't. You know that." I stare at my feet. "So, Amy just disappeared?"

"More or less. There was a note about running away."

A runaway note. What does that sound like? Crap.

The sheriff looks up as my mom comes home.

"Hello," she says hesitantly.

"Evening, Mam."

"Is everything okay?" she asks, checking to make sure I'm all right.

"Fine. Fine. We were just shooting the breeze about martial arts," says the sheriff. He gets up and walks away. "Have a nice evening. See you around, Marv."

I follow Mom into the house and wait for the sheriff to drive off. I give her a hug then tell her I forgot something and run to Venn's house.

I need answers.

I need them now.

CHAPTER FORTY

House of Games

The walk up Venn's driveway is intimidating. The house sits on the tallest hill in his neighborhood. All the homes look like mansions compared with my apartment. The forest looms over the back of the house, somehow blending in and not dominating the three stories.

The door opens as I step onto the porch. Venn is standing there with a raised eyebrow. Through the foyer I can see a Go board sitting on the floor.

"Hello, Marv. Come on in."

I step inside and try to frame my words. Venn looks over his shoulder then points upstairs. "My brother is in the kitchen. Maybe we should take this out of his earshot."

His brother, Lone Wolf. It's a strange thought that after

these two spend a day trying to kill each other they sit around eating frozen pizzas and playing Go. I remember Pressman saying something in class about how rival brothers would go home during the Civil War to spend time with their families.

I'd been to his house before, but had never seen his brother here. His father was a quiet man, but brilliant like Venn. He'd created a software company or something. His mother, where he got his slightly Asian features from, was half Japanese and usually doing rich-mom stuff like gardening or shopping.

Venn's room was lined with books. His bed was unmade and probably hadn't been slept in for weeks. He almost always slept out in the forest. However, I knew I'd find him here tonight because this was one of his playing-it-normal days. I wasn't sure how he and his brother worked those out.

Next to his window was a chest. Inside was a rope ladder bolted to the floor. He could get to the Rook in about ten minutes from here – in part because he was so fast and knew all the trails by heart.

His window overlooked the forest. It was hard not to imagine a younger Venn watching, waiting for the day he could rule the Game he knew was played out there. A cool breeze blew in through the window. The smell of pine drifted through the air. Even when he was here, he was living out there.

Venn sits on the edge of his bed. "Well?"

"Amy Davidson," I reply, waiting for a response.

"Oh." He looks down. "What have you heard?"

"Only what the sheriff told me."

Venn smiles. "So nothing then. Not any facts, at least."

"What are the facts?" I ask.

"She ran away."

"Ran away? Did she leave a note like mine?"

"Yes. I helped her write it."

Venn's response sends a chill down my spine. There's something cold and calculating about the way he's reacting. Like he's prepared for this...

"Why? Was she your girlfriend?" I ask.

"I liked her. She liked me. Amy had problems..." His voice drifts off.

"Problems?"

"Problems. She swore me to secrecy. Let's just say her domestic situation was so bad she preferred to leave home."

"She's fourteen."

"Fifteen, now. And yes, they were that bad. Did the sheriff tell you how many times Child Services came by the house? How many times the judge sent her back to that house? Not all girls in bad situations are fighters like Carrie. Amy was special."

I want to believe Venn. "Where is she?"

"I can't tell you. But she's safe." Venn's eyes drift around the room. "I have means."

I think he's trying to tell me that he's rich. Well, his parents are at any rate.

"Did the sheriff tell you that Amy calls her mother almost

every week and tries to tell her she's okay?"

"No..."

"The trouble is Amy's mother is bipolar and schizophrenic. She insists that it's someone playing a trick on her. She refuses to believe that it's her daughter. It's stressful for Amy. But she keeps calling."

"Why don't they trace the call?"

Venn shakes his head. "I've made sure that can't happen."

"Why does the sheriff think you killed her?"

"Did he say that?" asks Venn, somewhat surprised.

"Not in so many words."

"Was this an official inquiry? Was your mother present?"

"No..."

"Ah. Then there you have it."

"What do I have?" I ask.

Venn smirks. "You have no idea what this is about?"

"You."

He shakes his head. "No. It's about you, Marv. You and your girlfriend."

"Me?"

"Do you know who the sheriff's daughter is?"

No...

It can't be.

"Jesse?"

"Bingo. He finds out his daughter is dating the new bad boy over at Ellison. Maybe she wants to get a rise out of him, who knows. He comes knocking on your door bringing my name up, trying to insinuate us all into some kind of grand conspiracy. Jesse probably put the Amy Davidson notion into his ear."

I let the idea of me being a bad boy slip. "Why?"

"To stir things up. To make life difficult for us. For the Game."

"She's not even in the Game," I protest.

"You sure? They're all in the Game at Parker. They don't all carry shields and bows and go into the woods. But they're all into it. Even her, I'm sure."

"And Amy Davidson?"

"Safe. Just a ploy to manipulate you. I thought you were smarter than that. I thought you'd see right through it."

I try to find the words. "And Sparrow?"

"Now you sound like Richard."

I'm not sure if it's a threat or not. One entire wall of Venn's room is filled with weapons. If we fought, it would be messy. Venn is fast, I'll give him that. But I think I can take him.

"We don't know who we really are until we reach our breaking point, do we?" Venn crosses his arms. "I've been dying to ask you something, while we're on the subject of wanton violence. You know, I watched you and Jason take Black Tree. I saw the whole thing. I watched the arrow go in his shoulder. I saw his fall. I watched you go ballistic and start throwing people off the platform. Did you know...did you really know where the boxes were?"

I'd wondered the same thing myself. The fall could have killed them if they hadn't hit the boxes. None of them missed. But was that on purpose?

"We don't see ourselves when we're in battle, Marv. Some of us don't know our limits. We can't control our anger. I made you a knight too fast. I didn't teach you when to pull a punch. When to not go for the throat. And for that, I apologize. You could have killed someone. And that would have been my fault. Really my fault."

"I knew where I was throwing them," I reply.

"You don't sound convinced."

I'm not. I know I didn't want to see them really hurt. As angry as I was, they didn't deserve that. But I'm doubting myself.

Venn opens the door to his room. "Why don't you think it over, Marv. Ask yourself who here is really the one capable of murder."

I walk home trying to understand how he turned my accusation into an indictment about me. I came to find out what happened to Amy Davidson and leave feeling like I committed murder. Was this another one of his manipulations?

He says Amy is alive and calling her crazy mother. Her crazy mother who can't vouch for the story. It's circular. Amy is nowhere to be found...unless... I put that out of my mind.

The only fact I have right now that I can check is the one about the sheriff being Jesse's father. I could text her and just ask, but I already know the answer.

CHAPTER FORTY-ONE

Fall of Black Tree

Black Tree became my new home since Venn stopped sending others to help me guard the fort. Benny and Rhode were off trying to keep Skyperch and the other parts of our frontier together and rarely made visits. There was no one left to help me keep watch on Black Tree. I was in a kind of exile.

I did my best to make it look like there was always a presence here. When I left to go to class or to act normal around my mom, I placed cloaks over shields and kept a couple helmets bobbing behind the walls on black thread. It looked convincing from the ground.

My spirit soldiers couldn't fire arrows when I was gone. I toyed with the idea of setting up a booby trap, but gave up when I realized that someone seeing the wire would know why I'd set it there in the first place.

To get to Black Tree without someone to throw down the rope ladder was another challenge. I managed by using a grappling hook. It was scary as hell. The boards creaked as I pulled myself upwards. If one gave loose, it was a long way down. The only people to hear my screams would be the Centaurs.

Defiantly, I kept guard. I'd fought for the dead wood and iron planks. I wasn't going to give it up easily.

I sat up there and thought about things. About the Game. About Venn. About the markings in the trees. About myself.

Venn's words to me stung. Was I really a killer waiting to happen? In the judo ring I always kept cool. I even had a guy head-butt me in the middle of a match and I did nothing until he opened himself up. I threw him hard into the mat and then grounded his face into the floor as I pinned him and worked him in circles. All within the rules...

The crash boxes were on a small part of the ground when we took the fort. The fact that all the Centaurs I tossed landed on them couldn't be an accident. Could it? I was having my doubts.

Venn had worked his way under my skin. I wasn't sure who I was. I used to think of myself as a nice guy who only got rough when pushed into the corner, even then I was compassionate – sort of.

When Rhode first attacked me in the library, I had no idea what was going on. I thought I was about to be killed. I could have choked him cold. But I didn't. I used restraint.

Was that gone now?

It's a scary thought for me. I want to win the Game, but I don't want to kill for it. Nothing is worth that. Even the kid using the illegal bow didn't deserve that. He was just a scared jerk too afraid to play by the rules.

He was gone now. No one saw him since I made him quit. My punishment wasn't strictly by the book. He just left because he was afraid of me.

Good riddance.

But still. What if I had seriously hurt him? What if I had killed him?

A cold thought runs through my mind. Would the other Black Dragons have turned me in?

No.

They wouldn't.

They would have covered for me. There might have been some punishment I'd have to suffer, maybe even being kicked out. However, I don't think they'd have turned me in.

The fall would have been an "accident."

Or the kid would have become a runaway.

I'm not sure how that would work between clans. I'm sure something would have been worked out. That scared me.

Someone really could die out here and no one outside would ever know.

The bones.

The bones...

If someone did die, I'm sure they'd have covered it up –

like actually bury the body. No. They'd drag them out of the forest and call an ambulance and stick to an agreed-upon story. They wouldn't just leave a body.

They wouldn't. But would Venn?

A crime of passion, over in an instant. Someone panics. That's how it happens. What would someone do then?

Leave the body? Try to half-ass bury it?

My mind is a dark place.

I don't hear them approach until the first grappling hook comes over the edge. Then another and another.

I realize I'm under siege.

Dozens of Centaurs are below me. Lone Wolf is leading an assault. Further back, Cutter is on the ridge by the Keep watching me.

I grab my bow and start shooting down at the people climbing the ropes. They're using large coolie hats to block their heads. Not as formidable as a shield, but it's effective enough. They keep climbing.

I run to the nearest hook. It's stuck into the wood like a claw. A cable runs from the eyelet to the rope several feet away. Even if I could cut the cable, that would send the people below to the ground. I'm not a killer. I know I'm not.

"Surrender, Marv," someone shouts from below. "We know you're alone."

Crap.

"Then you know I'll throw the first person up here over the edge!" I shout back. I shoot two arrows at the closest person on the rope. One sticks into his leather armor. He keeps climbing.

A hand reaches over the edge. The first attacker is on the platform. He lunges at me.

I jump back and bring my hands down hard on his neck and send him to the floor. I struggle to tie his hand behind his back. He's strong. Real strong.

Someone lands behind me. I let go of the first one and face the other assailant as he cracks a shaft on my helmet. It hurts like murder.

I side-kick him in the groin. He stumbles backwards.

Two more are climbing over the edge. I run to the ladder and climb to the next level. I slam the trapdoor shut on the next level.

Red Fang crawls onto the first level. His war hammer is a giant sledgehammer. No more leather mallets. He slams the end into the deck under my feet. The shock travels up my ankles and stings. The hammer strikes again and a board starts to come loose.

They're breaking through. Red Fang is out for my blood.

The zip line is the only way left. I climb the ladder up to the small platform. I'm about to grab the handle when I see that a Centaur on a nearby tree has thrown a rope over the line. I'd get a few hundred feet then get stopped cold. Worse, I'd be stuck in the air. They'd riddle me with arrows until I dropped.

I'm trapped.

Damn.

More Centaurs are pounding on the platform below me,

trying to open the trapdoor. Red Fang's hammer shatters through a gap of rotten wood. They'll be through in a moment or climb over.

Black Tree is lost.

"Surrender!" shouts Lone Wolf from far below.

"Don't surrender," says Red Fang in a harsh whisper. "Let's see this to the end."

I climb back down from the zip line platform and rummage through the box of weapons. I find what I'm looking for then pour a plastic jug of used motor oil on the boards and through the cracks. They cry out as the gunk gets in their faces. I hear someone lose their grip and fall down the ladder onto the platform below. I hit Red Fang in the face as he pokes his helmet through his hole. Black goo sprays all over him.

"Had enough?" I shout.

"You have no idea what's coming for you," he yells back at me.

"You have to get me first."

Suddenly the tree gives a violent shake. I almost lose my grip on the ladder as I climb to the farthest part of the spike that will support me.

"How many of you pricks are on this thing?" I yell.

Below me I can hear Lone Wolf telling people to climb back down. So many of them had climbed up onto the platform, they made the whole tree tilt. It could come down. It could stay like this for a hundred more years.

Red Fang manages to make it through his rat hole

without slipping on the oil. He stands at the base of the trunk looking up at the plank handholds. He's going to either climb up or rip them out, trapping me.

I'm not going to wait to find out. I climb until the tree trunk is too thin and burnt to hold any more climbing spikes. The people on the ground are tiny below me. Even Cutter, standing on the ridge across the lake, looks a million miles away.

This is stupid. All I have to do is surrender. The Black Dragons could trade me back in a day. They need people right now.

Or do they?

Would Venn trade me back?

I'm afraid to find out.

And then there's Red Fang. He's not in a surrendering kind of mood. God knows what could happen before I get to the ground – or how I'll get there.

I only have one option. If this fails, I'll find out what they'd do if someone dies out here. Only in my case, they wouldn't have to call it an accident. Because this is suicide.

I take a breath. The tree sways in the wind. Below me they crack open the hatch. Lone Wolf, also covered in black oil, stands on the platform next to Red Fang. Red Fang aims an arrow at me. Lone Wolf puts his hand on the tip and pushes it down. He shakes his head. He knows what I'm about to do.

I jump.

CHAPTER FORTY-TWO

The Betrayal

The wind whips at my clothes. Somewhere a person screams. It's a high-pitched yell. I'm pretty sure it's not me. I'm falling fast.

When Benny and Rhode gave me the parachute, it got me thinking. You couldn't use something like that from here and expect to live. You'd hit the ground before it opened.

You could try to catch an open chute in the wind and pray that would work. In all likelihood, it would just blow you into the rocks, kill you and then drag you along the bottom of the ridge in one long red smear before you drowned in the lake.

All by myself in Black Tree, I began to devise all kinds of escape plans. Not really to abandon the fort, just to think of another way down. One way sounded less lethal than others. Theoretically...

I'd tried it out with weights. But never on myself. This was my first test.

The ground is growing real big real fast. Most of the Centaurs are still on the platform.

The ones on the ground scattered when they saw me jump. They didn't see the bungee cord attached to my belt...

Something pulls at my back and I'm jerked. The forest floor looks a little too close as my descent continues. I don't think I put enough rocks in the bag when I tested it.

I'm yanked back into the air. I pull at the rope tied to the end of the cord and manage to unhook myself. The ground grows close again. I let go and land on bent legs then roll across the ground.

I'm free of the harness and heading into the woods before they know what happened. If I didn't get the harness loose, I could have been stuck there, a party piñata, waiting to be beaten. Or worse, brain dead and limp.

There are shouts behind me. I ignore them and run full throttle. A Centaur jumps out at me. Before he can raise his shaft I leap off a rock and use his head as a pommel horse. He falls backwards and lets out a boyish cry. All the real knights are back up on the platform.

I tear through the forest and make it back into Dragon territory. The sentry at our front gate gives me a wave, but I keep going. I barge into the Great Hall, where Venn is holding court over the map and the oak table.

"Black Tree!" I blurt out. "They took Black Tree!"

"Then why are you here?" demands Venn.

"I'm telling you!"

"Who's defending it?" he demands.

"No one. They took it!"

"Then how did you get here?"

"I ran..."

"You abandoned it," Venn declares.

"There were twenty of them," maybe a slight exaggeration.

"One man could hold Black Tree!" Venn insists.

"Bull!" I reply.

Everyone is watching us tensely.

"There were too many of them," I explain. "I got to the top and had no choice."

"You could have held out."

"And done what? Wished angry thoughts at them?"

"They never should have got that far."

"What? Was I supposed to throw them off?"

"You did before."

"Onto boxes. BOXES I KNEW WERE THERE!" I scream at him.

"Whatever," replies Venn.

"Where the hell were you, Venn? Why was I alone?" my voice is hoarse.

"Evening the odds." Venn points out the doorway to the courtyard where a dozen Centaurs are tied up and sitting on the ground. Most of them are young kids.

"What are you at?" I ask.

"Winning. I know that might be unfamiliar to you. This is what it looks like." He slams his fist into the map. "Black Tree was important."

"Not important enough to you," I shoot back.

"How important is it to you?" he asks.

I storm away. Benny and Rhode come running into the hall. I walk past them.

"Where are you going?" asks Benny, hurrying after me.

"Taking back Black Tree."

Benny puts a hand on my shoulder. I shrug it off. Rhode stands in front of me. "Take a breath. It'll be there tonight."

I turn back and look into the dark hall. Venn is ignoring us. "Will you help me keep it?" I ask.

"We'll figure something out. First we have to get it back. Right now they're expecting a quick response," says Benny. "We need to wait it out."

"We also need a plan," replies Rhode. "Taking it with a dozen of us and a few defenders was hard enough. Venn isn't going to give us the people we need. We also made it harder to capture. How'd they do it?"

"Grappling hooks and big hats." I sit down on a log and try to think.

"Hats?" asks Rhode.

"Yeah," I mutter. "Big ones."

"Okay..." He just leaves it there. "How'd you get away?"

"Bungee jump."

"Christ," says Rhode. "Wish I could have seen that."

I nod back toward Venn. "What did he expect me to do?"

Benny shakes his head. "It's not you. He's just going a little ballistic."

"He's driving us all nuts."

Benny stands up. "I have an idea. Hold on." He runs back into the Rook.

"Watch out, a Benny original," Rhode says.

Benny returns with a duffle bag. He tosses it to our feet. Inside are climbing spikes, gas masks and smoke grenades.

"Explain?"

"If we toss smoke grenades up there, are even upwind of them, they're going to have to come down. While they're down, we go up," says Benny.

"How do we defend it?" asks Rhode.

"Vigilance and bolt cutters. Let them know we'll cut their grappling hooks. Maybe Venn will give us more ground support."

While that makes tactical sense, I have no idea what's going on in Venn's mind. There's no telling what he'll do.

"When?"

"Let's wait until a few hours before dawn. Everyone is at their thinnest then. That'll be the best time. With the smoke, they won't know how many of us there are."

It sounded like a reasonable plan – a reasonable way to get ourselves captured. The whole thing felt futile to me. We didn't have Venn's support. We were doing this to prove something. Scratch that, we were doing this so I could prove something.

I lost Black Tree on my own. Somehow that feels worse than if I had reinforcements.

Despite everything, Benny and Rhode are willing to help me. I feel guilty. This was about me and Venn. Or was it? Was this their way of defying him, too? Was defying him even smart?

I look over at the faces of the captured Centaurs, waiting to go home or sent back to Demon Keep. To Venn, they were just pieces on the game board to be traded for other pieces.

We were no different.

CHAPTER FORTY-THREE

Fallen

Venn glares down at me with contempt. With my face down in the muddy meadow, wrists bound behind my back, legs tied like an animal, the cold morning air doesn't blunt the feeling of my shame. Rhode and Benny are lying next to me, bound as well. Neither one of us can bring ourselves to speak.

Venn walks over to Lone Wolf, his brother, and negotiates for our release. All of this under Lord Cutter's watchful eye. Twenty Centaurs surround us, shafts pointed in our faces. The same squad that captured us. The same ones who tricked us into an ambush.

On our way to retake Black Tree, I had an idea. It

probably wasn't the one factor that got us captured, but it didn't help things either. I was thinking about Venn's squirrel analogy to defending the fortress. Our current plan was to use the smoke bombs to cause confusion and then climb up with our gas masks.

I thought I had a better way.

"What if we use the zip line?" I asked.

"If they haven't cut it," replied Benny, "I'm sure they're watching the landing platform."

"We don't need that. Remember when we laid out the line, the branch on the tree toward the middle? It's about three feet above the cable."

"You mean get onto the line in the middle?" asked Rhode.

"Yeah, then we drop in from the top."

He shook his head. "The line shakes like crazy. They'll hear us a mile away."

"No. We go slow. It's always swaying in the wind. Look."

We all stopped and listened to the wind. A storm front was shaking the trees around us.

Benny shrugged. "Fine by me."

"All right," said Rhode. "But I'm really not looking forward to this. I'd rather have just used grappling hooks like they did."

"That only worked because of sheer numbers and the fact that they knew I wasn't going to cut them."

Fifteen minutes later we were climbing the old sequoia

that hung over the zip line. The ascent took us longer than I expected. We kept to the side of the tree facing away from the landing platform. Benny said he heard someone back there. Probably a Centaur patrol keeping an eye out for us trying the thing we were about to do.

The tree limb seemed a lot sturdier in my mind. The cable a lot closer. The drop was more like six feet and not three.

We lowered a rope down from the branch and climbed onto the zip line one by one. The line could take a couple thousand pounds. Even still, with our combined weight, it drooped down more than I was expecting. We should have gone one at a time. We should have done a lot of things differently.

We tied loops around the cable in case we lost our grip. I led the ascent up the line with Benny and then Rhode following. It was slow-going. We tried to keep the line from shaking too much. Hanging upside down made everything disorienting.

The cable swung back and forth in the breeze. Every now and then we'd all feel a tremor come down the line like a signal on a telegraph. Black Tree was creaking.

The Centaurs' weight on the platform had already made the tree shift. This couldn't be helping. Nevertheless, we kept climbing.

As we passed through the branches that blocked our view ahead, two orange glows were visible on Black Tree – lanterns. One of them moved around the lower platform. The other one was still on the top.

One, maybe two people, sleeping in shifts. There didn't seem like any other movement. I paused and looked around the floor below. Nothing was stirring.

"If we were smart," whispered Benny, "we would have had one of us go on the ground and fake a ground attack. Then we could see how many were up there and who was below."

"You're telling us this now?" Rhode whispered harshly. "Jesus Christ." It was a much better idea than what we were doing.

Although it only looked like there were two Centaurs at most, a dozen of them could have been lying in wait. Actually...it was eight in Black Tree and fourteen more on the ground.

Ten yards out from the top of the zip line mast, Rhode handed me a smoke grenade from Benny's pack. I waited for the lantern to go to the other side of the lower platform, then pulled the pin and tossed it.

Sparks shot out of the canister as it flew through the air and landed on the deck. Dark smoke began to pour out from behind the large shields. Someone coughed, but that was the only noise other than the hiss of the grenade.

Something was wrong. We waited for more shouting. There wasn't any.

Suddenly the zip line shook.

"Oh, crap," said Rhode.

There was a snap. We were in free fall. I still wasn't used

to the sensation.

We had been so focused on getting to Black Tree, we didn't think about protecting our flank. The Centaurs had cut the end of the zip line.

The ground flew toward us. I held as tightly as I could to the rope. Our harness would keep us from flying backwards, but it couldn't stop us from crashing into each other or help us defy gravity.

The cable jerked and we swung like a pendulum. Rhode's feet were just a few inches above the ground. We arced through the air then swung backwards. There was another jerk on the cable and we fell again.

The momentum sent us sprawling in a line. I bounced to my feet. Rhode and Benny picked themselves up more slowly.

The Centaurs were on us like a horde. We tried to fight them off. There were just too many.

When I saw an opening, I ran for it. As I reached the edge of the clearing something hard smacked into my shins. I fell face first into the dirt.

Stars flew around my head. When I came around, Lord Cutter was standing over me. I tried to sit up. He kicked me in the chest, sending me to the ground again. Several more Centaurs stood around with their shafts aimed at my head.

My wrists were tightly bound behind me. Lone Wolf and Red Fang watched over Rhode and Benny. We'd been captured. We'd been outmaneuvered.

"Any other bright ideas, guys?" growled Rhode.

Benny and I were silent.

I was too ashamed to speak. Worse than not getting Black Tree back, or being captured, was the thought of Venn seeing me like this. I was the disappointment he said I was.

The yellow banner for parlay waves in the morning breeze. Mist clings to the muddy grass, blending the ground and sky in a dull gray. Through the legs of my captors, I see Venn talking to his brother. Lord Cutter watches from a distance, his gray shield strapped to his back.

I still don't understand the dynamics between Cutter and Lone Wolf. Sometimes Lone Wolf has the Centaur shield; other times, like in close battle, Cutter has it. I wonder if it's like Venn and Jason. Although Lone Wolf reminds me more of Jason in his quiet stoicism. Cutter seems like a behind-the-scenes plotter – the Centaurs' version of Venn. Whatever it is, the dynamic seems to be working better for them than for us.

Our complement of Dragons is half the number that showed up for the Centaurs. We look weak. I made us look weaker.

Venn points in our direction. Lone Wolf shakes his head then turns to Cutter. Cutter holds up two fingers. Venn nods his head.

Jason brings forth five of the captives Venn took yesterday. Sparrow is among them, too. They walk over to the Centaurs. Venn never gives Sparrow a second look. I guess that romance is over.

Lone Wolf walks over to where we're pinned to the ground. He pulls out a knife and cuts Rhode free and then Benny. They get up, rub their wrists and walk back sullenly to our side.

Lone Wolf puts his knife back and walks over to Cutter. Venn goes back to our end of the meadow. Rough hands pull me to my feet.

I'm being marched to the Centaurs' side!

I look back over my shoulder and shout at Venn's back. "Venn!"

He stops walking then wheels around. Pushing his way through the Centaurs, he brings his face toward mine. "Just quit the Game, Marv. Just quit."

"Why are you leaving me?" I ask.

"You cost me six captives, Black Tree and a lot more. Do the math. You're a bad bet."

The words hit me like a rain of fire. Each one burns. "I've only done my best."

"For who, Marv? For who? Getting Benny and Rhode captured? I should have seen it all along. I know what you are." He doesn't say the word, but he's calling me a traitor.

"I'm not."

"You might as well be, the damage you've done. Go with the Centaurs, your real masters. Or just leave the Game." Venn turns his back on me and walks away. The Centaurs drag me across the field.

Near the white rock and the yellow banner, Lone Wolf and Cutter watch the exchange. I stare at the ground and force all the emotion out of my face. I'm not going to let them have the satisfaction of seeing me like this.

A bag is placed over my head. I'm pulled and pushed until I lose track of time. Eventually we come to a stop and the bag is removed. Someone kicks me and I fall into a pit filled with muddy water. A wooden grate is lowered over the top. Centaurs stand around the top and look down at me. A few of them spit.

I'm in a muddy pit.

I've never heard of them treating prisoners like this.

I'm a special case.

CHAPTER FORTY-FOUR

Parlay

They yell at me for several minutes, taunting me to quit. Their wild dogs come to the edge and bark down at me. I'm called a coward and a failure. They tell me I'm gay. That I'm in love with Venn. They say I'm not worthy of the Game. They tell me to go home.

I can't go home. I'm tied up and in a dank pit. What they want is for me to surrender. They want me to give up the Game. They want to take me off the chessboard.

After Venn's betrayal, I want to leave. I want to get out of the damn forest. I want to leave Ellison. None of this is fun anymore. I hate everything about this place.

Eventually they leave and I'm left alone. The sun climbs higher in the sky as the morning turns into afternoon. It's a school day. I'm going to miss a class.

The ropes itch, and sitting in the muddy water only makes them tighter. I wait for someone to come get me. Nobody does. When I raise my head up, a dog trots over and snarls at me.

I sit and stew. At least I'm being left alone. Working the ropes doesn't get me anywhere. Cutter had been thorough and got my secret blade and all the other tools. The bindings are so tight they'll have to be cut off.

The sky grows dark as the sun begins to set. A glow approaches the hole as someone comes near with a lantern. Lone Wolf stands over the grate as two knights pull me out of the pit and walk me toward an opening in the Keep.

I'm brought into a room that's half dirt and half mud brick. A pillory stands in the middle. Lone Wolf pushes my head into the stocks.

"We're not going to untie you until we know you're secure."

Safe? They're treating me like a wild animal. "What are you afraid of?"

"Scared little boys who can't control their temper," he replies.

The pillory is locked around my head. Someone cuts the bonds from my wrists and places shackles on me. I'm now locked into the block in the middle of the room.

Lone Wolf pulls up a stool and sits down. He takes off his helmet for the first time since I saw him. He has Venn's face. It's a year or two older, but the two are like fraternal twins. Even his voice is a deeper version of Venn's.

My armor is piled in a corner behind him. They stripped it from me when I was captured, leaving me in a dirty T-shirt and jeans. Now they've laid it up for me to see. My helmet lies on its side as if I've been beheaded.

"You know the rules, Marv," says Lone Wolf. "If you agree to parlay, you'll be our willing prisoner. Any time you set foot in the Realm it will be to come to our paddock. Escaping would violate the terms. If you refuse parlay, you will be our captive. We'll hold you in the pit until you agree to parlay or you quit the Game. The Dragons don't want you back. Quitting is your only option. What will it be?"

"Screw yourself," I snarl.

"All right." Lone Wolf looks past me. I hear footsteps then someone punches me hard in the stomach. The wind is knocked out of me.

Out of the corner of my eye I see Red Fang. He gives me another punch then Lone Wolf waves him off.

"You're a fighter, Marv. Undisciplined and dangerous. Show some respect. What will it be? This every day? Or go home?"

I say nothing.

Lone Wolf nods to Red Fang. He walks around to the front of the pillory and starts slapping me. Not full force, but enough to smart.

"Come on, bitch," says Red Fang. "Quit. Quit, bitch."

I snap at his fingers and almost take a pinky off.

"Damn it!" he screams. He brings his fist back and

punches me in the jaw.

Someone screams. "Stop it!" It's a high-pitched voice. The one I heard when I leapt from Black Tree.

Cutter stomps into the room and stands in front of Lone Wolf. "Out! Both of you!"

It's a girl's voice.

Lone Wolf and Red Fang leave.

Lord Cutter sits down on the stool and faces me. She takes off her helmet.

"Holy. Crap," I reply.

"Hello, Marv," says Jesse.

Well this is awkward.

Her hair is pulled back in a ponytail and she isn't wearing glasses. She's still pretty, but there's a severe look to her, more mature.

She looks at the pillory and my bound hands. Blood trickles down my cheek from Red Fang's sucker punch. I stare back at her.

"We don't mess around here," she says.

"No crap," I reply.

"They're afraid of you."

"They should be."

"Marv, enough with the tough guy act. This isn't you. I've seen the real you. Too afraid to hold my hand in a theater. Too afraid to kiss me. That's the real you." She reaches a hand out and wipes away the blood. "Not this angry bruiser, mad that the world took away his dad."

I never told her about my father other than one or two

texts. Someone told her about me. Someone told her my deepest secrets. Sparrow?

It made sense. Sparrow wasn't there to pick up tactical information. She was there to pick up information about us. Who we were. Who was dating who. The kind of information a girl would know how to exploit.

I was set up from the start. "Why me?"

"What do you mean?"

"Why get to me? I'm nobody. Why you?"

"Are you talking about out there, Marv? Outside the Realm? That's real. I like you."

"You like me..." I say skeptically.

She lets out a small laugh. "You think all that was to get at you? Some plot? Why? What do you know? Did Venn tell you where he hid the shard?" She leans in and whispers into my ear mocking, "Ooooh, tell me Marv..."

My face turns red.

She sits back on the stool. "Oh, Marv. I'm teasing you. We all know Venn. He wouldn't tell you anything. He wouldn't trust anyone with that kind of information."

I think of the oak table we drag from the great hall and lock away in the map room – the way Venn absentmindedly touches it when he mentions the shard. The way he protects it...

"If you did know something," she leans in again and brushes her lips by my ear, sending a shiver down my spine. "Anything. Any small, tiny piece of information...I'd be grateful." She drags her lips past my ear, across my cheek and kisses me on the mouth. She pulls away with a trace of my blood on her face. "It'd be a secret between us. We could have lots of secrets. I'd also share with you anything we found." Jesse leans back in her chair and pulls a strand of hair out of her eyes. "Don't say anything yet. Just think about it." She lets out a small laugh. "I wish I had my camera. This is kind of hot."

Lone Wolf and Red Fang walk back into the room. Both of them give me angry glances. Red Fang, because he's a prick. Lone Wolf's glance is for something else. Is he jealous? Was there something between him and Jesse?

"Take Marv to the paddock," she says.

"The pit is more secure," replies Lone Wolf.

"The paddock is fine." She gives me a look. "Unless you want to parlay? I'll walk you to the perimeter myself. We could go grab a burger." She flashes me a smile.

Her offer is seductive. She knows how to manipulate men more than any other teenage girl since the Boleyn sisters.

I let out an exhausted sigh. "No parlay."

"We can't let you go home until you agree to parlay," reminds Lone Wolf.

"It's a Friday," I mumble.

Red Fang pulls my arms behind my back and ties my wrists. Jesse stands up and runs her fingers through my hair, like we were having a friendly board game. Maybe it is to her. "Parlay and we'll have more fun."

"I can't handle any more fun."

Red Fang and Lone Wolf walk me from the chamber. I stumble on the steps down from the interrogation room. Red Fang grabs the ropes holding my hands and jerks them tight.

"Watch your step, loser."

Lone Wolf stands back, watching me closely. He's holding a staff across his shoulders waiting for me to try something. He knows now is the only chance I'll have at escaping. Once I'm in their paddock, I have no hope.

CHAPTER FORTY-FIVE

Ronin

As Red Fang kicks me around and drags me through the dirt, Jesse's offer of parlay sounds attractive. I don't know how real it is. I'm sure they'll let me walk out of here. I'm not so sure she's going to keep acting like she's interested in me. At least until I tell her something she can use.

While Red Fang and Lone Wolf push me across their compound, I try to remember all the details from the time I spent watching it in Black Tree and everything else I've heard about Demon Keep.

The paddock is their place to keep prisoners. It's a separate hollowed-out hill toward the back of the Keep. The area is surrounded by a ridge and a crevasse filled with the ever-present painful thorns.

Red Fang has me tightly. He's not about to let me break into a run. Lone Wolf is ready to smack me down with his staff the moment I try anything. I'd never make it far with my hands bound.

I could cause them a world of hurt before they subdue me, but then they'd pay me back in full and with interest.

What's the point of running? Or even parlaying, for that matter?

Venn doesn't want me back. The Dragons feel like I let them down. Nobody wants me here. Jesse's invitation feels as paper-thin as the air it's written on. I'm an outsider.

I could just tell Lone Wolf I quit right now. He'd pull his knife, cut off my ropes and I'd be home in twenty minutes, never to be bothered again. "I quit." It's all I'd have to say.

Two words. No more crap. Screw them all.

Quit.

It's what quitters do. That's what my dad said.

I can't. Even if Venn doesn't want me around, I can't quit.

My father didn't quit. He let go so I could move on. He didn't do it for his feelings. He did it for me.

Never again.

I can't leave a situation just because it's unpleasant.

I have to play the Game.

There's Jesse's offer. I could see how far she'd take it. What would the oak table be worth to her? How grateful would she be?

Could I use that information to get back into the Game?

For a moment I imagine what it would be like if I tell

Lone Wolf to stop and let me go back to talk to Jesse. I could march in there and tell her I have the piece of information her clan has been fighting over for years. The one clue that could end everything.

I could make demands. I could lie low or I could ask for my own squad. I could go to war with Venn. I could do that right now.

The Game is in my hands.

Oak table.

Two words.

Traitor.

One word.

Liar.

Failure.

Betrayer.

That's what I would be – a betrayer. Two words said to Jesse to get some special favor and revenge on Venn. Then what? I live with the fact that I betrayed my clan? I sold out Rhode, Benny, Carrie and everyone else? To get back at Venn?

I'm not a traitor.

When a samurai is cut loose from his master he can seek out a new one or he can go rogue.

A warrior without a master.

I serve no one, only my honor.

A ronin.

Red Fang pushes me up the ridge. I stumble and lean forward. He yanks on my bindings. I know exactly where he is behind me. As his arms bend to pull me, I push back and use his momentum against him.

My head slams into his throat below his chin guard. Red Fang gasps. His hands let go to grab his throat, releasing me.

I don't run.

I turn and face him.

I head-butt him again, this time in the chest. I send him over the edge of the ridge. I dive down on top of him. I use his body like a sled to slide into the brush.

Lone Wolf will be on me in seconds.

My fingers pull Red Fang's knife from his waist and start hacking at the ropes. We practiced this a thousand times in Dragon Rook. It's why the Centaurs searched me over and over again for a blade. They knew I'd be free in seconds.

The ropes fall away. Lone Wolf is running down the ridge with his staff pointed at my head. He doesn't care if he lands on the gasping Red Fang. He wants to knock me out cold.

I toss the blade aside and take up a stance. Lone Wolf has the higher ground. He also has uncontrolled momentum. Rocks and gravel skid out from under his feet as he tries to slow himself. The tip of the staff is pointed at me like a lance.

I grab it with both hands and push it into the ground. Lone Wolf's inertia throws him forward like a pole vaulter. He falls into the brush head first. I give him a kick in the ass, sending him deeper into the thorns.

He swears as he tries to pull himself free. The Centaurs

will be coming soon. I have to get out of here.

Red Fang is still stunned. I yank his helmet free and pull his shoulder pads and chest plate free. I put them on as I climb the ridge.

When I get to the top, three Centaurs run toward me. I point in the direction of the interrogation room. They run away to help with the imaginary threat.

Using Red Fang's armor as a disguise, I run out the open gate and keep going. Before the meadow, I make a beeline and go through the uninhabited area.

Twenty minutes later I'm out of the forest. Behind me I can hear people running. As I get to the sidewalk that runs by the highway on the south end of the forest, someone is shouting at me.

Lone Wolf comes roaring out of the forest with six other Centaurs behind him. He comes to stop at the edge of the street. His eyes are filled with fury.

I rip off Red Fang's helmet and toss it to the ground. A tractor-trailer truck roars past. The Centaurs close ranks around me on the roadside.

I face down Lone Wolf. "You want to bring this outside?" I nod to the forest.

His eyes narrow and his fists ball up.

"Do you?" I taunt. "The rules don't exist out here." My voice is loud and rougher than it normally sounds. Lone Wolf is two years older than me and bigger, but I act like I don't care. Because I don't.

"You don't play by rules," he growls.

"If I didn't, your pal Red Fang would be dead. I wouldn't have left you in the bushes to get back up. Think about that. That's the thing about the Game. The ones on top punch harder than everyone else. They just don't like it when someone punches back."

Lone Wolf is almost nose to nose with me. It's uncanny how much he looks like Venn.

"You want to know what real war is?" I look around at the other Centaurs.

Lone Wolf turns away from me and marches back into the forest. The rest of the Centaurs follow after him. He looks back at me. "Step inside here and you're a dead man. DEAD."

I pick up Red Fang's battered helmet and carry it home like a severed head under my arm. Out of the corner of my vision I keep watch on the trees. I feel a hundred angry eyes watching me.

CHAPTER FORTY-SIX

Conspiracy

I stay clear of the forest the next day. Not because I'm afraid of the Centaurs. Actually, I look forward to encountering Red Fang and Lone Wolf again. The pit and the pillory were unnecessary. We've never treated people like that at Dragon Rook. At least not that I've ever seen.

Even Venn, in all his machinations, never treated people in such a brutal way. Except for maybe Richard. He asks for it.

It's a Saturday, so I don't have to worry about awkward stares at school. I want to talk to Benny and Rhode, but I can't bring myself to do it. When I got home there was one text message. It was from Carrie, wanting to know if I parlayed.

I sent her a one-word reply, **"No."**

"How are you texting me then?"

I didn't reply. If she couldn't understand that I escaped, there was no point in me telling her. People had to decide for themselves if I was a quitter or a traitor. Not that I could figure it out easily myself.

What was I?

The Dragons didn't want me.

The Centaurs wanted to kill me.

If I stayed out of the Game, what was the difference between that and quitting?

I was a free man. Free to stay home and eat potato chips. Free to march back into Dragon Rook and say, "Hey, what's up?"

Mom and I had lunch together before she went to work. She could tell something was bothering me. She promised to take me shopping tomorrow before she left. I knew she wanted to mean it.

After she left I sat down and read a book Benny had leant me. There's a knock on the door. Benny or Rhode would have just burst in the door if my mom's car wasn't there. They thought it was a hilarious gag. I guess it was.

Someone else is here.

I answer the door and Jesse gives me a smile. Before I can react, she reaches up and puts her arms around my neck and gives me a peck on the cheek. "Hey, fighter!"

I step back awkwardly. She marches in and helps herself to a seat on the couch. I didn't exactly invite her in. I didn't stop her either, I guess.

"Boy, Lone Wolf and Red Fang are PISSED at you," she smiles.

I cross my arms. "And you aren't?"

"No! I wanted you to escape. Don't tell them that."

"You wanted me to escape?" I'm confused.

"Why do you think I sent you to the paddock instead of the pit?"

"So you didn't have to hide my body after I died of hypothermia."

She shrugs. "You're such a drama queen, Marv."

This version of Jesse is all soft and girly. Gone are the hard edges in the interrogation chamber. She's even wearing perfume. Although there's another scent under it.

She takes off her jacket and sets it beside her. Underneath she's wearing a tight-fitting top. She looks like she's dressed for a date. I'm wearing my dad's baggy pants and an old T-shirt. The usual.

Her eyes rove around the apartment. "Your mom has nice taste."

Little by little, Mom had us settled into the place. Personally, I liked the moving boxes. They made the apartment feel less permanent – like we could keep moving on.

She pats the couch beside her. "Come on, sit down."

I take the chair across the couch.

She shakes her head. "Didn't your pal Venn explain to you that the outside world is different than the Realm?"

"He's not my pal and I'm not sure if they're that separated. Why are you here?"

"I wanted to see how you were. No one spotted you in the forest all day."

"That's something to be thankful for. And I'm fine. How's Red Fang's neck?"

"Not as bad as Lone Wolf's pride." She gives me a wink.

"Well, thanks for the update." I stand up.

"That's it? You can't keep both worlds apart? Still mad at me?"

"You threw me in a soaking black hole then had me tied to a pillory where your goons took pot shots at my face."

"All relationships have their ups and downs."

"You're psycho."

Jesse's voice gets serious. "No, Marv. You're psycho."

"Me?"

"You."

"Why am I the psycho one?"

"Because you think this is all a game. You forgot what it's about."

"And what's that?"

"The treasure. The treasure, Marv. Did Venn show you the gold brick? We have one, too. There's more out there. A lot more. Millions of dollars. Just waiting."

"Well, good luck to whoever finds it. I'm out. Venn doesn't want me back."

Jesse looks around the apartment again. "I meant what I said about your mom having good taste. She doesn't belong here. You don't either. Think about what the money could do."

The words sting. "What money? Are the bars even real? Even if they are, none of that is mine if I help you."

"I'll make a contract."

"A contract?"

"My dad can draw it up. He knows about legal things."

"Your dad? The sheriff?"

Jesse hesitates. "Come on, Marv. It's only a matter of time before someone finds the treasure. You guys know there are outsiders coming into the woods looking for it. Former students, people who heard about it."

Her dad knows all about the Game if she's willing to have him draw up a contract. Something fishy is going on here. "Did you tell him Venn may have done something to Amy Davidson?"

"Venn did do something to her," replies Jesse.

"What?"

"Do you trust him?" she asks.

"I don't trust anyone."

"You shouldn't trust him of all people. Venn doesn't see people as people."

"And you do?"

"I see you?"

"What do you see?"

"Something better for us all. Venn doesn't need the treasure. My family isn't rich like his. Parker is an expensive school. My parents work hard to put me there. Meanwhile, some rich kid is using you like plastic army men to play his game. That isn't fair. Is it?"

"It's the Game. It's the rules."

"It doesn't have to be. I know you know something. You're smart, Marv." She walks over to me and throws her arms around me.

I pull away. "You're worse than Venn!"

"Does he kiss as well as me?"

"What's real for you? Is this how you manipulated your way up into the Centaurs?"

She slaps me hard, right where Red Fang punched me. I go reeling and fall to the ground. The cut reopens and blood trickles onto the carpet.

Jesse falls down on top of me, cradling me. "I'm sorry! I'm sorry! You just don't understand. This game. It's...It's different at Parker."

I crawl away and put my hand to my face. "Just go, Jesse."

"Marv, I really do like you."

"Go!"

At the door she stops. "Ask yourself this. Do you trust Venn? Amy Davidson did. Where is she now?"

Jesse leaves me on the floor alone with my thoughts. The door closes and I finally get up. Her coat is still on the couch. I pick it up and walk to the door. Something smells funny.

I set it on the railing in front of the apartment and walk back inside, trying to place the scent. I put an ice pack on my cheek and go lie down.

As my head hits the pillow, I recognize the smell...

Clove cigarettes. Jesse was working with the outsiders.

CHAPTER FORTY-SEVEN

The Dead of Night

Was Venn evil? The thought ran through my brain as I tried to sleep. Not being able to roll over on my right side made sleeping even more of a challenge. The bruise still stung and oozed. Mom had put some ointment on my "hockey stick" injury before she left after lunch. That helped until Jesse smacked it open again.

Jesse...

Was she evil? All girls were a mystery to me. The ones who liked me were even more suspicious.

Venn. He had been a first-rate jerk to me. When I got caught at Black Tree he was livid. He didn't trade me back. He left me with the Centaurs. Venn had to know how they were going to treat me.

But was he evil?

Jesse and her dad sure make it out that way, with the talk about Amy Davidson.

But there's one problem: Venn's brother. He had to know what was going on. He and Jesse worked side by side. If anyone knew what Venn was capable of, it had to be him.

Unless he didn't know.

They slept down the hall from each other. In the forest they were worlds apart. Could Venn keep a dark secret from him? What secret?

The bones kept coming back to my mind. Every time Jesse or her dad mentioned Amy, I thought of the skeletal hand I saw back in the brush. It gave form to the idea Venn could do something truly awful besides lose it over my screwup.

He was wrong to yell at me for losing Black Tree the first time. I was stupid the second. Things escalated from there. Part of me was upset that we didn't get to hang out as much. He was the most interesting person I'd ever met. Venn was the cool and composed person I wanted to be – until he went ballistic. Then he was scary.

How scary?

The bones.

The bones...

The damn bones.

I'd believe Venn's story if I didn't fear there was something dark and rotten out there, an awful secret everyone was hiding. Ever since I saw them, I haven't stopped wondering about them. All my rationalizations fall apart.

I can't defend Venn when there's a huge piece of evidence I'm trying to ignore.

Either Venn is evil and murdered that girl, or he's just another hotheaded teenager like me who gets in over his head. He's not perfect. He's still a kid.

The bones...

Did he kill Amy Davidson?

I climb out of bed and put my shoes on. It's time to stop wondering. I have to go find the bones.

I take an alternate route into the forest and go to a cache of armor Benny and I kept hidden in case we couldn't make it to the shed by the school. I take the spade we used to bury it and tuck it into my belt.

The moon is out tonight, making it too easy for me to see and to be seen. I take a slow and careful path around the woods to the point where I'd gotten lost and found the bones. Orange lanterns glow in distant tree forts. From the highest part of the ridge I'm walking on, I can see a large fire over by Dragon Rook. They're having another bonfire. My invitation must have gotten lost.

The brush looks alien in the moonlight. I have trouble remembering where I crawled out from. The only thing I can do is get down on my stomach and crawl under it again like a rat. Fortunately, this time I brought thick gloves to keep my hands from bleeding.

Dark shapes scurry away from me as I crawl through the

thorns. Glowing eyes look back at me, trying to decide what kind of threat I am. I wonder the same thing.

The brush runs along a long, dried-out creek bed. I start at one end and work my way down. Every stem, stick and branch looks like a skeleton in the dark. The smell of dead things doesn't make the search any easier.

My lantern is only so helpful. I would have brought a flashlight, but the thought of a beam going up into the air like a searchlight scares me. Instead, I have to contend with the flickering of the candle behind the glass window.

I pull myself a few feet then look around. Then I pull myself forward again. Progress is slow. I decide to just find the muddy puddles and work from around there.

As I slide across the ground my body makes a dragging sound. I become used to the rhythm. So focused, I don't pay attention to the other noise at first.

Halfway into a drag, I hear something moving through the brush. I freeze. My lantern casts shadows that move in the distance. I blow out the light and wait.

Something moves again. Branches break. The brush shakes. I try to see past the thorns at what's out there.

A shadow moves by a dozen yards away. Something knocks a rock. Then there's a long silence.

I wait a few minutes before lighting the lamp again. It was probably one of the wild dogs, I tell myself. Not that fighting one off would be any fun.

I've never actually seen one of the mangy mutts attack anyone. They seem to be there just for their bark. Either way, I'd like to avoid them.

I'm about to give up when I see my light reflecting from a puddle. I slide my body into the middle and spin around in a slow circle, looking for the hand. Every forked branch looks like one. It seems futile, then a bleached white bone catches in the light.

The two bones leading to the wrist are unmistakable. Its fingers splayed open, like a challenge, the hand beckons me closer.

I slide up to it and give the hand a close inspection. Five digits leading from the wrist bones. This is not a giant dog paw.

I pull the spade from my belt and stab it into the dirt. Should I dig this up? If it is a body, I could be violating a crime scene or desecrating an Indian burial. I'll either break the law or be haunted by vengeful spirits.

Screw that. The only vengeful spirit I need to know about is Venn. I shove the blade into the dirt and begin to dig the bones out.

The forearm breaks free of the arm below the soil. I set it aside and begin digging out the other parts. I find a long femur. As long as my upper arm.

I lay it next to the forearm. The bones make a spooky impression of a fractured arm. The sight of them makes me nauseous. I'm tempted to just leave them be, but I have to know more.

I shove the spade into the dirt and hit something else. The earth is soft and gives away easily to my fingers. I start pulling fragments from the ground and setting them next to the lantern.

I know I'm ruining the crime scene or a future archeological dig. I don't care. I have to know.

I shove both hands into the ground and they feel something round. Round like the back of a skull. I pull away a massive clod of dirt and drop it down in front of the lantern on top of the other bones.

My fingers shake as I scrape away the dried mud. Bits of flesh and long hair fall away. Long dark hair.

Yellow bone reveals itself from under the dirt. The outer layer of mud falls away like a mold. The skull stares back at me.

I take a deep breath.

Angry eye sockets bore into my soul. Sharp incisors gnash at me in the lantern light. Big incisors. Fangs.

Bear fangs.

This was a big-ass bear.

Unless Amy Davidson lived in the woods, ate honey and stole picnic baskets, this wasn't her.

I fall backwards onto the ground in a wave of relief. The skull sits on my chest looking down on me. Laughing.

I hold it up in the light and point it at my head. "Well there Marv, now you know my secret!" I make it mock me.

"Sorry for disturbing you, Mr. Bear."

"No problem, prick."

"Yep. Christ, you're a big bear," I reply to my imaginary friend as I admire the size of the skull. "What the hell happened to you?"

Something moves in the brush. I aim the bear skull in the direction as I turn my head to look. Branches snap. Something grunts and charges toward me like a freight train.

Sawtooth is pissed and out for blood.

I know what killed the bear.

I don't care what anybody tells you about razorbacks and bears.

Sawtooth is special.

Sawtooth is a killer.

Sawtooth is coming for me.

CHAPTER FORTY-EIGHT

Sawtooth's Revenge

Sawtooth's tusks snap at the brush as he shoves his powerful bulk toward me. I abandon the bear skull and my lantern as I dive under the thorns and back into the puddle. Loud, angry snorts punctuate the air.

I claw through the mud and keep putting as much distance between us as I can. My knees slip in the muck and I flail for a moment without any forward motion. Sawtooth breaks free of the branch trapping his head and surges forward.

His massive hoof snaps one of the bones, making a cracking sound. He swings his head into them and sends the others scattering – one last taunt at the bear.

Crap. He killed a bear.

A bear could kill me.

I pull my knife from my belt and shove it into the ground to use as a claw. I pull myself free of the sucking mud and slide across the rough surface on my chest. The wet mud makes it a little easier to slide than before. Sawtooth chasing down my feet makes it more horrifying.

I crawl farther and reach a point where I can get up to my knees and look backwards. Sawtooth is stomping through the puddle. His whole left flank is wet.

Wait, it's not water. It's blood! A hundred bleeding pockmarks glisten in his side. He's been wounded – by a shotgun from the looks of it.

Damn. That explains his fury. The pricks with the shotgun tried to kill him.

They failed.

Now Sawtooth is on a rampage.

He's locked onto me.

I claw and pull at the branches and drag myself toward the edge of the brush. With Sawtooth's thick hide and tusks, the thorns are little match. He strides across the puddle and blows hot air at my feet as he yanks free of the thorns.

Moonlight is just beyond my fingertips. Something touches my feet. I kick out. I'm pushed out of the underbrush.

I don't look back as I scramble up the bank. Rocks slide out from my fingers and boots as I climb on all fours. The wall feels like it's a mile high.

I reach the top and roll over. I pick myself up to see

where Sawtooth has gone. Red eyes jump toward me as he leaps out of the ravine.

Holy crap!

I fall backwards and land on my ass. He swings his massive head toward me. I slam my fist down on his neck.

Sawtooth lets out a grunt and a gasp. The handle of my knife sticks out from the barrel-like neck. Blood trickles down. Not a life-ending stream. Just a slow bleed.

Oh crap.

I don't wait for the second strike. His tusks are like scimitars ready to rip my flesh from my bones. I run.

I keep running.

I don't look back.

I can hear him.

Hooves hit the ground like metal hammers on a drum.

I pump my arms and navigate the dark terrain as best I can. When I run past the orange glow of lanterns in tree forts, people call out challenges. They're ignored.

As I go past one fort, I hear someone yell for me to stop. When they see the massive shape chasing me, they scream out, "HOLY CRAP!"

The lights of Dragon Rook glow through the trees. Shadows are running around the walls. This is no bonfire. We're under siege!

Rhode is chasing after two Centaurs. He shouts to me, "Where the hell have you been?"

"Sawtooth!"

"Bullcrap," he yells back.

"No!" I point behind me. "SAWTOOTH!"

Rhode looks to the trees behind me and sees the wild boar kicking up dirt in the moonlight as he grunts and snorts after me.

"CRAP!" shouts Rhode as he breaks into a run with me.

In front of the Rook, a swarm of Centaurs are attacking our weakest wall. They've formed a barrier like a Roman legion and are fighting off anyone who gets near. Archers shoot Dragons at point blank, while deep inside their barrier something heavy pounds away at the castle.

"We can't get near them!" Rhode yells to me.

"If I break them up, can you take them down?"

"Yeah..." Rhode looks behind me at Sawtooth. "Oh, Christ. DO IT!"

I turn my head to check that the razorback is still chasing me. He hasn't slowed down. Red eyes flash back at me.

I run straight toward the shielded attackers. Arrows whiz past my face. Someone yells at me to yield. I run straight into them and push myself between the shields.

Hands reach out to grab me and punch me. I cover my head and work my way farther through the mass of bodies. Somebody lets out a scream.

More people scream as Sawtooth runs into them like a line of bowling pins.

"RUN!" someone shouts.

The Centaurs drop their shields and battering ram and take off toward the open gate. I hear a cry as Sawtooth knocks a Centaur knight to the ground.

Sawtooth starts to charge the other boy. He cowers on the ground. I grab a shaft and hurl it at Sawtooth's head.

He snaps his red eyes toward me and swats the shaft to the side. The Centaur picks himself up and limps away.

Dragons chase off the others while a few gather near me. Someone hands me another shaft. Sawtooth paws at the ground and lets out a snort.

I give the shaft a spin and wish it had a spear on the end. I keep moving to the side, keeping Sawtooth outflanked. His hoof claws at the ground again. He takes a step toward me and lets out a low grunt.

Then he falls over.

Dead.

After an anxious moment, we stand around his body, fascinated. Sawtooth lies on his side as still as the night. Blood spurts from his wound then comes to a stop. Rhode and Benny finish tying up the Centaurs they caught fleeing and walk over to Sawtooth's body.

The pool of blood is larger than he is. The moon reflects in the puddle. It's a strange image. Almost serene.

Rhode puts a hand on my shoulder. "Holy crap, Marv. You killed him."

I'm about to deny responsibility. It was probably the shotgun blast that did it. Although my knife handle is the only wound they can see. Sawtooth's heart simply gave out. It had to be the run that did it.

"Well it's settled then," says Benny.

"No crap," replies Rhode.

"What," I mumble.

"The debate," says Rhode.

"What debate?"

"What's the fiercest animal in the forest."

"It ain't me. I ran."

I turn away from Sawtooth. "What the hell happened here? Where's Venn?"

Rhode shakes his head. "Benny, set up a perimeter. Let's not let them through again? Okay?"

"Where's Venn?" I repeat.

"Venn is trapped inside Demon Keep," replies Rhode.

CHAPTER FORTY-NINE

Machinations

"We think Venn got captured," says Rhode.

"Captured?" I look around the compound. "Here?"

"No. He went on a raid at Demon Keep. Jason and Carrie are holding a defensive position. Venn isn't anywhere to be seen."

"A raid? What the hell? While this was happening?" I point to the battered wall where the Centaurs had tried to get through. Two kids with trowels and cement are trying to patch it up.

"A counter-raid to this one. Venn expected Cutter to lead a full assault on the Rook when they found out whatever secret Venn told you."

"I didn't say anything!" I protest.

"No crap. We know that now." Rhode points to the damage done. "This was a feint. They only sent in the smaller guns to attack us. They wanted Venn to come at them. Cutter figured Venn would assume you ratted us out. Especially after we saw her go to your house.'"

"You watched me?"

"Not me. But Venn had you watched."

"I kicked her out. So explain this to me again? Why is Venn in Demon Keep?"

"Venn set you up. He told you something he actually wanted you to tell Cutter. That way she'd launch a full attack. While they were doing that, he was going to sneak into Demon Keep, this time with a bigger force. But apparently, you didn't tell Cutter what she wanted to know. She figured out that Venn was up to something anyway, so she made a feint...to his feint."

My head is about to explode. "JESUS CHRIST! CAN'T YOU PEOPLE DO ANYTHING SIMPLE???"

Rhode shakes his head. "That's Venn."

The mind games were too confusing. "Now he outmaneuvered himself. Cutter...I mean Jesse...just made him step on his own prick."

"He thought you were going to squeal."

"I didn't!"

Rhode holds his hands up. "Easy. Don't blame me."

"Great. Just great. Now this is all my fault because I didn't open my mouth?"

"Well..."

"Why didn't he tell me in the first place?"

"Nobody can act that well. He figured you'd be emotionally vulnerable. The abandonment of a secondary father figure would make you willing to tell everything to them."

"Secondary father figure? Venn?"

Rhode holds up his hands. "His words. He also let the whole Amy Davidson thing get blown out of proportion so you'd think he'd be capable of killing someone."

"For crying out loud! I was neck deep in mud trying to dig up a skeleton I thought Venn may have buried in the woods! That's where Sawtooth found me."

"Christ," replies Rhode. "Skeleton?"

"Yes. It was a bear."

"The claws look like hands."

"I know this now. Anyway, back to Venn! Where were you on this?"

"He only told us the plan a few hours ago."

"And you guys agreed to this insanity?"

"It's Venn..." says Benny.

"Yeah. Yeah. Christ. Now what?"

"We wait for Carrie and Jason to pull back."

"What about Venn?"

"What do you mean?" asks Rhode.

"We need to get him."

His eyes widen. "You want to get him after all this?"

"Yes. He's one of us. Let's just say I had a very cathartic experience tonight."

"Cathartic...?"

"I figured some stuff out. Venn was a prick to me. But he's not evil. He's fifteen and full of himself. Now he got his ass caught in a trap."

"We could wait for him to parlay."

I shake my head. "He won't. Besides, they're playing by a different set of rules over there. I don't think it'll be that simple. I think Cutter and them are working with ghosts to try to find the treasure."

"Seriously?" asks Benny.

"It's a hunch." I rub my bruised face. "I know what they did to me when they were just screwing around. I can only image what they'll do to Venn. It goes beyond the Game."

In the back of my mind I think about the possibility of them trying to frame Venn for something to do with Amy Davidson's disappearance. They could be setting him up, trying to get him to tell them where his part of the shard was.

"We have to get him," I decide.

"How? Last we saw, he was inside Demon Keep."

"Let's get a map."

Benny stretches the map of the Realm out on the ground. He points out where Carrie and Jason are holding part of the ridge. "They're blocked in over here." It's on the ridge near Black Tree. "They can shoot arrows and keep the Centaurs back. But there's not much else we can do. After Venn went inside the Keep, the Centaurs closed in their perimeter."

"Have they caught him yet?"

"None of our runners say they've seen him marched out to the pit," explains Rhode. "Last I heard smoke was pouring out of the inside. He brought a crapload of smoke bombs inside there and a gas mask."

That'd be Venn. He figured out a way to negate their home-field advantage. While they're coughing up a storm and waiting for it to clear, he'd been searching inside. Clever plan – if he didn't get his retreat smashed.

"Do we have any more gas masks?" I ask.

"Yeah," Benny replies. "But how are you going to get inside there? They've called up all their reserves. No one is getting inside or out. Don't forget the dogs. They're running loose all around. The Centaurs are up on the ridge while the dogs chase us down near the gate. The Centaurs keep them mean and hungry."

"I got the dogs covered." I point to Sawtooth. "Think they'd like a leg of wild boar?"

"Who wouldn't. How are you going to get in?"

"Find me our biggest ax."

"For Sawtooth?"

I shake my head. "No. For Black Tree."

"Holy crap."

"Yep. Get us a squad. Just a few of the stronger ones we don't need to defend the Rook. Let's leave as soon as we can." I turn to Rhode. "You should stay here and keep the Rook. I don't want to get you captured twice in one week."

Rhode nods to me and starts calling out orders. Three of our bigger knights come running. Rhode gets them axes we use to chop wood and cut logs. I carve a big haunch off Sawtooth and shove it into a sack.

We line up and run to Demon Keep. Benny and his archers lay down defensive fire for us along the way once we pass the meadow. Deep in Centaur territory, we make a run for the ridge by Black Tree.

Donovan jogs up next to me. "What are the axes for?"

"We're building a bridge."

"Tonight?" he asks.

"In the next ten minutes."

CHAPTER FIFTY

Black Tree Bridge

Charred splinters of the tree chip away as I swing my ax at the trunk. The Centaurs holding the fort try to shoot arrows down at me, but can't reach me under the shadow of the lower platform.

The trunk is massive. I've only managed to cut into a few inches. I persist and keep swinging. The two other knights follow my lead and keep hacking.

The Centaurs above us holler down. "What are you idiots trying to do?"

"This is going to take forever," grumbles Donovan.

I ignore him and keep hacking. The Centaurs pile to one end to get a better look at us and try to shoot arrows by leaning as far out as possible. Carrie and Jason shoot up at them from their position nearby.

Carrie watches us hack away and finally shouts, "It's not going to..." Her voice is stopped cold.

CRACK!!!

Black Tree moans. The trunk begins to shift. The Centaurs scream. Ropes drop down as they abandon their posts.

After they climb down, I shout, "Pull on their ropes!"

Jason comes running from the trees. He grabs a dangling rope and pulls. Carrie and the others take hold and begin a massive tug-of-war with the giant.

CRACK!!!

The tree shifts and the ground begins to shake. My fellow ax men look at me with wide eyes.

"RUN!" I yell.

We dive clear of the tree as it makes a deafening sound like thunder. The giant tilts. Splinters the size of men fly away from the trunk. Coal dark pieces shatter like broken obsidian. Black Tree breaks from its base and comes crashing down.

The world shakes and I'm knocked to the ground by the upheaval. We're all flattened by the force.

I pull myself to my feet. Black dust is everywhere. Finally it settles. Black Tree is no more. The towering behemoth no longer scrapes at the sky, it bridges the gap between the two ridges and over the lake; it's now Black Tree Bridge.

Across the gap, Venn's streams of red smoke pour out of

a massive ghoul-faced mound. The black trunk stands out against the blood-colored mist. I pull myself onto the massive base and charge across the chasm.

Carrie and Jason form up a line behind me to breech Demon Keep. The Centaurs who aren't still stunned begin to form a defense. I run over the gully and jump off the edge of the tree before they can block me.

Black Tree was so tall, I land midway up the earthen fortress. The defenders are twenty yards behind me, scrambling to climb after me. Carrie and her archers take pot shots from the top of the trunk, throwing them into disarray.

A girlish voice shouts orders. Jesse, in her Cutter armor, is staring from across the compound. She grabs a squad leader by the neck and points him in my direction, then turns to yell at someone on the hill. She whistles and mangy dogs begin racing toward me.

Lone Wolf leaps through a cloud of red smoke and lands just feet away. He charges, using his gray shield to try to push me down the hill. I dodge to the side and try to lose him in the smoke.

The Black Dragons and the Centaurs clash on Black Tree Bridge. I run from the skirmish and toward the back of Demon Keep, trying to find an entrance by searching for an air shaft bigger than my arm.

Lone Wolf's staff swings at my head, barely missing. I reach for my own and feel something strange on my back. I swing it forwards and knock him aside with Sawtooth's haunch.

Lone Wolf stumbles backwards, then catches his balance before falling off the hill. Barks and growls come running toward me as the pack of wild dogs single me out. Still holding the haunch, I throw it into the middle of the pack. Poorly trained, mostly hungry, the dogs stop their pursuit and leap onto the huge treat.

I put more distance between myself and Lone Wolf. He closes the gap quickly. Now unarmed, I bring myself into a defensive crouch. He swings his staff in the air and breaks into a fighting stance.

He make an impressive jump and brings the end of the staff down hard through the space where my skull had just been. The swing follows through and the end of his staff slams into the ground, leaving a dent. He quickly snaps the staff back into an attacking posture.

I step backwards again.

Lone Wolf's shaft lashes out at me.

I fall backwards.

Everything goes dark.

CHAPTER FIFTY-ONE

Demon Keep

I see stars against the blackness. It's hard to breathe. For a moment I think Lone Wolf knocked me out cold. There's a small disk of light in the dark, shimmering like a puddle. Disoriented, coughing, I crawl to my knees.

Tears stream as I try to catch my breath. It's the smoke. I pull my gas mask from my belt and pull it over my head. Breathing becomes a little easier.

Somehow I managed to fall down one of the air shafts when I jumped clear of Lone Wolf's strike. I paw at the darkness and find a wall to steady myself as I stand. The light is no longer visible. Either the smoke covered the shaft back up or someone is coming down after me.

I move away from my landing spot. I have no sense of

direction as to where I am. My fingers slide along the earthen walls while my other hand probes the space in front of me, keeping me from walking into a wall or impaling myself on some unseen danger.

Our maps of Demon Keep are incomplete guesses based on Jason and Venn's forays and estimates from what we've see above ground. Beyond the mouth of the skull, there's the great chamber where Venn pissed on the throne. Past there are more corridors and then the vast network of tunnels we know almost nothing about. The spot where I fell was to the back of the hill – a complete blank spot on any of our maps.

My thighs bump into something and I feel the edge of a table. I spread my fingers across the surface and feel the surface of a textbook. There's an apple core and a half-empty can of soda. Just like us, they have homework.

At the end of the room the wall opens into a corridor. Footsteps echo as people go running back and forth. More familiar with the layout than I am, the Centaurs are able to traverse their lair with less stumbling.

"Armory, clear!" shouts a voice.

"Checking study room!" calls out another voice followed by a cough.

They're searching the Keep in the dark. Boot steps run down the hall toward me. I duck down and grab my knees. Someone passes right over.

"The asswipe fell down here, somewhere," yells a cruel voice. "Dumbest thing he ever did."

Red Fang.

They know I'm down here.

I hear the sound of something hard hitting the table in the study room. Red Fang is slashing his staff at everything around him. Cans get knocked over and chairs fall to the ground. He's thrashing around violently. Occasionally the air is punctuated by a cough.

"Damn it!" he screams. "Checking the hall," he shouts to the others.

He runs toward the doorway. I kick my leg out and trip him as he exits. I hear him hit the opposite wall hard, then fall. I leap on his back, pinning him to the ground. He's out cold.

Footsteps run toward me. I feel around on the ground for his staff and take it.

"Find him?" shouts a voice.

In my most petulant and angry voice, I reply with a cough. "Here. COUGH. On the ground. Take him out. COUGH. I'll check for the other. COUGH."

Hands grab Red Fang, thinking he's me, and drag him toward the front of the Keep. That takes care of two of them...

I follow the wall into the next room and use my hands to reach into the darkness. There's a footfall. I'm not alone. Someone kicks me in the back. I let out a groan.

"Marv?" calls out a familiar voice.

"Venn?"

"What are you doing here?" he asks.

"I came to rescue you."

"Rescue me?" He says the words like I just said I was going to fart us to the moon.

I touch the coiled rope at my side. "I brought a rope..."

"Is it a magic rope, Marv? Are we going to climb up it like Aladdin?"

"Um, no. I was going to lower it down to you. Never mind. I came to get you out."

"I see...Feeling guilty?"

"For not ratting everyone out? I should kick your ass for your stupid plan." I argue into the dark, not sure where he is.

"How do I know you didn't tell your girlfriend where the map was hidden?"

"Why would I be here? And by the way, I don't know."

"I gave you all the clues. I tapped the table. Made you help me carry it."

"But it's not where the map is."

"You didn't know that."

"No. But I wasn't going to tell anyone."

"Are you sure?"

"I could kick your ass right now."

"Fine. I believe you. You're a better man than I thought. Apology accepted."

"Apology? Apology? ARE YOU KIDDING ME?" I want to kick him.

Venn grabs me by the shoulders. "Quiet."

"Are you crazy?" I whisper. "You betrayed me. I trusted you."

"I thought..." Venn searches for the words. "I thought you

were vulnerable."

"If I was? You can't treat people like that, Venn."

"I would have shared the reward with you. I don't even care about that."

"I know, Venn. But that doesn't mean you can't ignore what this game is about."

"Even if it means you'll become rich, faster?"

"Even if. And how's that plan working out? We're not chess pieces. And that's a good thing. Right now Jason and Carrie are out there trying to help get you out. Pawns don't do that. Friends do. Friends don't play these dumb mind games and try to turn us into double agents. Christ, man. I thought we were friends."

"I'm sorry, Marv," says Venn in a quiet voice. "I'm truly, deeply sorry. It's the Game."

"No, Venn. It's not the Game. It's the way you play it. The war between you and your brother. Crazy Jesse's manipulation."

"We want to win."

"Venn, you can't win this game if there's nobody left to share it with. Are you going to pat yourself on the back? Carry yourself around in a victory lap? This game is about winning as a team. Maybe it involves huge sacrifices and brilliant ploys. But it's not Venn against the world. It's us against them."

"I can beat this thing."

"I'm sure you can. But can't you share it with us? Don't treat me as a chess piece to be sacrificed. If I have to take a fall, I will. But if there's a better way, I'd rather do that."

Venn says nothing. We both listen for Centaurs in the halls. Footsteps run past the entrance and fade away.

"You're a better man than I realized, Marv. Your dad would be so proud of you. I'm sure he was."

Something clicks. "This is about your father, isn't it? You and your brother?"

"Let's not go there. Let's just say it's always a competition, Marv. We're fighting for his love. Who's the better son."

"Screw that, Venn. Know why I loved my dad? Because he was a great guy. If you'd have met him, you'd have felt the same way. He'd have treated you like a son."

"You and me brothers, there's a thought."

"So do we get out of here?" I ask.

"Not without their shard."

"Seriously?" I protest.

"Marv, you saw the people in the forest. You know Jesse and her dad are up to something. We have to find it before they steal it. That's part of why I did what I did. The Game was changing. They're cheating. If we don't get it now, we may never have a chance."

"What do we do?"

"Help me find it. It's got to be here somewhere close."

CHAPTER FIFTY-TWO

The Shard

I reach out blindly into the dark and feel row upon row of helmets lying on shelves. At first I think it's an armory, then realize it's a trophy room. This is where the Centaurs keep all of the captured helmets. My fingers feel the textures of hard plastic, metal and leather. As the Game evolved, so did the ways of defending ourselves.

Crashing sounds fill the room as Venn throws them to the ground in his frustrated search for their piece of the map. "Feel for a secret door. Something out of place."

"This was your plan? To search blindly around the Keep?" I pointlessly whisper under the sound of clanging helmets.

"They kept digging further and further back," says Venn.

"They were trying to create a space deep inside the hill. We're as far back as it goes."

And as far away from the entrance as possible, too, I realize. Behind my gas mask and the suffocating smoke, it was easy to forget that we weren't just in the dark; we were deep underground – trapped inside their lair.

"You have a plan for getting out?" I ask.

"Lose faith in your magic rope?"

"Suicide is always an option."

"I got it covered," he says without offering an explanation. His words are punctuated by the sound of an entire shelf being ripped from the walls. "Damn it!"

I duck out of the way as it crashes. I notice I can see part of the room in the dim light from a torch in the hall. "Your smoke is clearing. Have any more?"

"One." Venn gets on all fours and starts inspecting the floor. "Look for a trapdoor."

I search for a few minutes, wary of someone coming through the entrance. Finally I ask, "How long are we going to give it?"

"Until we find it. Leave if you want."

"I'm not leaving you," I grumble. I wouldn't know how. "I should, though."

"It's close quarters here. We can take down a bunch of them before they get to us. Take hostages, too."

Oh Christ. That's his plan? Venn is going to start taking hostages and wall himself up back here? "You're a menace."

"I'm whatever it takes."

"What about the Rook? What if they attack in full force?"

"They won't. If they do, we'll kick them out when we need to."

"You're not worried about our shard?"

"Nope," he says with certainty. "Damn it," he says, getting to his feet. "Theirs has to be around here somewhere."

"Where would you put it?" His talk of secret compartments and trapdoors has me wondering how many secret passages are in Dragon Rook.

"That's not the same."

"Well, I know where ours isn't. But where you wanted me to think. Or rather you wanted them to think it was." I didn't say the words "oak table" out loud. It still felt like treachery.

"That's different."

"How do you know? Assume they're clever. They are. Your brother may not be as smart as you, but he's smart enough. And he knows how you think. Plus Jesse is clever. Just give them some credit. Maybe this is all a deception."

Venn tears down another shelf. Someone shouts from down the hallway. Footsteps echo around us. The Centaurs are closing in.

"Crap," says Venn. He pulls a canister from his belt, yanks the pin and rolls it down the hall. Black smoke fills the chamber. "Fine. Let's go."

"How?"

"Black Tree," he replies.

"Black Tree has fallen."

"I know, remember?"

"No. I mean literally fallen. I cut it down to get to you."

"Really? Wicked! What I meant was the reason I had you capture it."

"Offense?"

"No. So I could see where the red smoke was coming out of. I mapped out all the air holes and shafts."

"Where is this map now?"

"In my head. I have a photographic memory."

Of course he would. "So, uh, where's our exit?"

"Fine. Fine. This is our last chance to find it, I'm telling you. Oh, crap!" Venn shouts as shapes begin to push into the room.

We fight our way through the blind mob and run down a corridor. I keep a hand on Venn's shoulder because he's the only one who knows how to get out. I bet he knows the corridors better than the Centaurs by now. The only thing he doesn't know is where their map is.

"Venn!" I shout.

"What?" he comes to a stop.

"I know where their shard is!"

"Where?"

"Not here. Let's go and I'll explain."

Venn turns a corner and we step into a room with a shaft of light cutting through the smoke. He grabs a table and drags it under the hole in the ceiling. A Go game is laid out on a board. Venn stops to look at the pieces.

"Venn!" I shout.

"Sorry." He helps me up, then I pull him into the narrow passage.

After climbing twenty feet we emerge in a clump of tall weeds near the side of the hill. We duck as a Centaur goes running by to form up in a line.

"Come on," shouts Venn.

We make a run for Black Tree Bridge. A line of Black Dragons are standing on the trunk holding off the attackers. I count more than fifty of our people, plus more on the far ridge.

"Where did they come from?" I ask as he knocks over two Centaurs facing away from us.

"They're our reserves."

"I thought membership was down."

"No, bitching was just up. I knew what I was doing."

On top of the trunk, Carrie shouts to us. The other Black Dragons cheer us as we come running. A hand grabs at my shoulder then falls away as Benny sends an arrow past my head.

We reach the end of the spire and fall in with the rest of our clan. With bows drawn and shields up, there's a kind of detente going on. The Centaurs are holding back. Jesse is cornered with a group of her knights defending her. She uses the Centaur shield to push back at them.

"What's going on?" Venn asks Carrie.

"They've got Jason pinned up. We've got Cutter. It's a stalemate."

Lone Wolf comes striding toward the end of the trunk. He gives me and Venn an angry glare. "If you want to talk terms, that ain't happening." He taps his gray shield with his staff. A line of Centaurs forms up behind him.

"Duel him," I whisper to Venn.

"What?"

"Call a duel!"

"I'm not so sure, Marv."

I prod him. "Just cut and run when it's time. You'll know. Just do it!"

CHAPTER FIFTY-THREE

Last Stand

Venn and Lone Wolf face each other down on the back of Black Tree Bridge. The Centaurs have moved forward to where the top platform lies sideways. We've moved back toward the opposite ridge and fanned out in a line.

The Centaurs on the opposite side have lined up across from us. Archers on either side have their arrows drawn. Jason and Jesse are still penned up in their holdouts.

"All right, little brother," says Lone Wolf as he strides down the black trunk. He smacks his staff against his shield. "It's been awhile." He shoots me a look. "Your boyfriend teach you any new tricks?"

"Not as many as he taught your girlfriend," taunts Venn.

Oh, crap! Jesse is Lone Wolf's girlfriend. Lone Wolf

gives me a glare.

Venn shoots me a look over his shoulder. "Ex-girlfriend."

Somehow I'm not relieved. Jesse is shouting something at us. She's too far away to understand. One of her Centaurs tries to break free and is knocked down.

Venn swings his staff at his brother. Lone Wolf knocks the blow easily. "Lame," he replies, not realizing Venn was distracting him.

Lone Wolf swings the staff in a wide arc and comes to a stance. Venn holds his shield up and hold his staff like a javelin. Lone Wolf lunges and the two of them exchange blows.

Lone Wolf is taller and heavier than Venn. He doesn't quite have Venn's speed, but he has greater strength and skill. When his blows hit Venn's shield, they make a loud crack we all can feel.

The two go back and forth several parries. Venn loses several feet of ground and retreats toward the trunk. He narrowly misses a wide swing and has to jump to the ridge.

Lone Wolf leaps off the trunk and does a forward flip before landing on his feet. He swings at Venn, who then does three backflips before landing in a stance.

Somebody claps.

It was that impressive.

The two go at it again. Venn keeps dropping back. He ducks as Lone Wolf's staff knocks over the black spike of a trunk that sat next to Black Tree.

"You're not doing a good job, brother," says Lone Wolf.

"Running home isn't how you win."

"Fine!" shouts Venn. He rips off his helmet and throws down his staff and shield. He raises his fists. "Let's do it like this. Let's get it over with."

Lone Wolf hesitates. A line of Centaurs forms behind him. He sees Red Fang standing there and nods. "Take this," he hands him his shield and staff.

Venn throws a kick at Lone Wolf's head then does another series of backflips. Lone Wolf runs toward him and leaps into the air. He misses Venn's head by inches. Venn tries to grab the leg, but Lone Wolf retracts it.

I pick up a large rock and look at Red Fang. "Why don't you suck on this?" I hurl it at his helmet.

Red Fang screams and charges at me. I break out into a run away from the ridge. Behind me, Venn and Lone Wolf are still at it.

Red Fang shouts some unintelligible obscenity at me. Two of his Centaurs chase behind him. I hear them hit the ground as Benny and Carrie take them down and bind them.

I come to a stop at the end of the ridge. Red Fang looks around. We're all alone.

"This ends now," he says. He throws down Lone Wolf's shield and pulls a dagger from his waistband.

"Seriously?" I reply.

Red Fang grips the handle with the blade pointing to the ground. His other hand comes up in a stance. "Seriously."

"How many times do I have to kick your ass?"

"You never..." Red Fang falls to the ground.

Carrie lowers her staff and pulls the knife from his hand. "What an ass."

I take the gray shield. "Call the retreat!"

Carrie takes out a whistle and gives it three long bursts. The Black Dragons abandon their positions and come running.

I sprint back to Black Tree Bridge. Venn runs past me in the other direction. I chase after him. "Where's Lone Wolf?"

"Out cold!"

"You did it!"

"No. He tried a backflip and hit his head on a rock. Fat bastard!!!" Venn laughs as we hurry back to Dragon Rook. "Is that it?"

"If you kept the shard where I think you did, then this has got to be it."

Behind us I hear Jesse screaming in rage, calling the Centaurs to all-out war.

CHAPTER FIFTY-FOUR

Siege

Venn and I race to the top of the Rook and watch as the Centaurs storm our compound. We've pulled all of our forces behind the walls. The Centaurs know they've lost. The rules of the Game no longer apply. We don't want anyone getting hurt in their lust for revenge.

"Will the walls hold?" I ask.

"Long enough," says Venn. "Rhode is reinforcing them."

Benny and Carrie come running up the steps. "Is that it?" asks Benny.

I hold out the shield. "I think so."

Venn raises an eyebrow. "You're sure?"

I hand it to him. "I think they're just as clever as us in their own way. It was how you hid it that made me realize what they were doing."

"Okay..." replies Benny.

"Cutter's shield. What does it look like?"

"It's the Centaur shield. The bright red one." He looks down at the gray shield Venn is holding. "That ain't it."

"What does Cutter never carry into battle?"

"She has the Centaur shield all the time," replies Benny.

"No. Only in battle. She gives it to Lone Wolf whenever we parlay or she's walking around their territory – where she knows she'll be safe. Then she holds this shield. This is her personal shield. You'd think she'd want Lone Wolf to protect the Centaur shield in combat? Right? But she takes it instead. If we were going to steal a shield, we wouldn't bother with the gray one."

"Maybe she just doesn't like carrying the big one," says Benny.

"Could be. But I've seen Red Fang with the Centaur shield. Never with this one. It's special."

"All right," interrupts Venn, "I buy your reasoning. Let's open this sucker up." He hands it back to me. "You have the honor."

I take the shield and look at Carrie and Benny for approval. They nod to me. I raise the shield and smash it against the ground. The edge cracks. I bring my heel down and stomp on it. We all take turns cracking the shield. The inner layer breaks open.

"Hold up," says Venn. He leans down and pulls away a wooden veneer. "There was probably an easier way, but good effort, guys..."

Underneath the wood is a clear plastic sleeve. Venn pulls it free. A large piece of parchment is sandwiched inside. There are two fragments of a map. Below the map are several rows of numbers.

Throughout the map are symbols like the ones I saw carved into the tree. Venn's eyes scan over the map inch by inch. "Interesting."

"Is it like ours?" asks Benny.

"It's the missing part."

"Do you need to go get our shard?" asks Carrie.

"Nope," says Venn.

"He can't," I reply.

"What do you mean?" asks Benny.

I give Venn a look. He nods.

"It doesn't exist."

"I burned it," Venn explains.

"You did what?" hollers Jason as he walks up the stairs.

"Well, we can't take it out of the Realm? Right? The rules say nothing about destroying your own map."

"What have you done?" yells Jason. "If you can't have it, they can't have it?"

"We have the map." I point to Venn's head. "Up there."

Venn hands the Centaurs' map to me. "I'm done."

"Like that?" I ask.

"No. I need to sort things out a bit. The number sequence is a code. I know you guys think I'm awesome and all, but I can't just decipher it all at once. I'll need some time."

Benny looks out over the edge. "They've literally got pitchforks and torches."

"Marv!" screams Jesse over her jeering army.

"Your girlfriend is here," replies Venn. "She's pretty pissed."

There's a loud crash as a group of Centaurs smash into the outer door with a battering ram. More of them keep piling into the compound. Instead of wooden staffs and bows, they're carrying pry bars and axes.

"We can fight them back," says Jason.

Venn disagrees. "I don't think they're in a taking-prisoners kind of mood. It was inevitable."

"Inevitable?" I ask.

"Of course. Didn't you guys think this through? The Game works up until one side actually gets both pieces of the map. Then the losing side has nothing to lose by breaking the rules. This is how it devolves into anarchy."

"You saw this coming?"

"Yes. If my plan had worked, though. It wouldn't have."

"They'd have let you walk out of Demon Keep with the map?" asks Jason.

"No. I would have looked at it then put it back." He taps his head. "They'd never know I had the map. We'd carry on a friendly war. Not this." He points to the Centaurs rioting at our walls.

"Well, great. I'm sorry your plan didn't agree with reality," Jason grumbles.

Rhode comes stomping up the stairs. "All clear."

"What's all clear?" I ask.

"Our people. They're gone."

I look around the perimeter of the castle. All I see are angry Centaurs. An arrow whizzes past my face. I pull back. "Gone?"

"Away from here," says Venn. "Back to their homes. Safe. I didn't want anybody getting hurt."

"How?"

"Secret escape tunnel," replies Venn. He points toward a distant cluster of trees.

"I didn't know about it."

"We wouldn't call it a 'secret' if everyone knew. It was a backup plan. In case of this."

The Centaurs suddenly begin to scatter. We move to the edge of the parapet to see what's going on.

Jesse and Lone Wolf are still standing in the courtyard looking up at us. Blue lights flash through the forest down the road that leads to our front gates.

"Crap," mutters Rhode. "They called the cops."

A police SUV comes to a stop in front of the compound.

Venn turns his back to the car and faces us. "It looks so out of place here. Doesn't it?"

The sheriff's voice calls out over the PA. "Come out with your hands up. Drop any weapons." The door opens and he steps out and pumps a shotgun.

"It's Jesse's dad. Cutter, I mean," I explain. "He's in on it. He's trying to find the treasure, too, I think."

"What do we do?" asks Carrie.

"I'll turn myself in," says Venn. "What is he going to charge me with? Well, what have I done that his daughter hasn't?"

"You can't. You're the only one with the other half of this," I hold up the map. "They'll make up some bullcrap story about Amy Davidson and keep you while they search here. Meanwhile, they'll probably call this whole place a crime scene or something and keep us out."

"Amy was trouble," says Carrie.

"Amy was troubled," defends Venn. "I'll sort that out."

I can't let that happen. "Venn, you take the tunnel. We'll turn ourselves in."

"What?"

I slip the map back into the shield. "I'll give them this back. They don't know what you know."

"It makes sense," says Carrie.

"But I know everything now," replies Venn. "I could go get the treasure and keep it to myself. I could have it all. I could take it and leave you out of it."

"You could, Venn. You could have it all. I trust you."

"Seriously? After, you know...everything?"

"Yeah. I trust you to be you. My trust should mean something to you. If all your talk about character was real when we met."

"It was."

"Then go."

Venn heads down the steps. He stops and looks back. We already have our hands above our heads as we step into view of the sheriff.

"You guys seriously trust me with this?"

"GO!" we all shout.

"Just don't let Hitler win," I yell.

Venn's boot steps fade away as he runs down the spire for the tunnel.

"We're never seeing him again," grumbles Rhode.

I step to the edge of the tower as a spotlight splashes on my face. Jesse is standing next to her father, eyes locked on me, looking very, very pissed.

I shout down, "Is this because I didn't ask you out on a second date?"

CHAPTER FIFTY-FIVE

Treasure

It's been four days since I last saw Venn. After he ran into the tunnel, we all walked down the stairs and out the front gate into the blinding light of the spotlight. The sheriff made us all get face down on the ground.

Jesse ripped the shield from my hands, then her father cuffed us. We laid there for twenty minutes while he searched the Rook. Finally he came back out and kneeled down by my head.

"Where'd he go?" he asked.

"I honestly don't know," I replied.

"Where's your map, son?"

"I don't know either. Venn never told us."

The sheriff walked over to Jason and the others and

asked them the same question. We could all honestly say we didn't know. He went back to his truck and made us wait in the dirt. I could overhear him talking to someone on his phone.

Jesse came over to me, holding the shield. "You guys take a picture of it?"

"No. Search us. Oh, wait, your dad already did."

"Venn did, didn't he?"

"No. We never got a chance." It was the truth.

"You're lying."

I looked up at her. "I've never lied. About anything."

"Why did Venn run?"

"Because he thinks you and your dad are going to make up something about Amy Davidson, to frame him. He probably went home to call his lawyers. I'd watch out. His family is rich."

"Lone Wolf is his family."

"Don't forget it. Whatever bad blood they have between them is stronger than what pull you have on him."

"It's not like that," she protested before walking away.

"You got it?" her dad asked.

"Yeah," she muttered, pushing the map into a pocket.

The sheriff finally released us from the cuffs. I got the feeling this wasn't an official call. I sat down and looked up at him, but didn't say anything. He walked back to his SUV and drove off. I couldn't see if Jesse was with him or not.

We kept up appearances at the castle for the next few days, waiting for Venn. No one saw a sign of him. We kept the map a secret from the other members because we wanted to keep up the illusion of the war.

In the back chamber I gather with Carrie, Jason, Rhode and Benny. We had to decide what was next for us. How long would we keep the battle going?

"He's gone," Jason says. "In his mind, he won. So he took it and left."

"Left his family?" asks Carrie.

"I'm sure he was waiting for the chance to do that," grumbles Rhode. "Maybe went off with Amy or something. Used the money to start over somewhere else."

"Venn? It doesn't sound like him," I reply.

"You don't know him as well as we do," Jason says.

"Don't I?

"He treated you the worst," Carrie frowns. "You of all people should be the one most angry with him."

"I trust him," I insist. I was surprised to hear Carrie of all people lose faith.

"That's what makes you an innocent," she says softly. "That's why he manipulated you."

"Venn did what he did because he forgets that his chess pieces have feelings. He thinks in the long run we'll see how he played the Game and congratulate him and we'll all be friends." I'm trying to keep the faith. I want to believe my version of Venn is the real one and not the conniving one they see or the sociopath Jesse tried to make me see.

"Marv..." says Benny.

"Not you too?"

He waves his hands in the air. "I don't know."

"Listen, my dad told me something I'll never forget. We're two people. Who we are in the moment and who we want to be. Good people do bad things. Bad people do good things. Venn may be devious at times, but he wants to be a good person. I know it."

"I hope you're right," says Jason.

"What now?" asks Rhode.

"I like the Game," says Benny. "Maybe Venn ran off with the Nazi gold. This place, the Rook, you guys, that's what's important to me. I'd defend it even if there was no prize."

"Me too," says Rhode. "Venn may have won the prize, but he doesn't have the Game."

"So we keep going?" asks Jason.

"Why not?" says Carrie.

"What about the treasure?" asks Rhode. "I don't care. But we can't keep telling people it's out there."

"I agree," says Jason. "We'll figure something out."

After the meeting broke up, Carrie pulled me aside when we were out of earshot of everyone else. "You know, Marv, Jason is leaving this year..."

My face begins to blush. "Yeah. Uh, listen. I'm sorry I didn't say anything to you sooner. My mind has been in a lot of crazy places. This whole Jesse thing. I mean, there was really nothing between us...not really...I'm not even sure if she stopped seeing Venn's brother. Really, it was just some trick...I mean, nothing happened. I wish I'd asked you out. That would have made things different. 'Cause, like, when I first saw you I thought you were cute. Whew, I said it."

Carrie gets a funny look on her face. "Um, Marv, I was about to say that since Jason is leaving and Venn is AWOL, we're going to need a new leader next year."

I want to die.

I want to die right now.

My red cheeks turn into nuclear lava and I hope I die.

Right. Now. Die. Please.

Carrie's ice queen face breaks into a sly smile. She leans into my ear and whispers, "I'm glad to know I have options."

After not dying, I hiked back to my favorite spot on Skyperch and went to sleep under the stars. In the distance, the lanterns of Demon Keep glowed as they plotted away, planning their next attack. Somewhere, two men with a metal detector and a shotgun tried to decipher clues and locate the treasure that they were sure was out there.

The trees sway and I notice a shadow on the railing.

Venn is looking down on me. His clothes are ripped and his face is scratched and dirty. He looks like hell, but he's grinning in the moonlight.

"Want to see the most awesome thing you'll ever see?" he asks.

The last time I said "yes" I went on the greatest adventure of my life.

I didn't need to answer. I followed him down the rope

and chased after him as he ran through the woods.

"The forest is behind us," I shout as the trees thin.

Venn turns to me. "Not the one we're headed to..."

We ran all night.

* * *

A note from the author

I'd like to thank you for taking the time to read this. If you're new to my writing, thank you for taking a chance. If you've already read one of my other books, thank you for the continued support!

Your support is vital to independent authors such as myself.

If you enjoyed this book, please write a blurb on Amazon.com.

Thank you,

Andrew

I can sometimes be reached on email here: andrew@andrewmayne.com

You can follow me on Twitter here: @AndrewMayne

My website with more books and audiobooks: AndrewMayneBooks.com

Printed in Great Britain
by Amazon

23401228R00218